Labels *won't* define us.

"I feel so duped," I said. "We're making a yearbook that only has popular kids in it."

Venice shook her head. "It's not over. We haven't even sent anything to the printer yet."

I read down the list of names. Anya had scribbled notes beside some of them. *Tate Lloyd—Volleyball. Nicole Salazar—Debate. Rocky DeBoom—Track. Pia Bell—British accent. Jeff Hannah—Dirt bike. Danny Wild—Snowboard. Darcy Hart—Ballet.* It seemed that Anya thought people in middle school could be described in one or two generic words. I wondered what she'd scribble next to my name. I didn't feel I could be reduced to two words. Seriously. I had about a thousand interests.

"We need to do something," Venice said. "It's up to us."

"Yeah," I said. "But what?"

PROJECT (un)POPULAR

BOOKS BY KRISTEN TRACY

FOR TWEENS

The Reinvention of Bessica Lefter
Bessica Lefter Bites Back
Too Cool for This School
Project [Un]Popular
Project [Un]Popular: Totally Crushed

FOR TEENS

Crimes of the Sarahs
Death of a Kleptomaniac
A Field Guide for Heartbreakers
Hung Up
Lost It
Sharks & Boys

FOR KIDS

Camille McPhee Fell Under the Bus

PROJECT [UN] POPULAR

✦— Kristen Tracy —✦

FIC
T
Tracy

A YEARLING BOOK

Text copyright © 2016 by Kristen Tracy
Cover art copyright © 2016 by Lisa Ballard

Yearling and the jumping horse design
are registered trademarks of Penguin Random House LLC.

randomhousekids.com

Educators and librarians, for a variety of teaching tools,
visit us at RHTeachersLibrarians.com

The Library of Congress has cataloged the hardcover edition of this work as follows:
Tracy, Kristen.
Project (un)popular / by Kristen Tracy. — First edition.
pages cm
Summary: Sixth-graders Perry and Venice, photographers for their
middle-school yearbook, are frustrated to learn that only pictures of popular students
are welcome, but when Venice gets involved with a boy Perry doesn't like, Perry puts
their friendship at risk by siding with Anya, the editor-in-chief.
ISBN 978-0-553-51048-5 (hc) — ISBN 978-0-553-51050-8 (ebook) —
ISBN 978-0-553-51049-2 (glb)
[1. Popularity—Fiction. 2. Photography—Fiction. 3. Middle schools—Fiction.
4. Schools—Fiction. 5. Best friends—Fiction. 6. Friendship—Fiction.] I. Title.
PZ7.T68295
[Pro 2016]
[Fic]—dc23
2015016264

ISBN 978-0-553-51051-5 (pbk.)

Printed in the United States of America
10 9 8 7 6 5 4 3 2 1
First Yearling Edition 2017

☆

**For Judy Blume.
Thank you for your stories.**

PROJECT [un]POPULAR

1

Spirit Day Photos

In a perfect world I would've digitally removed the booger from Derby Esposito's nose days ago. Because if you didn't zoom in close and look for the booger, it was arguably the best picture anybody on Yearbook staff at Rocky Mountain Middle School had taken on Spirit Day. It totally captured the mood and the moment. I'd framed Derby perfectly beneath our school banner, and caught him jumping off the stairs near the trophy case in midflight, his smile in perfect focus as his noodle-hair wig and full-body cape swirled around him. I mean, it told a story: *Nerdy caped boy with noodle hair enthusiastically loves his school.*

"Nobody will see it. And it might not be a booger," Venice said, leaning forward to inspect the computer screen. "I think it looks like cupcake frosting. Maybe other people will think so too."

Venice was sweet like that. She always assumed the best about everybody. Nobody was going to think that was frosting.

"All these rules really hold me back artistically," I said. "Without them, I could be delivering much better work."

Venice gave me a hug. She felt the same way. But there really wasn't anything I could do. Seriously. Removing that booger would have meant automatic detention. I mean, even though we were the yearbook's junior photographers, Venice and I didn't have much power. We weren't allowed to change any of the photos without getting written permission from three people: Anya, our yearbook photography editor; Ms. Kenny, our yearbook faculty advisor; and the person whose image we wanted to alter. I thought getting written permission from three people to remove a single booger felt lame. But Yearbook had a firm image-editing policy. Last year some of the junior photographers had gone rogue and used high-quality image-editing software to adjust a few seventh graders' facial expressions. Also, somebody added a tiger to three basketball game photos. It wasn't like they made the tiger a jersey and turned it into a player. The tiger just sat in the stands, holding a soda and waving a foam finger. But the edited photos hadn't gone over well. Fingers were pointed. People got blamed. And that was why my best Spirit Day photo had to include Derby Esposito's booger.

It's amazing how a couple of people who came before us and behaved crazily could make it so we had to follow terrible rules.

"You need to stop stressing out about every little detail," Venice said, clicking on a photo I'd taken of Drea Quan.

"Look at how amazing her hair looks upside down," Venice said.

I'd caught Drea mid-cartwheel at last week's pep rally.

She played the flute in the band. I was really surprised and impressed she could hold her instrument and do gymnastics.

"Your work is magical," Venice said. "It belongs in magazines."

I leaned my head against Venice's shoulder. She was the most awesome best friend ever. Seriously. I couldn't imagine sixth grade without her.

"Don't forget to fill out your performance evaluations," a voice said. "Ms. Kenny will collect them right after the bell." But I didn't even respond to that statement. Because I was really focused on looking at a photo that Venice had taken of a bunch of eighth-grade boys trying to climb the flagpole.

"Thanks, Leo," Venice said.

I rolled my eyes when I heard that. I didn't need Leo Banks to remind me of anything. Venice and I were both excellent students. We weren't going to blow off turning in our first self-evaluations. I looked up and watched him wander off to join his friends at the business table. Why couldn't Leo be more like them? Javier, Eli, and Luke never bugged us. I think it was because they were normal seventh graders who looked cute and worked hard on their advertising and financial assignments. Unlike Leo, who, for some reason, was a seventh grader who didn't look cute and tried to offer annoying input almost every class.

"I bet Anya takes a bunch of these," Venice said, clicking through the last photos in the folder.

"I hope so," I said. So far she'd been a superharsh judge of our work. She had found something wrong with every single photo Venice and I submitted. Weird shadows. Improper centering. Low-flying birds. Her reaction surprised me a ton. Because Anya, along with Ms. Kenny, had been responsible for picking us to be on Yearbook in the first place.

When Anya whooshed into the room, you could totally feel the energy change. Instead of taking her assignment folder and hanging out with Sailor and Sabrina like she usually did, she walked right over to where we were sitting and bent down to look at our computer. When I say that Anya whooshed, I mean that she actually went *whoosh*. Every time she arrived somewhere she let out a dramatic breath.

"Hi, Anya," Venice said, adjusting the brightness on her flagpole photo, trying to lighten the sky.

"Okay," Anya said, leaning in a little bit closer. "Please don't freak out, but we need to talk about something that's not very pleasant."

I immediately thought about Derby and his booger. I looked at Venice. Why had she let me include that photo?

"Is it about our photos?" Venice asked.

Venice was bold like that. She always wanted to get straight to the point.

"Venice," Anya said, frowning a little at the flagpole photo on the screen. "Perry," she said, looking down at me with a serious face. "I want to help you guys get to the next level. And do you know what I see when I look at the photos you submitted this week?"

All I could think about was Derby and his unfortunate nose contents.

"What?" Venice asked.

"Room to improve," Anya said.

Ring.

Those were pretty crushing words. Maybe it was a sixth

grader/eighth grader thing. Or maybe it was because she acted like my disappointed boss. But Anya O'Shea made me really nervous. Even her clothes made me feel that way. Once a week she liked to wear a bright white double-wrap crocodile-skin belt. Usually she wore it with jeans. But today she was wearing it with an electric-pink skirt. I'm not saying it looked bad. Or that she wore it too much. It's just, I never would have considered buying an accessory that had once been a white crocodile.

Venice and I dropped our evals into the wire basket on Ms. Kenny's cluttered desk and then hunkered down at the back table. We had given ourselves fairly positive reviews. We were great at labeling and stickering all our materials. We turned everything in on time. We consistently worked extra hours after school and on weekends. Plus, our first signature unit was 80 percent complete.

Venice reached out and looped her pinky around mine. Looking down and seeing our matching fingernails felt pretty reassuring. We'd taken turns painting each other's nails two days ago, following some very detailed instructions I'd found online. So our fingertips looked really stylish, and also like caterpillar heads, except for our right pinkies, which were emblazoned with a cool squiggly triangle called an Akoben that Venice said was an African symbol for strength. Anya sat down across from us and glanced at our nails but didn't give us a compliment. Her nails were plain. So I figured she was the kind of person who didn't know how to fully embrace nail art. She tucked a piece of her ridiculously shiny blond bob behind her ear and set two folders down in front of us. One was labeled *Venice* and the other was labeled *Perry*. "You know

I'm a fan of your work," she said. "That's why you guys are here."

Things felt really formal all of a sudden. Usually Anya sat next to us. Did she really need to sit across from us and present us with labeled folders? I mean, did we really need to pretend we were in a business meeting?

"Let's pretend we're in a business meeting," Anya said.

I felt Venice reach out and gently touch my leg with her right pinky. I knew what she was doing. She was sending me secret squiggly strength. Venice was so good at sending me tiny messages. Seriously. She was the most awesome friend ever. Plus, she always smelled like cinnamon.

"Okay. Some people show up to Yearbook thinking that it's an arts-and-crafts free-for-all." Anya picked up a black marker and wrote the word *fun* on a piece of paper. Then she crumpled it into a ball and tossed it onto the big rectangular desk next to us.

Venice and I both watched as Anya picked up a stapler and dramatically pounded the paper ball a few times. I thought Ms. Kenny would come over and say something. I mean, it's very intimidating when an eighth grader starts slamming around office products. But Ms. Kenny didn't interrupt anything. She actually gave Anya a thumbs-up and said, "Check back in with me when you're finished."

"Absolutely," Anya said. She picked up the flattened *fun* paper and threw it on the floor. Then she crushed it under the heel of her ankle boot. "This isn't playtime anymore."

"Crap," Venice said.

This really surprised me. Venice hardly ever used that word. She was classy.

"You shouldn't say *crap* in a business meeting," Anya said, reaching for the folder labeled *Venice*.

"But I think I just sat in gum," Venice said.

I felt terrible for Venice. Because she was wearing awesome gray jeans. And a butt-gum mark would definitely ruin the look she was going for.

"That's nuts," Anya said loudly. "Everybody knows that gum is banned from the workroom."

The room grew quiet.

"Who put gum on the chair?" Anya asked.

Everybody looked our way. Even Ms. Kenny.

Venice stood up, revealing a wad of something dark brown stuck to her behind. I couldn't believe it. The wad looked exactly like a dog turd. But I didn't want to say that out loud. Poor Venice. The whole class was looking at her butt and it had something unspeakably gross stuck to it. Other than being hit by a school bus, this was basically the worst thing that could happen during the first month of school. She swept her hands over her rear end to try to dislodge whatever was attached.

"Don't touch it!" I said, jumping to my feet. "I need paper towels." I had to save my friend. The faster we cleaned her pants, the better.

"Oh, that's mine," Leo said in a very calm voice.

I stopped looking for the paper towels. What kind of weirdo jerk brings dog turds to school? Seriously. Who does that?

I watched Leo hurry over to Venice. He looked super tall in his extra-dark jeans. I felt so annoyed watching him. Venice looked very unsure of what to do. Which made sense. When we'd talked about how awesome being a sixth grader was going to be, we never imagined anything would get stuck to our butts.

"We shouldn't let art supplies migrate from the art supply area, Leo," Anya said in a friendly but stern voice.

"Sorry," Leo said. "I must've dropped it."

He swiped his long bangs out of his eyes and then stood in front of Venice for what seemed like a year.

"Um, can you hand me my gummy eraser?" he asked, looking down at his sneakers.

I'd never even heard of a gummy eraser before, but I wasn't startled by the fact that they existed. Because I was in middle school now—a place filled with stuff that was totally new and different and possibly weird-looking.

Venice started to turn pink. She pulled the glob off her butt and thrust it toward him. The wad was indented with the stitching of her butt seam. I thought maybe she should have squashed it in her hand before she gave it to him. It seemed overly personal to give the yearbook's advertising manager an imprint of your rear end. But she handed him his gummy eraser just like that.

"That was so weird," Venice said, making a goofy face at Sabrina, who was making a goofy face back.

"We don't have time to mess around today," Anya said. "Let's move forward."

As soon as Anya opened the folder labeled *Venice*, I felt so much more fidgety. The folder was filled with photos Venice had turned in when we applied to be junior photographers. Venice and I didn't really take pictures to be evaluated. We did it to express ourselves. Even applying to be on Yearbook staff had almost given me full-body hives. I mean, assembling my photos for other people to judge made me feel almost naked. And Venice totally understood. She felt the same way. Taking pictures was fun. But sharing them with other people for critical viewing made us feel super nervous and fragile. Hopefully, Anya would understand that.

"Is Ms. Kenny part of this?" Venice asked.

She sounded hesitant. Which made sense. It felt like we were about to get slaughtered.

"Ms. Kenny is tied up with business stuff today. She already knows what I'm gonna say. Cool?" Anya asked, sliding a stack of Venice's photos onto her desk.

"Um, cool," Venice said.

But I didn't say *cool,* because I didn't feel entirely cool about this. Sometimes Anya felt more like the teacher than Ms. Kenny. Which was a little weird, because Anya might not have even been thirteen.

"I want to talk about strengths and weaknesses," Anya said. Her eyes scanned Venice's photo of a barn with incredible intensity. Deep down, we really wanted to work with Anya and hear her advice. She was super talented and had won a bunch of photography competitions. One picture she'd taken of a jellyfish had been a finalist for *National Geographic Kids* magazine and appeared on their website.

"I love your black-and-whites. You do such a good job with landscape," Anya said, pointing to a row of pine trees lining a hiking trail near our favorite park.

"I have a real passion for trees," Venice said, leaning in closer to look at her own photos for the thousandth time.

Anya nodded and went to another photo. "Do you want me to tell you your strength here?" she asked.

She didn't even give Venice time to answer before she blurted it out. "You really consider the sky." She pulled out another picture. One Venice had taken of a field of brown cows with long clouds stretching over them.

"Totally gorgeous, and I don't even like cows," Anya said.

Venice nodded. "I prefer horses."

"Are you ready to hear your weaknesses?" Anya asked.

I thought that felt pretty advanced. But it seemed like it was gonna happen whether we were ready or not.

"You need to move in closer," she said. "It's a common weakness. But think about how much hotter this hot guy would look if we saw more face area and less bicycle area."

"Um, that's my brother," Venice said.

"Congratulations," Anya said. "You clearly come from great genes."

Then Anya turned her attention to me. "Okay," she said. "We're actually running out of time because we need to go shoot some shots. So I'll skip the stuff I loved and get to the other stuff."

I guess it was a positive that she had loved some stuff. Too bad I didn't get to hear about it.

"I'm not going to lie. Sometimes your photos totally freak me out."

"In a good way?" I asked.

"Let me put it this way," she said. "You're super great at action shots. And animals. Especially combined. But we aren't going to take any pictures of leaping cats. Ever. I'm telling you right now that you can't put your cat in the yearbook."

"I wasn't planning on doing that," I said. It surprised me that I was even being accused of such a thing. I mean,

I liked Mitten Man, but I wasn't obsessed with getting him into print. I'd only included four pictures of him because my mom and dad and Venice had said they were prizewinning and amazing. It's not like I was obsessed with Mitten Man. Did I look obsessed?

"We didn't think any of our portfolio photos were going to be included in the yearbook," Venice said. "We just turned in our best work."

"Yeah," I said.

"Please don't interrupt," Anya said. "During critiques it's best just to absorb all the comments."

But I wasn't sure I agreed with that. Because some of her comments felt completely wrong.

"Back to Perry. You're pretty good with posed photos. These ones of Venice and her ridiculously cute brother are pretty fab." She looked at Venice and made a kissing sound. I guess to let us know she would be interested in kissing Victor. "But your doll photos are beyond creepy. I mean, I'm taking them out of your portfolio and giving them back to you and you should never show them to anybody again."

"Okay," I said, totally embarrassed that I'd even included the doll photos. I thought they looked dramatic and showed my ability to zoom in on facial features at interesting angles. But clearly, that wasn't what Anya saw. I took the doll photos from her, but I didn't have a place for them to go. So I just held them.

"Are you like really into horror movies or something?" she asked. "Is that what your nails are about? Why do you have a war horn on your pinky?"

I looked at my pinky. Was my symbol for strength a war

horn? Did Venice know that? Why had she suggested some-thing so violent? "Um," I said, suddenly feeling much weirder about myself than I had two minutes ago. "No, I don't go to the movies much. And this is an African symbol for strength."

"Right," Anya said, nodding at me. "It's a total war horn. Warriors blow it before they jump into battle and slaughter village people and/or other warriors."

I glanced at Venice, but she just looked at me and shrugged. At this point, I was feeling pretty attacked and I sort of wanted Venice to defend me. I'm not sure what she could have said. But anything would have made me feel better.

"Do you stay home a lot?" Anya asked, sounding both suspicious and sympathetic.

"Not too much," I said, covering my war horn with my thumb. "I go out. Movies aren't my thing, I guess. Especially violent ones."

"So what is your thing?" Anya asked. This question felt so intense. Like she was going to use my answer as a way to define me for the rest of my life. I had to say something in-teresting. Something that made me look smart. And curious about the world. And not creepy. Or war horn–obsessed.

"What's your thing?" Anya said again.

I could feel her breathing on me. I saw Sailor and Sabrina scribbling on the giant school calendar fastened to the wall. They looked so happy and relaxed. I wished I had the confi-dence to feel that way in Yearbook. Because feeling unsure all the time sucked a ton of my energy. I closed my eyes and took a deep breath. And the answer just popped into my head.

"The Internet," I said.

Anya blinked at me and then tilted her head. Like she was trying to figure out if that was a good answer.

"The Internet is your thing?" Anya echoed. "Okay."

Venice looked so worried for me. But I thought that was a pretty good answer. Because it made me mysterious and hard to define.

Anya flipped through my pictures until she got to the third one of Mitten Man. When I submitted him curled up in the bathroom sink, I thought it looked adorable. But in this context it made me feel lame.

"Do you watch a lot of cat videos?" she asked, straight-faced. "Don't answer that. Okay. I think we've covered the ground we need to cover. What I'm trying to say is that every single photo you submitted from Spirit Day is plagued with your weaknesses."

"So we're not using any of them?" Venice asked. Her voice sounded really tragic.

"Don't be so depressed," Anya said. "I've given you a road map to the future. Focus on your strengths and your photos will make the cut."

I couldn't believe she wasn't taking any of them. Had she looked at them close enough? I had to say something.

"What about Venice's flagpole photo?" I asked. That one felt really special.

"Everybody is too far away in that one. And she cuts two guys off at the shins. You can't cut people off at the shins. Ever. We'd have to crop them at the knees. Then we lose the ground. Then we lose the pole base. It doesn't work."

She sounded so certain. And also sort of right.

"What about Perry's picture of Derby?" Venice asked.

I watched Anya bite her lip as she closed the folders and slid them under her arm.

"Wow," she said. "You guys really don't take rejection well."

But I didn't agree with that. Because neither of us was crying.

"There was actually a lot of cool stuff in that photo. But here's the thing: I don't like Derby. I don't think anybody really does. We're not going to waste valuable space on people like him."

And I was sort of in shock when I heard that. Because basically she hadn't said anything negative about my photo. She hadn't even brought up the booger. She just didn't like Derby.

"So are you ready to go get some awesome shots?" Anya asked.

I felt a little stunned by what had happened, but I didn't want to turn down the chance to leave class and take photos. That was the whole reason I'd signed up for Yearbook.

"I guess I'm ready," Venice said, standing up.

I followed her lead and stood beside her.

"Cool," Anya said. "I hate being late."

Leaving the classroom with a lanyard that said STAFF always made me feel incredibly important. I loved walking past the classrooms and watching people look up as we passed by.

"Where are we going?" Venice asked.

That was a good question. Because on the schedule it said we were going to write Spirit Day photo captions. And we certainly weren't doing that.

"Spirit Day photos," Anya said. "Here's the hit list."

Venice and I both quit walking down the hallway to read it.

"Keep moving," Anya said. "Reece will be by the vending machine any minute."

Wow. This was a surprising list. Not only did it name about a dozen popular seventh and eighth graders, but it also listed locations of where to find them.

"Are there any sixth graders on the list?" Venice asked.

Anya unscrewed her lens cap and shook her head. "Don't get all weird on me. We're not building the perfect yearbook in one day. It's a process."

"But Spirit Day was last week," I said.

"Yeah," Anya said. "But we need some retakes. I just don't love what we've got."

I looked at Venice in horror. Anya was retaking photos of her friends. That seemed really slimy. Because if we gave everybody a chance to show their spirit a second time, maybe they could have made the yearbook too.

"Reece!" Anya cheered as she hurried to the vending machine. "Perfect shirt. We'll shoot these in color. Yes. I love that face."

Click. Click. Click.

Venice and I looked at each other.

"That's exactly what she wore on Spirit Day, except her hair looks better," Venice said.

"This feels so dirty," I said.

"Maybe we should fight harder for your Derby photo," Venice said. "Maybe I should take a picture of you all dressed up again and submit that."

I shook my head. Neither of those options seemed like the right way to fight back against what was happening.

"I feel so duped," I said. "We're making a yearbook that only has popular kids in it."

Venice shook her head. "It's not over. We haven't even sent anything to the printers yet."

We watched popular Reece Fontaine purchase several items from the vending machine, striking many exaggerated purchasing poses. I read down the list of names. Anya had scribbled notes beside some of them. *Tate Lloyd—Volleyball. Nicole Salazar—Debate. Rocky DeBoom—Track. Pia Bell—British accent. Jeff Hannah—Dirt bike. Danny Wild—Snowboard. Darcy Hart—Ballet.* It seemed that Anya thought people in middle school could be described in one or two generic words. I wondered what she'd scribble next to my name? I didn't feel I could be reduced to two words. Seriously. I had about a thousand interests.

"Let's go!" Anya called to us as she hugged Reece goodbye and began walking toward the gym. "Tate Lloyd's up next."

"We need to do something," Venice said. "It's up to us."

"Yeah," I said. "But what?"

2

Home Life

One tragic thing about Venice was that she lived at 524 Falls Drive, which was almost two miles away from me (and school), which meant she had to take the bus home while I walked alone. Making my way home, I couldn't stop thinking about Anya O'Shea. It bugged me that she'd rejected all my Spirit Day photos. It bugged me that she'd rejected all of Venice's Spirit Day photos. And it really bugged me that she said she didn't like dweebs or want them in the yearbook. But the thing that bugged me the most was that Anya had all the power.

As soon as I got home I took out all my photos. I spread them out on my bed. I pinned them to my walls. I taped them to my mirror. I arranged them on my floor. I probably looked like a crazy person. When I heard a knock on my door and my sister, Piper, walked in, I was sort of surprised to see her, but I wasn't really surprised by her reaction.

"Dude, you look like a total crazy person," she said. "What are you doing?"

The reason I was sort of surprised to see Piper was that she technically didn't live with us anymore. She lived in Pocatello in a dorm room with three other college students. The only time she came home was when she needed to do her laundry or take our food.

"What are you doing here?" I asked. Because that was an easier conversation than talking about why I was acting like a crazy person.

"Mom called and said I had a package, so I decided to swing down and pick it up," she said. She walked into my bedroom and started to really examine some of my photos.

"Are these from Spirit Day?" she asked, pointing to the photo of several band members arranging themselves on the gymnasium floor to form the letter *M*.

"Yeah," I said.

"Some things in middle school never change," she said. She leaned in closely and looked at the photos of Drea and Derby.

Piper had gone to Rocky Mountain Middle School too, years ago. She hadn't been on Yearbook, though. I guess she was more focused on being an athlete. She played volleyball and ran track. She'd always had really powerful legs.

"What do you think? Do you like them?" I asked. I think it was pretty clear that I was bummed out and fishing for a compliment.

"Yeah," she said. "Is there a reason why you only took pictures of the nerds?"

That question really surprised me. Because I didn't think it was true. "That's so rude," I said. "Only about half of them are nerds."

"Right," she said. "Is that a mop on his head?" She tapped Derby's photo with her finger.

I shook my head. "It's noodle hair and it's super judgy to say they're all nerds."

Piper shrugged. "It's just that our yearbook focused more on the athletes, club kids, and school officers. People with obvious boogers and noodle hair weren't really featured."

I couldn't believe she'd zeroed in on Derby's nose so quickly. It was like he had the most visible booger on the planet.

"I can image-edit anything unflattering," I argued. I didn't like the direction this conversation was going. Couldn't Piper just tell me they looked awesome? That was what Venice would do.

"You'd have to remove this girl's entire mouth," Piper said, pointing to Drea's upside-down-handstand-grimace face.

And that was when I completely lost it. It's one thing to have an unkind eighth grader tear me down, but it's a totally different ball game to have my own sister show up unannounced in my bedroom and judge my work so harshly.

"Holy, holy, holy," she gushed as she hurried to my side and gave me a hug. "I didn't mean to make you cry. I thought maybe there was a nerd feature you were working on."

And when she said that I started shedding way more tears. Because I realized that until I started taking flattering pictures of popular kids, none of my photos were going to get picked. Ever. And that seemed so depressing.

"Stop," Piper said. "Don't melt down on me. Did you have a rough day? Tell me about it."

But I didn't even know where to start. So I just focused on upsetting stuff that popped into my head and felt important.

"How much do you know about crocodile accessories?" I asked with a sniffle.

"Um," she said, stroking my hair. "You mean, like, stuff made out of crocodile, or stuff people use to dress up their pet crocodiles?"

I sniffled and thought about that. "You know somebody with a pet crocodile?"

She shook her head. "No, but Bobby's uncle raises them on a farm in Florida. I've seen a ton of videos on his phone."

Of course Piper had seen that. She had a pretty interesting life. She even had an interesting boyfriend named Bobby, who showed her interesting things on his phone and also took her to all kinds of amazing concerts in Utah and Nevada.

"I think killing animals for accessories is cruel," Piper said.

"Yeah," I said. "It is."

"But what does that have to do with your day?" Piper asked.

I sniffled a little more and wiped my nose on my shirt sleeve. "Anya O'Shea wears a white and frightening crocodile belt and she's the yearbook photography editor and she basically has rejected all my photos and it's because the people in them aren't popular enough."

Piper nodded. "Well," she said. "I think that's how the yearbook mostly works."

I was shocked to hear my sister say that. I mean, it sort of seemed like she thought it was okay to do this.

"But that's wrong," I said. "Yearbooks should include everybody."

Piper glanced over at the photos spread on my floor. "Wow. You've taken a ton of pictures of Mitten Man. Was that an assignment or something?"

That remark made me feel even more self-conscious. I mean, didn't everybody take lots of pictures of their cat?

"None of these were assignments," I said. "I mean, I guess the Spirit Day photos were sort of an assignment." I looked over at those pictures longingly. Maybe I should have snapped a few photos of athletes and class officers.

"Right," Piper said, giving my leg a sympathetic pat. "They look great. They kind of buck the trend."

By now, I'd stopped crying and was trying to formulate an argument for why my pictures belonged in the yearbook as much as Anya's did. "I think the yearbook is about taking a snapshot of the school. Doesn't that mean the entire student body?"

Piper smiled at me and gave me a hug. "You are so adorable. And you have a strong sense of justice."

Finally, it felt like Piper was on my side again. "Right," I said. "So what should I do?"

"Well, if I were you, I'd probably just do what Anya said and get the best possible grade in the class. Then, next year when you have more power, you can build the yearbook the way you want it."

What a terrible answer. I mean, I understood what Piper was saying. But it felt like a very fake and wrong way to handle things.

"But I want to make the yearbook fair *this* year," I said.

"In my English class we've been reading a ton of Walt Whitman, and he has this line, 'Peace is always beautiful.' And I totally believe that."

"So what are you telling me?" I asked. Because it sort of seemed like Piper had suddenly just started talking about her homework instead of my problems.

"Anya sounds fierce. I'd go along with her and be peaceful. Anything else sounds like too much work," Piper said.

I took a hard look at Piper. She wasn't like me at all. She streaked her dark-blond hair with lighter blond highlights and lined her lips with a pink pencil every morning to accentuate her delicate mouth. She always had a boyfriend and had recently become a vegetarian. Of course she wouldn't fight against injustice. Dating Bobby, learning yoga, wearing makeup, making three salads a day . . . Piper didn't have time.

"Well, I've got to do something," I said. "I can't sit by and watch Anya stomp on the little people."

Piper frowned. "She's probably not a villain. She's probably just trying to make the best yearbook she can."

And that statement really offended me. Because Anya was attempting to build that yearbook without using any of my great photos.

"Let's talk about something else," I said. I wasn't in the mood to hear my own sister defending Anya O'Shea. "Where's your package?"

"What package?" Piper asked.

"Didn't you say you came home to pick up a package?" I asked.

Piper exhaled really dramatically. She sounded almost like Anya, and it made my skin break out in goose pimples.

"It was just junk mail," Piper said, standing up and walking to my closet.

It seemed like a complete waste of gas to drive all the way from Pocatello to pick that up.

"So, let me be totally honest. The package isn't the only reason I came," Piper said as she poked through my folded jeans. "Mom showed me something last week and it got me worried about you."

"What?" I asked.

She turned around to look at me. "A photo of you on the first day of school."

I thought back a whole month and tried to remember what I'd looked like and how I'd felt that day. I vaguely remember thinking my hair had too much frontal poof. But when you have naturally wavy, medium-length brown hair with sideswept bangs, sometimes that happens.

"Considering my day, I don't know if this is the best time to judge me," I said.

"I'm not here to judge you. I'm here to help. Your outfit that day was eighty percent orange," Piper said, working her way through my shirts one by one.

When she said that I vividly remembered my first-day-of-school outfit. I'd worn my new orange Hamburg Hoodie. I'd thought it looked awesome, and I said so.

"That outfit's a hit. Everybody at school is wearing Hamburg Hoodies," I said.

"Orange ones? I thought Hamburg Hoodies were pale yellow," she said, sounding really skeptical. Then she flipped around and held up the offending hoodie. "Other than you, the only thing I've ever seen covered in this much orange is a traffic cone."

"You are being so mean," I said. Her criticism really stung. I mean, sure, the trend was pale yellow today. But when I bought my Hamburg Hoodie that color was sold out. So the clerk had encouraged me to get in front of the trend and buy a bold color.

Piper dropped the hanger to the floor. "Everything I'm saying is out of love. Guess who was named Best Dressed all three years of middle school?"

"You?" I asked. I wasn't too surprised to learn this. Piper was trendy and back then she wore a ton of jewelry.

"No. Melanie Soto. But do you know who went shopping with her every week? *Moi.* And do you know who convinced her to get brow-skimming bangs? *Moi.* What you look like matters. I mean, don't judge me based on what I'm wearing now. Since I've embraced yoga, I only wear flowy clothes."

I stared at her. I didn't even know what to say. Everything she was telling me made me feel extra lame. I couldn't wait for her to leave so I could call Venice and recount all my sister's crazy insults.

"Don't look at me like that, Perry," Piper scolded. "I'm here because I want to help you."

I walked over and picked up my Hamburg Hoodie. "But I don't think I need this kind of help," I explained. Until Piper showed up, I had actually planned on wearing this outfit tomorrow.

"Perry," Piper said. "If you want to topple the popular kids and save the nerds, you need to dress the part."

I didn't say anything to that. Because I wasn't sure I wanted to do any of those things. We stood there in silence, with me holding my orange hoodie and Piper looking at it in horror.

"All I want is for Yearbook to be fair," I said.

Piper rolled her eyes. "If life was fair, we'd all own yachts and have butt-length hair and awesome boyfriends like Bobby. But life isn't fair. Less than one percent of us will get those things."

Sometimes Piper really lost me. Because I didn't even think I wanted a yacht or butt-length hair or a boyfriend named Bobby. My face must have had a confused look on it, based on what Piper said next.

"I really am giving you good advice. If you want to help the nerds, that's great. But if you dress like a traffic cone, the popular kids will see you coming. They're not interested in changing the system. It works for them. Do yourself a favor, Perry, and try to blend."

And I wasn't sure if Piper was telling me this because she thought it was the most peaceful solution or because she thought it would work. But it sounded pretty bogus to me.

Luckily, I didn't have to respond to her, because my phone started ringing.

Venice had saved me. I knew it was her calling me, because we made each other's ring tones "Axel F" by Crazy Frog over the summer.

"Venice?" I said. "I'm so glad it's you."

"Hi, Venice," Piper yelled as she backed out of my room. "I love you, Perry. I'm only trying to help you. Tell Mom I took the bread."

I let out a big breath and whispered into the phone, "I need to tell you one million crazy things."

"Actually, I can't talk right now. One of my mom's catering assistants canceled and I need to go skewer antipasto kabobs," Venice said.

"You've called to tell me you can't talk to me?" I asked. Because that seemed like a wasted call.

"I'm calling to give you some great news," Venice said.

"What is it?" I asked. I really needed some great news.

"My brother Victor knows Derby Esposito's sister Rose, and so he called Rose and got Derby's number, so you can call him now."

I didn't say anything right away. I think I was still waiting for the great news.

"Perry?" Venice said.

"Why would I want to do that?" I asked. I really didn't understand why Venice would think calling Derby was even close to great news. Sure, I wanted to include his picture in the yearbook. But I didn't want to call him.

"So you can ask him if you can remove his booger. Once you get written permission I think you should send that photo directly to Ms. Kenny. That should be our new plan. We bypass Anya and we take back the yearbook one great photo at a time."

"Um," I said. "You think I should just call Derby up and

start asking him questions about his booger? That's your great idea?" I couldn't picture myself doing that.

"We need to get our best photos in front of the decision makers. If we present that photo without Derby's approval, we risk Anya talking Ms. Kenny out of it. Let's face it. Yearbook has gotten political."

Venice's voice sounded so enthusiastic and certain. I wish I could have felt that way. "Well, maybe after I finish my Idaho History homework," I said. "I have to draw a really complicated map for tomorrow that includes forts and rivers."

"We're in the same boat! Duh. I sit right next to you," Venice said. "FYI, Mr. Falconer *loves* Meriwether Lewis."

"Right," I said. It sort of bugged me that she sounded so jazzed. And also that she said the word *duh* to me.

"Let me know how it goes," she said. "Bye!"

I walked to the kitchen to see if Piper was still there. She wasn't. And all our bread was gone. Home life. It was as hard on me as sixth grade.

Since my mom worked late on Thursdays as a receptionist at my dad's dental practice, I decided to get started on the map. I went back to my room, pulled out my Idaho History book, and began looking for forts and rivers. Mandan. Clatsop. Missouri. Clearwater. Snake. Columbia. I tried very hard not to think about Yearbook, or Derby, or anything Piper had said. I turned my focus to finding all the map's blue winding lines.

I was glad I wasn't born in a time when people had to be explorers. I would have hated doing that. All that walking in uncomfortable boots toward the unknown. Plus, you had to carry your own canoe. And sometimes you had to eat dog meat. And not everybody survived. Nothing about it sounded appealing or fair. Sketching the squiggling rivers into place, I wondered if anybody else at my school making this map felt the same way.

3

Assembly Photos

I decided to wear my orange hoodie after all. Because it didn't seem logical to let a college student who wore tribal-print palazzo pants and tank tops tell me how to dress.

"Snappy look," my dad said as I sat down at the table and joined him for breakfast.

"Thanks," I said, glancing at his outfit. I didn't really feel like I could return the compliment, because he was wearing a dark-brown shirt and light-brown pants and it wasn't a very flattering look. Like it or not, being a photographer had changed the way I looked at people. Because I didn't look at them like people as much as I looked at them as potential photographs. And if I took a picture of my dad right now, he would look like a possibly dead tree trunk.

"Where's the toast?" I asked, staring down at my bowl of dry cereal. Then I remembered that Piper had stolen all our bread.

"Cereal today," my mom called from the kitchen sink. "Toast tomorrow."

I wondered if all college students stole their family's food or if Piper was a special case. I poured my milk and tried not to feel bitter about it.

"I went online last night with TRAC," my dad said.

"Why?" I asked. TRAC was our school's online grading portal. It was also where teachers put their teaching philosophies and syllabuses. It surprised me that my dad was checking it, because I checked it all the time and I'd never had any late assignments or low grades. He didn't need to be on there.

"Have you finished your Idaho History map?" he asked. He'd finished eating his cereal and was slowly peeling a banana.

"Yes," I said. But really I thought he should have asked me that question much earlier than the morning it was due.

"Did you know that in English you're spending the whole semester reading literature about the Great Depression?" he asked.

Of course I knew that. Other than the Great Depression, the only other subject Ms. Torres talked about was how to format an essay.

"She must be tough," he said. "She's making you write six essays this semester."

This made me choke a little bit on my apple juice. Because I didn't like thinking about future homework while eating.

"And have you checked out your major assignment in Idaho History?" he asked. "Your teacher actually lists useful power tools to help you complete it."

My dad really didn't understand what a sixth grader wanted to talk about at the breakfast table. "Venice and I are only reading the syllabus a week ahead so we don't freak out at all the work we have to do," I explained.

"Sounds smart," my mom said.

"Shouldn't you look at the whole semester? What if you've got two essays due the same week you've got exams in math and science?" my dad asked. "Isn't it better to know that now?"

"Did you see that on TRAC?" I asked. Because that basically sounded like a week that would kill me. And Venice and I hadn't seen any week that looked like that on TRAC.

"Let's not stress Perry out before school," my mom said. "I'm sure the teachers coordinate major assignments."

Breakfast was making me feel really anxious.

"Well, I hope you have a great day," my dad said, totally ignoring that everything he'd said to me to this point was designed to make the opposite happen.

I swallowed. "I hope you have a great day too, and that nobody shows up with a traumatic gum injury."

My dad laughed at that. "Thanks. Everything on the books looks pretty basic. Cavities. A crown. Removing a permanent retainer. Nothing too exciting."

I really didn't like to hear about my dad's work. It's not that I thought teeth were disgusting, but sometimes he talked about mouth diseases and those were completely disgusting.

"If we can't talk about classes, can we talk about the assembly today?" my dad asked. "Do you know who's coming? It's listed as TBA."

My dad wanted to be involved in my life. Which should've made me feel tremendously loved but sometimes made me feel pestered.

"A snake is coming," I said.

"What?" my mom asked in a concerned voice.

"What kind of snake?" my dad asked, in a curious, excited, and very unconcerned voice.

"A python," I said. "They announced it last week. It's from Southeast Asia."

"Why couldn't they bring a turtle?" my mom asked. "Kids love turtles. And they don't constrict around people's chests and squeeze them to death." She clenched her fist really hard until it shook a little.

"Eww! We need to stop talking about lethal homework and snake death grips," I said as I loaded up my backpack.

"If they let students hold the snake," my dad said, "do you think you'll volunteer?"

That question made me squirm. Of course I didn't want to do that. I was going to be too busy anyway. "I'm on Yearbook," I explained. "We'll be taking pictures of the snake."

My mother grimaced when I said this. "Don't crowd it. Snakes are springy. They can lunge without warning."

But I rolled my eyes at that comment, because I was sure that Principal Hunt would never allow a springy python that could lunge without warning to enter the gymnasium.

"I'm not worried about it," I said. "Love you guys." And I was gone.

Walking to school, I thought a lot about what Venice had said the night before. I hoped she wasn't going to be disappointed that I hadn't called Derby. Maybe if Venice hadn't been skewering kabobs, I could have talked to her more about what I needed to say to Derby and then I would have felt more comfortable making that call. Venice was sensible. I hoped she'd understand why I hadn't done what I hadn't done.

As soon as we got to Yearbook, Anya sought me out and said something that improved my mood quite a bit. "You have great animal energy. So you'll shoot the snake."

"Really?" I said. I'd been sort of prepared to hate Anya for the rest of the year, but this made me like her a little. I loved taking pictures. "Have you told Venice?" Because I didn't want Venice to think I was hogging the camera.

"Yeah," Anya said. "She's totally cool with it. Let's come up with a game plan with Ms. Kenny. I want to give you the best opportunity to get the best photos."

Ms. Kenny quickly joined me and Anya and Venice to create a game plan. It felt pretty awesome. I liked the idea that we were all on the same team. Because until this moment, it hadn't felt that way.

"You'll definitely want to show up to the gym with your wide-angle lens on and the lens cap off and ready to shoot," Ms. Kenny said.

"Right," I said. That seemed like a no-brainer.

"And don't overfocus on the python. You want pictures of the crowd, too," Anya said.

"Exactly," Ms. Kenny said. "And don't forget the teachers. And the principal. This is a great chance to get colorful reaction shots." Ms. Kenny looked really crisp and happy today. She was wearing a gray jersey shirt with zippers near the shoulders and a black skirt that flared at her knees. Maybe she'd worn such a cute outfit because she wanted me to take her picture today. I made a mental note to look for Ms. Kenny during the assembly.

"The handler, Mr. Mortimer, is expecting a photographer, but he's asked that we not approach the snake's head area unless we see that he has secured the snake's mouth between his hands. And no sudden movements. He says this one can be nippy," Ms. Kenny said, making pinching motions with her fingers.

"Nippy?" I asked. I started to wonder if Anya knew about that and maybe didn't want to take the snake photos.

"He says she's never nipped anyone before," Ms. Kenny said. "Oh, dear, you look nervous. Do you want me to take the pictures?"

Did I want that? Not really. I felt like any chance I had to take school photos was a shot to get them into the yearbook. "I'm fine," I said. "I'll do it."

"Great! I think we're set," Anya said. "The bell will ring in a few minutes."

I decided to shove any fear I had about the nippy python out of my brain and focus on the positives. Ultimately, I was pretty happy. That was the great thing about my life. One minute it looked pretty hopeless, and the next minute I was in charge of photographing our principal reacting to a python.

Venice pulled me aside, into the room's back corner. She looked really concerned. She was probably worried about me and the nippy snake. I tried to give her a reassuring smile, but before I could do that she blurted out something alarming.

"So I asked Derby if he'd talked to you and he said, 'What are you talking about?' " Venice stared at me hard, her wide-eyed gaze filled with disgust and disbelief.

But I stared right back at her with an equal amount of disgust and disbelief in my own eyes. Because I couldn't believe Venice was asking Derby about me not calling him. That felt like a total invasion of everybody's privacy.

"I didn't know what to say. It felt too weird to call him up and ask if I could image-edit his nose," I said. "I think there must be another way."

"Perry, if we're going to actually fix the yearbook, we're going to have to make our move right now. And that might mean we have some weird conversations. It's just how it's going to be," Venice argued.

"Yeah," I said. I felt so conflicted. I wanted to change the system. But I didn't know how. Because the system was bigger than I was. And since even Piper knew all about it, it meant the system had been around at Rocky Mountain Middle School for a long time.

"Maybe we can find him at lunch," Venice said.

Getting his phone number. Finding him at lunch. It was beginning to feel like Venice wanted me to stalk Derby Esposito. Was that really the solution?

"Hey, Perry," a voice said from behind me. "Make sure you don't take off your shoes. My uncle saw a guy get bit by a python during a special feeding session at a zoo. I think it thought his white socks were rats."

"What?" I asked, flipping around to see Leo. Why was he always giving me advice I didn't want?

"The python isn't going to bite me," I said. "No part of my body looks like a rat." And then, to let him know I was super offended by what he'd said, I snapped my fingers and turned my back to him.

Leo walked off and joined Eli, Javier, and Luke by the door.

"You totally just bit his head off," Venice said. "Are you okay?"

That was when I realized I wasn't okay. I felt really stressed out. I didn't want to have to think about anything except taking totally awesome pictures of the snake and the audience.

Ring.

I walked up to Anya, because I thought she'd want to go with Venice and me to the auditorium so she could oversee the photos.

"Cool," Anya said, leaning down so she could whisper something in my ear. "Sailor, Sabrina, and I are going to sit in the front row near the center. That way you can get our boots in the shot. If you give us a countdown, we'll give you a surprised reaction every take."

I pulled away from her. "Huh?"

And then she didn't even bother whispering as all the students filed past us to get to the assembly.

"I want you to take our picture," Anya said. "It's Sabrina's birthday tomorrow. I told her we'd do it."

And that seemed totally wrong. Because you couldn't go around promising people that we'd put them in the yearbook just because their birthdays were tomorrow.

"Come on," Venice said. "You need to get down there." She tugged on my arm and pulled me out the door.

"What did she say?" Venice asked as we walked down the hall. "You look really angry."

I looked behind me to see if Anya was there. And she totally was. Anya, Sabrina, and Sailor were clacking behind us in their matching boots. I felt full of rage.

"Tell me," Venice insisted.

But then I got this amazing idea. It was very brilliant and it took away my rage and filled me with hope. "I need you to help me locate certain people during the assembly," I said in a soft voice.

"Like who?" Venice asked in an equally soft voice.

"The nerds," I said, with an evil grin. "We're going to start fixing the yearbook right now."

As soon as we walked into the auditorium, there was total chaos and a million people talking all at once. From the corner of my eye, I watched Anya, Sabrina, and Sailor peel away from the class and sit in the front row.

"You should go up and introduce yourself to Mr. Mortimer before he takes the snake out of that rubber tub," Venice said, pointing to a giant blue plastic bin on a table next to the microphone stand.

"Wow," I said. "How big is that python?"

"Nine feet," Mr. Mortimer said as he walked toward me with his hand extended. He was a skinny man with short brown hair and giant glasses, and for some reason it was easy for me to picture him holding a huge snake.

"Did Ms. Kenny explain that you shouldn't rush up on the snake or approach its head unless I have both my hands around her jaws?" he asked, powerfully pumping my hand a few times.

"She did," I said.

"Fantastic," he said. "This looks like a fun crowd."

I looked around at the mayhem in the gym. I didn't know if I saw "fun." Everybody around me looked like they'd just eaten a ton of sugar and were going nuts.

"Do you need us to help you do anything?" Venice asked in a chipper voice.

To my surprise Mr. Mortimer nodded. "Toward the end I like to let a few people hold the snake. When the time comes, can you help me pick out some volunteers?"

"Totally," Venice said.

"Then let's get started," Mr. Mortimer said.

I stood off to the side, on the foul line, while Principal Hunt introduced the guest speaker. She went on and on about his snake credentials. Apparently, in addition to speaking at schools, Mr. Mortimer had a job extracting venom from deadly snakes. And he'd been bitten by a cobra and a green mamba. And sometimes when people got bitten by snakes and the hospitals couldn't get any antivenom, Mr. Mortimer would donate his blood to help save them. I was pretty sure he was the most famous person to ever enter our gymnasium. And I thought it was surprising that our school could afford him.

When he finally reached the microphone, the students erupted in applause. I took a few pictures of people clapping like mad and cheering. I found Drea Quan freaking out. And Fletcher Zamora. Leo also had an amazed look on his face, but I refused to take his photo because I really couldn't stand him. I took a ton of shots of Mr. Mortimer. And a few of Ms. Kenny. When Anya started shooting me hate daggers, I decided to click a few shots of her and Sabrina and Sailor. Their jeans and lavender tops practically matched. And their brown boots looked nearly identical. It looked like they were in some weird eighth-grade-girl gang that dressed alike.

I paused from taking photos, because what I really wanted was a picture of the snake. Mr. Mortimer called it a carpet python. He said this type of snake was semiarboreal, which meant it liked to climb trees. In the wild it ate lizards, bats, birds, and mammals. But in captivity this one ate one medium-sized rat every seven to ten days. I took a shot of Rocky DeBoom when he said that, because he looked shocked and grossed out. That was when Venice started whispering the names of other students I should take photos of.

Winnie Dusenberry looked extra pasty and frightened. If I were that naturally pale, I probably wouldn't wear so much black. *Click*.

Chet Baez had his eyes covered. That made sense. He liked birds. And didn't snakes eat those? *Click*.

Sasha York needed to learn how to smile. Because her mouth was open so wide I could see her bottom retainer and that was not very attractive. *Click*.

Hayes Ellsworth looked hilarious. I liked how much expression was in his face. Even though it looked freaked out and red. *Click*.

I had taken so many great nerd photos. I could feel myself smiling. I bet at least six of them would make it into the yearbook. Six nerds! At this rate the yearbook would be super inclusive of everybody in no time.

"And now I'd like some help from the audience with holding the snake," Mr. Mortimer said. "She's not heavy, but she is long."

Venice raced out into the crowd and grabbed three perfect nerds: Winnie Dusenberry, Chet Baez, and Derby Esposito. It was like a dream come true. But then I saw something awful. Anya, Sabrina, and Sailor had walked up as volunteers. How had that happened? They didn't even wait to get picked. And what really drove me nuts was that Mr. Mortimer invited them to be part of the snake-holding line. As I watched them arranging themselves through my lens, I realized I wasn't going to get an amazing picture of everybody. The shot was too big. It made sense to focus on the snake's head. And that was when it hit me. We needed to position the nerds as close to the python's head as possible. If anyone were to fall into the fuzzy background, let it be Anya, Sailor, and Sabrina at the tail.

"The head!" I shouted to Venice, who was helping arrange the volunteers.

But she shook her head and looked freaked out. She must've thought I wanted her to make one of the volunteers hold the snake's head. But I wasn't insane. I didn't want that.

"Get Derby closer to the head!" I yelled.

Derby heard that and looked at me in a very horrified way. I guessed that made sense. But he needed to change that facial expression because it did not read well in my lens.

Click. Click. Click.

Then I saw things start falling apart. Anya realized what

I was doing. She refused to hold the snake's tail and began passing people, going under people's arms and the snake's own body to get closer to Mr. Mortimer and the python's head.

Venice had done such an awesome job arranging the nerds that Derby was holding the snake right behind her brightly colored black-and-yellow head. Even though Mr. Mortimer held the snake's mouth closed, she kept flicking her dark and wet-looking tongue. It sort of looked like she was flicking Derby's wrist. He kept trying to turn away from the snake, and he had this weird facial expression, like he was in pain. Was he having a panic attack? My aunt Patrice had had one of those at a picnic once when a bunch of bees landed on our sandwiches. I hadn't been sure what to do then. And I wasn't sure what to do now. So I kept taking pictures.

Click. Click. Click.

Derby's skin looked pale and pasty. He started to lean against Mr. Mortimer.

Click. Click. Click.

I started to worry that he was going to get sick.

Click. Click. Click.

I think other people started to worry about that too, because Principal Hunt grabbed him by the elbow and removed him from the line. It was awful. My hope of taking the perfect snake photo with Derby had been ruined. And what was I left with? Anya O'Shea standing right next to Mr. Mortimer, holding the snake right below her amazingly colored yellow-and-black head. Sailor stood beside Anya, followed by Sabrina. And then came my great group of nerdier kids.

Click. Click. Click.

Tragically, they looked nerdy. Anya, Sabrina, and Sailor boldly stood right next to the snake, no fear in their faces, and they also looked cute. From what I saw in my lens, this project had been a complete failure. Winnie, Derby, and Hayes had their faces so squished up in fear that it was hard to recognize who they were. Also, Derby looked like he was on the verge of puking.

For a final flourish, Mr. Mortimer invited Principal Hunt to kiss the snake's head. The gymnasium erupted in applause. I wasn't sure she was going to do it. I mean, even with her jaws being held shut, the python still had a flicking tongue and looked like a totally deadly snake.

The kiss happened so fast that I missed it. I couldn't believe it.

Click. Click. Click.

I barely captured an unflattering blur of Ms. Hunt's curly brown hair approaching the python. My angle was wrong. It was completely out of focus. Nothing looked right.

The next thing I knew the snake was being placed back into her plastic case and everybody was dispersing. They flooded down the bleachers in a giant mob. The noise bounced off the floor and walls. I felt an arm on my shoulder and I expected to turn and see Venice. Instead, I came nose to nose with Anya.

"Send me the photos you took," Anya said. "I'm so going to use one of those for my Christmas card this year."

And then she was off. With her friends. Practically galloping across the polished wood floor in victory. Across the gym I could see Derby shaking as he drank from a water bottle that had been handed to him by Ms. Donna, the school nurse.

Everything was over. I felt like such a failure. Even with Venice's amazing help, the kinds of changes we needed to make were beginning to feel totally impossible.

4

More Unwanted Advice

The hours that followed the python assembly felt brutal and unending. After sixth period, I felt totally dazed as I dragged myself down the hallway to my locker and out the front door. I didn't see Venice anywhere. People began to blur as I made my way down the front walkway and across the street.

Halfway home I looked down at myself and realized I had four stains on my Hamburg Hoodie. I didn't even remember getting one stain, let alone four. Being locked in a battle with Anya O'Shea was turning me into a stressed-out zombie of a person. I scratched at the first stain. Mustard. I must have spilled some on myself during lunch. Both Venice and I had eaten corn dogs. The second stain was blue and it flaked off easily. Ms. Stott had asked me to hold a breakaway sphere during her lecture on the layers of the Earth. Maybe some of the Earth's crust had gotten stuck to me. The third stain looked like dirt. And I guess that happens. But the fourth stain was purplish and oily. I had no idea where it had come from.

I probably would have stood on the sidewalk scratching at my stains all day if I hadn't heard the sound of "Axel F" by Crazy Frog blasting out of my backpack. I unzipped my pack as fast as I could and pulled out my phone.

But for some reason Venice wasn't speaking. "Are you butt-dialing me? Should I hang up? Hello? Are you there?" I asked.

When she finally started speaking, her voice was barely a whisper. "I'm still on the bus. I sat too close to the back. And I learned something awful."

I wasn't too surprised to hear this. Total perverts with farting issues and sometimes rubber-band weapons sat at the back of the bus.

"Maybe you should move forward," I suggested.

"No. It's good information. It's something we need to talk about right away," Venice said.

In the background, I heard the bus door gasping open.

"Are you about to gross me out?" I asked. She sounded so freaked out about what she was going to tell me that it was freaking *me* out. I mean, I'd already had a pretty terrible day.

"Leo rides my bus," she said in a voice barely audible. "He told me something terrible."

"Who's Theo?" I asked. I wasn't sure why Venice was suddenly riding the back of the bus and talking to strange people who wanted to tell her terrible things. I would never do that. It was like after I said goodbye to her in Idaho History, my friend had become a totally new person with a death wish.

"Leo Banks. Our advertising manager in Yearbook. Remember?"

Of course I remembered Leo. How could I ever forget that creep?

"What's wrong with him?" I asked. Whatever he told her had to be pretty alarming for her to sound this upset.

"Leo's awesome. Don't hate on him. This is about Anya. I know why she picked us for the yearbook staff."

That wasn't very alarming news. "So do I. She loved your black-and-whites. And my animal shots are good." It was sort of like Venice had forgotten everything that had happened during our sit-down critique.

"You couldn't be more wrong," Venice said. "Okay. I'm getting off the bus now. Call me later, Leo!"

"Wait. Why do you want Leo to call you?" I asked, making a gagging sound. Did she like him? I didn't think he was cute. And even if he was, no guy was so cute that you should start risking your life by riding at the back of the bus and having terrible conversations with him.

"You're not listening to me, Perry! I'm saying that Yearbook is way more rigged than we realized. We're the only sixth graders in the class for a reason. And Ms. Kenny is totally hung up on the budget and she lets Anya run the creative side."

"We're fixing this with our great nerd photos," I said, hoping that at least some of them had turned out.

"That's not enough," Venice said. "We're going to have to do way more."

And that was the moment when I started having a ton of doubts. About everything. I mean, was Leo even telling the truth? And did I really want to spend the rest of the school year battling a superpopular eighth grader who had a very powerful will? What if I simply turned in a few nerd photos and followed Piper's advice? I could build a better yearbook next year. I mean, I had so much on my plate anyway.

PE with Ms. Pitman felt brutal because I had her second period, when her legs were still fresh. And English with Ms. Torres required all of my brain because she was way too enthusiastic about poetry written during the Great Depression. And Science with Ms. Stott often involved chemicals and dead stuff. I mean, having to learn *and* smell terrible odors at the same time wasn't a picnic. And Idaho History with Mr. Falconer was a memory marathon. Because I didn't find the state of Idaho interesting enough to remember stuff about it naturally. So I drilled everything into my short-term memory with flashcards and hoped for the best. Last period I had Math in Focus with Mr. Pickering. Which required real work. I just didn't know. I wasn't sure how much of my life I should devote to Yearbook.

"Are you listening to what I'm saying?" Venice asked.

"If we let Anya build the yearbook the way she wants it, we'll still end up doing something and we'll probably get an A."

"Shut up!" Venice said.

Wow. "Did you just tell me to shut up?" I asked. Venice never told me to do that. She loved hearing my input and ideas.

"I did. An easy A isn't why we applied to Yearbook. Remember? All the photos you took? You stalked Mitten Man for days to capture him perfectly curled up in that sink."

I stopped walking. Why was Venice being so mean? "I did *not* stalk Mitten Man! Take it back!"

"You followed him around for—seriously—half a week," Venice argued. "I'm not judging you. I'm just reminding you that your pictures matter."

I wasn't sure why this conversation was turning me so angry and paranoid. To calm myself down I started walking along an invisible balance beam on the sidewalk.

"Leo said that Anya said she wanted to pick sixth graders so she could boss us around," Venice said.

Based on what I'd seen today, that did sound an awful lot like Anya. But it bugged me for some reason that Leo was the source of all this new news.

"And Leo said that Anya said she's been planning her perfect yearbook since last year. And that she's already got it laid out. She actually has a dummy yearbook already made, and she's filled in everything with pics of her friends. And that's what our yearbook is going to be," Venice said.

That did sound pretty terrible. "Really?" I asked.

"Yes. And Leo also said that she's obsessed with the boys' volleyball team and hates the theater club," Venice added.

"Hmmm," I said, trying to process everything Venice was telling me. I was really surprised when I looked up and saw that I was standing in front of my neighbors'. Never in my life had I balance beam–walked that far.

"We need to do way more than take pictures of a few nerds!" Venice said.

"Um, we don't really have a ton of options," I said.

Clearly, Anya had been positioning herself for this opportunity her entire middle school career.

"We need a new plan!" Venice said.

Venice was acting like such a mess. She needed to pull

herself together and remember what was most important here. Our friendship.

"Perry, are you paying attention? We have new information."

Venice sounded so panicked that it started to panic me. She had never gotten this upset in elementary school unless we were both freaking out about something together. Leo was basically a stranger. Why should he have this kind of power? Why was she trusting him 100 percent? I didn't like the way this felt. "How do we know Leo is telling you the truth?"

That was when Venice's voice totally changed and she started yelling, which was rare for Venice because she was basically the most supersweet person ever. "Why would Leo lie about any of this? Of course he's telling me the truth!"

When I felt this anxious, I had to keep moving. So as I thought about Venice's pro-Leo argument, I gently kicked at my neighbors' mailbox post and decorative brown mulch. It really bothered me that Venice was yelling. I was her best friend. I just thought she should have been handling this differently. It made me really suspicious of Leo. "Maybe he doesn't like Anya and he's trying to get us to gang up on her." *Kick. Kick. Kick.*

"Of course he doesn't like Anya," Venice spat back. "She's a jerk! Weren't you paying attention today?"

Double wow. This was one of the meanest phone calls I'd ever had with Venice. I was starting to get worried that she was going to say something really unforgivable to me. So I tried to let her know I appreciated what she was saying, but that I also didn't like Leo's influence on our friendship. "Thanks for calling me, but I think you're acting crazy and that you should stop talking to Leo on the bus. I think he's trying to start a toxic triangle."

Piper had taken an AP psychology course in high school and had warned me about toxic triangles at my birthday party last year. "Watch out for kids who try to start toxic triangles," she'd said. "Boys especially. They do it for the extra attention. They find a pair of really cool friends and then try to insert themselves and get them to fight by starting drama."

"Are you quoting that weird thing Piper said at your birthday?" Venice asked.

That was when reality finally hit me. I was probably already in a toxic triangle. Leo was that good. I mean, Venice had yelled at me and basically called my sister weird. What was going on with that? I kicked my neighbors' mulch a little harder. "Okay. Everything Piper said came from a psychology textbook. And I can't believe you're not asking me about how my day went. I feel like a total moron for screwing up the picture of Principal Hunt and the snake. And I gave Derby a panic attack. I've felt awful about myself all day. Seriously, Venice. I might not be strong enough to do what you want me to do here." I started walking toward my driveway.

"Don't crumble on me," Venice said. "Do you think you can have your mom bring you by tonight so we can come up with a plan? Leo's free to talk anytime after six."

I couldn't believe that Venice thought I would be willing to have a toxic phone call with toxic Leo. "This call needs to end right now," I said. The timing was perfect because I was at my front door.

"Wait!" Venice shouted. "Don't! We've got to figure out a way to get Ms. Kenny involved. If we don't have a plan in place by Friday, when the sections are finalized, Leo thinks we're sunk."

"You're breaking up," I said, cupping my mouth and making static noise.

"No! No!" Venice said.

Click.

When I walked through my front door, all I wanted to do was sit in front of the television and zone out. But that didn't happen. Because when I walked through my front door, my mom was unexpectedly standing in the kitchen instead of being at work. And she started taking pictures of me.

"Stop that!" I said, putting my hands up to block my face. "I have stains all over me."

My mom ignored me and kept snapping away. "I need them. The ones I took on the first day of school are too dark."

My mother had become super obsessed with scrap-booking. It happened when I was in the third grade. So for the first eight years of my life I had one photo album. And for the next three I had six. And those suckers included every-thing from report cards, to pieces of my hair, to napkins at fancy restaurants, to every stinking movie ticket stub we'd purchased since she took her Scrapbook Survival 101 course at the Idaho Falls public library.

My mom liked to think that her interest in scrapbooking and my interest in photography made us similar. But I didn't see it that way at all. My interest in photography meant I was an artist who wanted to capture moments of time that would never happen again. And my mom's interest in scrapbooking meant she was a mom who had a really tough time throwing stuff away, and who also enjoyed collecting evidence to prove to other moms that she was a super-interesting person. Because she loved showing our scrapbooks to other moms. I hope that didn't sound mean. My mom was an interesting mom. I think that working as a receptionist at my dad's dental office made her feel boring. Because when people asked her how she liked that job, she usually said, "I like it when it's not boring."

My mom handed me a plate with baby carrots and pickles and a scoop of hummus.

"Tell me all about your day," she said, sitting down next to me on the couch. "How did things go with the snake?"

This was not the conversation I needed to be having right now. I didn't want to talk about how I totally bombed the photos.

She rubbed my shoulder and took one of my carrots. "Was it super long? How close did you get to it? Did you learn any interesting facts?"

"Mom," I said. "I'll talk about anything but the snake."

My mom smiled at me. "You are your mother's daughter. I knew you'd think it was creepy."

I couldn't believe she was still talking about it.

"Mom," I said in a huffy voice as I stood up from the couch. "I'm gonna eat these in my room."

"Okay," she said. "Sorry. No more snake talk. Sit down. Next subject."

I sat back down.

"How are things going for Venice? Last time I talked to her she was really stressed about her math class."

I couldn't believe how insensitive my mom was being by asking me about Venice, even though she didn't know anything about our drama. So I decided to pretend that we weren't having any drama so I could avoid talking about it.

"Venice loves math," I said. "The reason she was stressed is that Geometry is a combined class and has seventh graders and probably some dumb eighth graders in it."

"Let's not call them dumb," my mom said, stealing another carrot. "You don't even know them."

"You're right," I said. Because I really didn't want to call random people I didn't know from a combined class dumb. I was just in a terrible mood.

"Come on, Perry. Don't be grumpy. Let's keep talking. I saw you've hung up a bunch of pictures in your room. How are things in Yearbook?" she asked.

And that was when I stared at my hummus for a whole minute and started to lose my mind. "Yearbook isn't awesome. My class has a jerk in it and Venice has become friends with him." It turned out that I was terrible at faking not having drama with Venice in front of my mom.

"A jerk?" my mom asked. "You mean a boy?"

I pictured Leo. His awful face was burned into my brain. "He's a jerk!" I said.

"Let's not call anybody a jerk," my mom said. "Middle school is hard. Nobody's perfect all the time. What did he do?"

And when my mom said that, I realized she was never going to be on my side. She was going to make me try to be friends with awful-face Leo.

"It's important to give people second chances," she said.

That was when I snapped and decided to get real with my mom. Because dancing around the topic of hating Leo wasn't helping my situation. "Okay. So Venice has started talking on the phone and hanging out with this jerk. And he's not just a jerk. He's a seventh grader who rides at the back of the bus," I blurted out.

My mother dropped her carrot. "What? She's dating?"

That was when I realized that my situation was even worse than I realized. Venice was on the verge of going out with Leo. "Nobody dates in middle school, Mom. They go out." I could feel myself breathing faster and faster.

"Well, let's talk about it," she said, picking her carrot back up.

"That has cat hair on it now," I said, pointing to her carrot.

My mother picked the hair off and ate it anyway. Which felt a little unsanitary. Because when my food had Mitten Man hair on it, I either washed it off or threw it away or fed it to Mitten Man. *Meow. Meow. Meow.* Mitten Man entered the room and nuzzled my leg.

"Look who missed you today," my mom said, picking him up under his fluffy belly and setting him between us.

"He's just a cat," I said. "I don't think they even understand how time works."

I felt so miserable. And seeing Mitten Man didn't help. I kept thinking about Venice. I wished our conversation hadn't ended that way. Because what I really wanted to do right now was to go into my bedroom and talk to Venice about my day. But I didn't want to talk to the Leo-loving, mean version of Venice I'd talked to ten minutes ago. I wanted to talk to my normal best friend.

"Have you ever met somebody and realized after one

minute that you couldn't stand them?" I asked. I pictured Leo's round face and his stupid long bangs.

"Well, I try to give people more than a minute," she said, sounding like a mother.

It bummed me out that my mom didn't automatically side with me. Because under normal circumstances I tried to give people more than a minute too. But Leo was different. "Do you think Piper is in class?" I asked. I mean, I didn't really have time to waste trying to convince my mom to hate Leo with me. What I really needed was to find out how to survive a toxic triangle.

"Give her a try," my mother said.

I dragged my backpack to my room and flung myself on the bed. The sad thing about calling Piper was that I had to decline an incoming call from Venice twice. I just didn't want to talk to her until I knew what I was supposed to say. And that wouldn't happen until I talked to somebody who knew psychology.

"Piper," I said, when she finally picked up. "You were right." That was how I started a lot of conversations with Piper. Because that was what she liked to hear.

"Holy, holy, holy," Piper said. "You wore that orange hoodie today, didn't you."

I sniffled. "Yes."

"And you had the worst day of your life?" she asked.

I felt myself holding back tears. "I've got a huge problem now," I said.

I heard her take a deep breath. "First, let's just agree that some outfits are totally cursed."

I wasn't even worried about that hoodie anymore. "Okay,

but my huge problem is named Leo." And then I told her very quickly about Leo making all kinds of trouble in my life and asked her for advice.

"He sounds crafty," Piper said.

"Totally," I said. "He literally spends most of class in the craft corner."

"Don't worry too much at this point," Piper said. "It doesn't sound like a toxic triangle. Yet."

And when she said that I felt so relieved I almost started crying. Because the word *toxic* sounded so deadly.

"But you do need to figure out a solid plan," she said. "You can't let a seventh-grade conspiracy theorist derail your friendship."

"A what?" I asked. She made Leo sound like a dangerous criminal.

"A conspiracy theorist is somebody who believes that other people are always involved in secret plots even though they don't have proof."

That definitely sounded like Leo.

"But I don't want you to worry about this," Piper said. "I'll come by tomorrow and help you figure out a plan."

It felt really exhausting that sixth grade required so many plans. I mean, when was I supposed to do my homework?

"It would be better if you came by tonight, because I don't even know if Venice and I are still talking," I explained.

"Yeah, I wish I could," she said, "but Bobby's picking me up in five minutes. He bought us tickets to a monster-truck rally."

This was so depressing on many levels. Couldn't she see that I probably needed her more than Bobby and those monster trucks?

"But what should I do about tomorrow? I feel so weird about everything," I whined. "How should I act around Venice? What about Leo?"

"Relax," Piper said. "Just behave around Venice like you always do. Be nice. As for Leo, go ahead and listen to what he has to say."

"But I don't believe him!" I said.

"That's fine, but you don't need to waste energy engaging him," Piper said.

"I was never planning to engage Leo! That's so gross!" I said.

"Right. I don't know what you think *engage* means, but what I'm saying is that you shouldn't waste energy challenging him. Let him say what he has to say, and then go about your day. Don't let him influence your mood. Okay?"

That sounded reasonable. "I really don't want to be in a fight with Venice. Sixth grade is going to suck without her."

"You and Venice can make up in an instant. It's not like you two are dunzo. Don't worry about that. Go and do your homework. Get a good night's sleep. Have a great day tomorrow. And I'll come home for dinner."

But I'd never heard the word *dunzo*. So I asked a simple question. "What does *dunzo* mean?"

"It's like when a friendship totally dies and the whole thing is wrecked and you never speak again. My friendship with Ally Malloy went dunzo in fifth grade. It was the pits."

I didn't really remember Ally. "Did she move away?"

"Yeah, after we were dunzo her family moved to Wisconsin. But don't worry about that. Do some homework. Go to sleep. Have a great day tomorrow," Piper said.

"But I just declined two of Venice's calls. I think she'll be mad at me if I don't call her back," I explained.

"Maybe you *should* call her back," Piper suggested.

This was terrible advice. "I can't do that. I don't know what to say to her. She told me to shut up! She yelled at me! I absolutely do not want to talk to her right now," I said. "But I also don't want her to get mad at me. And I want everything to feel normal tomorrow."

"Listen," Piper said. "You're making this much harder than it needs to be. Send her a nice text. Throw in some cool emojis. Tell her you've got homework and you'll see her to-morrow."

That sounded like a good idea, because it was the truth and I could do it from a distance.

"You give really good advice," I said.

"Yeah, life should be about finding peace and love," Piper said.

I didn't know if I agreed with that. Because I thought life should also be about having fun and learning stuff and visiting the beach once a year.

As soon as I hung up with Piper, I got out my notebook and started writing practice texts. Because I didn't want to practice on my phone. Because once I had accidentally sent Venice a practice text that I meant to send my cousin Paloma about her sick dog and it put a lot of confusion into our friendship.

Crazy day! Sorry I didn't pick up but I needed some time to think. I'll finish thinking tonight and talk to you tomorrow! 🐼 🖤

That was a bad text because I didn't need to remind her that I didn't pick up.

> Crazy day. I hope you don't hate me for hanging up on you, but it really hurt me when you told me to shut up and then gushed on and on about Leo (who I think might be a secret conspiracy jerk) so let's talk tomorrow. 💜 🐼 👍 🔔

I knew that was terrible even as I was writing it because it mentioned Leo and was longer than a text should be.

> Crazy day. Let's catch up tomorrow. You're great! And my best friend. 💜 🐨

Right before I sent the text, something weird happened. I got a text from a number I didn't recognize.

> **Stranger**
> What are you doing?
>
> Me
> Who is this?
>
> **Stranger**
> Where are the photos?
>
> Me
> WHO IS THIS?
>
> **Stranger**
> Anya. W/Sailor and Sabrina.
> Dying to show them.
>
> Me
> [stared at phone]

Anya

Hellloooo?

Me

Left them at school.

Anya

Bummer! 😕 😕 😮

I waited for my phone to buzz with more texts. But it didn't. I was really surprised that Anya had my number. And I was also surprised by her emojis. Wink. Wink. Kiss. I wasn't sure what it all meant. I thought back to what Piper had said about Anya probably not being evil. Maybe she was right. Maybe she was trying to just build the best yearbook she could. And maybe I shouldn't try to sabotage her with nerd photos. Nerds probably enjoyed not being photographed. Based on what I had seen during the snake-holding photo, they didn't know what to do when the lens was on them anyway. Was it my job to teach them? Did I have time to do that? Should I do what Piper said and wait until next year? Maybe I did need to work with Anya. Could I do that? Should I do that? I sent the text to Venice. Right now, almost anything seemed possible.

5

Final Page Count

Final page count was a big deal in Yearbook. Once it was set, you couldn't change it. Not even by a single page. And it wasn't like you could guess at the number. You had to plot out every single section. And that meant you had to think of everything. Home and away games. Student and teacher portraits. The school play. Clubs. Student council. Spirit Day. Signing pages. Assemblies. Dances. Index pages. And anything else we wanted in this year's book. Today was the day it all got decided.

I was so nervous getting ready for school that I kept going back and forth about what to wear. Obviously, I wasn't going to wear my cursed hoodie. At first, I thought I'd wear my stripy-stitch sweater and twirly skirt. But then I worried I'd be too hot. And it would probably feel awkward to act normal with Venice and potentially sweat at the same time. So then I thought I'd wear denim leggings and a long shirt. But then I worried that Venice was going to wear her denim leggings, because those were her favorite pants. And if I had a crush on a guy who was in my first class, I would probably wear my favorite pants to school. Then I realized I was thinking about my outfit all wrong. I shouldn't be worried about what other people were wearing. I needed to dress defensively. Because today, wearing cute clothes wasn't the point. My clothes needed to send a clear message.

When I walked out to the kitchen to join my parents for breakfast, it was clear that my clothes were sending exactly the message I wanted. People needed to stop messing with me. I was my own person.

"Whoa," my dad said. "That's a dark look."

My mom frowned when she saw me. "Why all the black?"

I'd decided to wear my black footless tights and black skirt. And a dark-gray slouchy T-shirt. I didn't want to look too fierce, so I wore my magenta ballet flats. Also, I pulled my hair back into a ponytail.

"It's how everybody dresses," I explained. "Black is really popular." Because I didn't really want to explain my social situation to my parents.

"Aren't you going to be hot?" my dad asked. "Black clothing absorbs the sun."

I rolled my eyes. "Middle school doesn't have sun. We have fluorescent light."

"You are so cranky," my mom said. "I hope you're in a better mood for dinner and Piper."

I slathered my toast in orange marmalade and took a giant bite. "Oh, I will be. I love her to death." Now that she didn't live in the house anymore and hog the bathroom, I really liked Piper.

"Your mom says you don't want to talk about the snake assembly," my dad said. "Did something happen?"

Wow. My parents really didn't know how to switch topics. I'd stopped talking about this yesterday. But I didn't want to make a huge deal out of it. Now that I wasn't planning on changing the system, what happened yesterday didn't matter as much.

I shrugged. "The snake was huge. I staged a photo. I gave a kid a panic attack. And I missed a big shot of the principal kissing the snake."

"Wow," my dad said. "Principal Hunt did that? I'm impressed."

But his comment made me feel bad that I'd missed that shot.

"You sound so negative," my mom said. "Don't be so hard on yourself. It's really hard to take pictures of moving targets."

She gestured to my dad with her toast. "Phil, tell Perry about the time we went to that animal safari park near San Diego." She rolled her eyes at me. "He couldn't get a picture of anything."

"That's not true!" my dad said. "I got a great shot of the red river hog. But your mother destroyed it."

My dad stood up and brushed crumbs off his lap.

"It was indecent," my mother said.

"I think I've heard enough," I said. Because I had no desire to hear my parents talk about an indecent photo of a red river hog.

"We should've framed that baby and hung it right in the

living room," my dad said. "I think it was the safari park's main hog."

My mother looked like she was about to lose it. Which surprised me, because she was the one who'd destroyed the photo. And no matter how bad the picture, I thought it was sort of a crime to do that.

"The only reason the hog stopped long enough for you to get a photo was because it was taking the world's biggest poop," my mom said. "And that doesn't belong in the living room."

My dad looked legitimately upset by what my mom was saying. It felt weird to be listening to this conversation. "Exactly what that hog was doing by the tree stump is up for debate," my dad said. "It was probably one of the best photos I ever took."

"I think I'm done," I said.

I didn't know what other sixth graders' parents talked about at the breakfast table, but I doubted it was about whether or not a red river hog had pooped in a safari park by a tree stump fifteen years ago. I got up and took my backpack and got out of there.

Walking to school, I practiced what I would say to Venice over and over. I would not get mad about Leo. I would listen to his crazy theories. And I would try to remember as much as I could, word for word, so I could tell Piper and get her expert advice.

Be calm. Be calm. Be calm.

As soon as I walked into Yearbook, I thought I was going to blow it. Because Venice and Leo were hanging out in the craft corner. And it sort of looked like Leo had dressed defensively too, because he had on black pants with shredded knees that felt very hostile to me, and a T-shirt with a shark on it. If I were asked to pick out an outfit that a toxic jerk would wear, I would have selected those exact clothes. I couldn't figure out what Venice saw in him. Bleh. Venice waved as soon as she saw me walk in, and so of course I made my way to the craft corner so I could pretend to be polite and say hello.

"How's it going?" Leo asked me.

It was hard for me to even look at him in that crazy costume of an outfit. And even though every cell inside me wanted to freeze him out and pull Venice into a different corner, I decided to follow Piper's advice and behave normally and listen to what Leo had to say.

"It goes well," I said, taking a seat next to them.

"So is everything okay with us?" Venice asked, scanning my outfit up and down.

Ugh. I thought it was so rotten for Venice to ask me that with Leo sitting right here. How could I be totally honest? How could I tell her how much I didn't like him and his clothes and his face and his hair and his breath when he was sitting two feet away from me?

"Yeah," I said. "I think so."

Venice smiled huge and gave me a hug. And it felt really good to get hugged by Venice.

"So," Leo said. "Do you guys want some friendly advice on how to approach Ms. Kenny?"

When Leo spoke, the sound of his voice made me want to throw up all over his knee-shredded pants. I mean, I really did not want any of his advice. And it really surprised and even hurt me a little that Venice did. Because the way our friendship had worked until this point was that Venice and I agreed about everything. Even which people were nice and which people were annoying. Why was this situation suddenly different?

"That would be great," Venice said. The way she smiled and blinked at Leo made the answer become clear: Venice was into him.

"Here's your biggest problem," Leo said. "Ms. Kenny loves Anya. So it's not going to do you any good to complain about her. You need to come up with a way to get your ideas approved by Ms. Kenny and not Anya."

I didn't think that sounded like too big a problem. We'd just give our ideas directly to the teacher. How hard would that be?

"Anya is probably going to tell you that there's a chain of authority and all the ideas need to go through the editor in chief. But if you follow that, your ideas will never see the light of day."

"Got it," Venice said.

I couldn't believe that the starting bell hadn't rung yet. This was the longest conversation I'd ever had before class. And just when I thought it was over, Leo kept talking.

"Don't be afraid to make waves," Leo said. "That's my best advice. She's counting on you two to be total followers. Today when we finalize the page count, push for sections you want to build, not the ones she's already got in mind." Leo moved his hand through the air like he was drawing waves, because I guess he thought we didn't know what waves were.

"Well, she's in for a surprise!" Venice said. "Right, Perry?"

Did listening to Leo's ideas mean that I had to follow

them? Piper hadn't covered that part with me. I mean, even though I wore my power outfit, I certainly had not come to school today prepared to make waves. I tried to think of what Piper would suggest but it was impossible to do that, because I was sure what she'd learned in her AP psychology class would be much better than anything I could imagine.

Before I could worry about whether I should make waves, the bell rang and it was time to get to our assigned spots. Venice and I made our way to the long table next to Anya. Even seeing Anya made me feel anxious. Because I wasn't sure if she was my friend or my enemy or a combination of the two.

"Cute shoes," Anya said to me as I slid into my chair.

I carefully considered my answer. "They get the job done."

Anya laughed at my response. And I think it was her laughter that helped calm me down. Piper was probably right. She wasn't evil. She was just an eighth grader with a strong vision.

"So today is the day of all days," Ms. Kenny said. "And after today, the next few months are set in stone. No changes. What we decide today we learn to live with for the rest of the year. Got it?"

All sixteen of us said that we got it. I think Leo said it twice.

"Anya turned in an outline last night that includes all our page counts, and I have to admit, I think it's basically perfect," Ms. Kenny said. She fired up her laptop and projected an index onto the screen.

"You are amazing," Sailor called from her stool near the paper cutter.

"I totally agree," Sabrina said. "Woot. Woot."

"It's an improvement over last year," Javier said. "Because you give us three signing pages."

"Yeah," Anya said. "Having one autograph page was ridiculous. Mine got way too crowded."

Venice looked at me like she was hearing the worst news of her life. But I didn't feel that way. Because the index did look pretty solid. She had even included a page for the drama club, which Venice had said Anya hated. So clearly she was somewhat of a team player.

"Is there a reason we're giving the boys' volleyball team two pages?" Leo asked.

Oh, snap. I guess we all weren't going to agree with the index. I waited anxiously to see what Anya would say.

"I gave the boys' volleyball team two pages because Coach Battle is retiring this year and I thought we might want a tribute page. I mean, he's been here for over forty years," Anya said. "And he's won five state championships. Also, I think he's scheduled for kidney surgery."

That really shut Leo up. Because it was basically a totally great answer.

"Are you sure the count for eighth-grader portraits is right?" Eli asked. "We need eight pages? That's two pages more than the seventh graders."

"Based on attendance records we need eight," Anya said. "Unless you don't want to keep the portrait size uniform from grade to grade."

"We absolutely want to keep the size uniform," Ms. Kenny said. "We fiddled with that a few years ago and it was a disaster."

"Nice job, Anya," Luke said. "You've saved us a ton of work."

Luke Willard was one of the copy editors, and it surprised me to hear him say something positive because he'd been so negative about everything. Even when Ms. Kenny brought doughnuts.

"Do we have enough space for all our ads?" Venice asked. "Javier and Leo have been working overtime to sell space."

Wow. She was really grasping for anything to complain about.

"Absolutely," Anya said.

"Yeah, it looks good to me," Javier said.

Like it or hate it, I think we all had to accept the fact that Anya had delivered the perfect index.

"Looks good to me," I said. I glanced at Venice and she was scowling at me hard. Which hurt my feelings. I was just speaking the truth.

"I do see one problem," Ms. Kenny said, moving the arrow on the overhead screen to the last page number in the index.

"What is it?" Anya asked. She sounded so shocked.

"We actually have an additional four pages. We have some money left over from last year. So we get to add another section. Maybe two more."

From what I knew about Yearbook so far, four additional pages was a crazy amount of extra bonus pages. Some of our short sections, Look-Alikes and Field Trip Day, were only two pages each. So this meant potentially two new sections!

"Yes!" Anya cheered. "This is so fantastic. I know just what the yearbook is missing."

"Hold on," Ms. Kenny said. "I run this class like a democracy. I want to give everybody the chance to brainstorm and come up with a plan. Either we'll add a section, or we'll lengthen a preexisting section."

"Add a section!" Anya cheered. "Let's put our own personal stamp on this year."

"Add one," Sailor echoed.

And then something sort of weird happened. The whole class started chanting, "Add one. Add one. Add one." I think Anya started it. And Sailor and Sabrina followed. And then everybody was doing it, except for Venice and Leo. I mean, even I did it. Adding a section seemed pretty harmless.

"Okay," Ms. Kenny said. "That's overwhelmingly decided."

The class erupted in cheers. We were so dorky. Only a dedicated Yearbook staff would care so much about getting four extra pages. Venice and Leo had a different reaction and they frowned at each other. They were such downers. Seriously. It was like the rest of the class was happy, so they had to go form the bummer zone.

"Moving on. You know we can't leave a section untitled. It's just not in my DNA to do that. So by the end of class today, we need to decide what section we'll be adding."

Venice shot her hand up. "I thought you said there might be room for more than one section."

Ms. Kenny turned off the overhead and closed her computer. "If you can think of two sections and the class votes that way, we can absolutely add two sections."

"I really think one amazing section would be the way to go," Anya said, speaking directly to Ms. Kenny.

"Don't convince me," Ms. Kenny said. "Talk it out among yourselves. We'll take a vote at the end of the class. Feel free to look at these." She set out a box of old yearbooks. They looked dusty.

Suddenly, the room became electric. Anya made a bee-line for Luke. Other students headed straight for the box.

"Dude," Javier said. "I think I found my dad in this one."

Venice took the green yearbook emblazoned with gold mountains and our school name and then began to scour over the pages. It was like she thought we were going to have a test on it or something.

"This will really give us a chance to make our mark," I heard Anya say.

Anya continued to work her way around the room while Venice and Leo and I looked at old yearbooks. I was surprised by how much eye makeup some girls wore. I mean, they looked like meerkats.

Finally, Anya made her way to our table. "Okay," Anya said. "So I was thinking it might be fun to have a section for What's Hot. We could totally use all four pages. Think about it. It could really tell the story of our year."

Venice looked mad. And so did her sidekick, Leo. "Don't the popular kids get enough space?" Venice said.

Yikes. She really wasn't holding back.

"I don't look at it that way. I mean, so many students at Rocky Mountain Middle School are on the brink of fame. Reece Fontaine will probably be in the Junior Olympics next year. And Fletcher Zamora has been in three national commercials. And Hannah Jones just won a regional chess championship. I mean, there's a ton of talent in our class."

It seemed reasonable. Those people probably were going to be famous.

"And we can include lots of topical stuff too. We can get the school to vote on stuff they think is hot. Fro-yo flavor. Song. Movie. Book. Dog breed. Pizza place. Ski slope. Dance move. Inspirational quote. This section could be fantastic."

Venice acted like she hadn't even heard what Anya just said. "Our theater club has a ton of talent too. Maybe we could shine a light on them?"

Anya didn't comment and rolled her eyes.

"What do you think, Perry? Do you have any ideas for the additional section?" Venice asked.

I couldn't believe she would put me on the spot like that. I'd sort of already agreed with Anya.

"Um, her idea about hot stuff sounds good," I said, pointing to Anya.

Then I looked at Venice. She wasn't smiling at all.

"Maybe we should get the whole class to talk about this," Leo said.

They were being so difficult. Anya had a great idea and they knew it. Those people Anya mentioned were probably going to be super famous. Plus, things that are hot are topical and they matter to everybody. Why not dedicate part of our yearbook to a few people's super accomplishments and a bunch of hot stuff?

"Do you not like the idea?" Anya asked. "Because it's fine if you don't. But this is a democracy and you and Leo are only two votes, so unless you can get half the class to agree with you, it feels like we're wasting time."

Snap! Anya wasn't fooling around.

"Okay," Leo said loudly. "Venice and I want to bounce a few ideas around about the additional section. Cool?"

At first there was silence. Even though (for some crazy reason I didn't understand) people in the class liked Leo, we weren't used to him trying to lead the class.

"Go for it," Ms. Kenny said. "You've got twenty minutes until the vote. I need to run to the office. Don't miss me too much. Anya, you're in charge while I'm gone."

As soon as the door shut behind Ms. Kenny, the room grew super quiet.

"Venice?" Leo said in an annoyingly sweet voice. "You had an idea."

Everybody turned to look at Venice.

"Maybe we can feature the theater club in a fun way," she said, playing with the drawstring on her pink hoodie. She looked nervous.

I was surprised that Venice had suddenly become obsessed with the theater kids. She didn't even know any of those people very well. In fact, I think she'd referred to a bunch of them as dramatic attention-seekers. I guess she'd focused on them because Leo had said that Anya had said she didn't like them. It was as if Venice and Leo were becoming the same person and they'd only known each other for a month!

"We do club pictures for all the clubs. And theater will have their own," Anya said.

Venice kept flipping through last year's yearbook. The way she turned the pages was beginning to feel aggressive.

"That sounds right," Sailor said, nodding. "A What's Hot section still works for me."

Numerous "yeahs" mumbled through the room.

"Maybe we could do something with the sixth graders?" Venice offered.

Her idea was so vague I almost felt sorry for her.

"Can you be more specific?" Anya asked.

"Um, maybe have captions about, um, what they thought middle school would be like," Venice said.

I looked down at the desk. Total silence followed this suggestion. I could hear the clock in the room next door ticking.

"I have an idea," Leo said. "Have a section that features clubs that haven't been made official at the school. Like botball robotics club or the Ultimate Frisbee club or Crafts for a Cause. Those guys made wallets out of duct tape that they sold for Alzheimer's patients," Leo said.

I watched his hands to see if he'd make any lame gestures to sell his suggestion. He didn't.

"Isn't botball robotics planning to build a robot that can pick up a Nerf football *and* do a backflip?" Venice added. "I heard that."

Weird. Where was Venice getting her botball information? I hadn't heard that. I didn't even know our school had that club.

"Yeah," Anya said, trying to sound polite. "We've got clubs covered."

"But these are unofficial clubs," Leo pressed. "And unofficial clubs weren't covered at all last year."

"Crafts for a Cause is a great suggestion," Venice added.

Because apparently her favorite activity in the world was agreeing with Leo.

"Or maybe you could feature fall harvest," Leo said, clearly ignoring that his ideas were terrible and unwelcome.

"How would we feature fall harvest?" Anya said, finally sounding as annoyed as I felt. "It's a nonschool activity that involves heavy machinery."

"Let's not shoot down any ideas. This is a democracy," Venice reminded us.

This was really too much. Watching my friend defend Leo's barfy ideas was driving me nuts. I needed to remember all this to report back to Piper.

"You could visit farms where kids are helping out with harvest. Hayes Ellsworth helps his grandpa put up the biggest grain field in the county. And Sasha York helps with her family's potato harvest. Their sorting facilities are huge. I think one of the biggest in the state," Leo said.

Anya's mouth had fallen open. She couldn't believe Leo's nerve or terrible ideas, and neither could I.

But before Anya could say anything, Leo's number-one fan leaped to agree with him. "I bet those pictures would be stunning."

"Sorry to be negative, but Future Farmers of America gets a quarter page already. Last year they squandered it on a prize pig and a group photo in front of a spud cellar. They're not getting their own section. They're a club and they're going to be treated like a club. That's it."

"But if you consider the regional relevance—" Leo said, before Anya cut him off.

"Farm photography has zero to do with middle school. You should stick to coming up with good ideas on the business side," Anya said. "That's where you belong."

A chorus of "oohs" floated through the room.

Ms. Kenny swung open the door. "I could hear you guys halfway down the hall," she said. "It's nice to know you all care about the additional section so much, but let's try to respect everybody and their ideas. This really is a democracy. We vote in ten minutes."

And I didn't think it was too rude to tell Leo any of that, but he certainly looked stung by Anya's words as he walked off.

"Wow," Anya said as she scribbled on her legal pad. "Some people cannot take a hint."

"Oh, he took it," I added, sounding a little snarky.

Anya smiled at my comment and drew an exclamation point next to her idea about adding a section for What's Hot. Then I watched as Leo grabbed the hall pass and left the room. I wondered if he was going to go to the boys' bathroom and cry. I wondered if he was crushed that his rotten student-harvest idea got rejected. I mean, his unofficial club suggestion made sense, but I really didn't feel I could support it, seeing as how I couldn't stand Leo.

"I need to use the bathroom," Venice said, popping up.

"The hall pass is taken," I said. Because it was. Plus, I couldn't stand the idea of Venice running off to go comfort Leo.

"Can't I just use a staff lanyard?" Venice asked.

"Absolutely," Ms. Kenny said. "If nature's calling."

I watched as a flustered Venice raced after Leo. It was pretty sickening. I mean, I could understand Venice racing after me. But as far as I was concerned, Leo was still basically a stranger.

"That was intense," Anya said.

I nodded. It suddenly felt awkward to be at the table alone with Anya. I wasn't sure what we should talk about.

"Okay," Anya said. "I normally wouldn't call attention to this, but I'm going to help you fix your number-one problem right now."

I couldn't believe that Anya knew I had a number-one problem.

"Let's go get some duct tape," she said, making her way to the craft corner.

I wasn't sure how duct tape could solve my problem. I mean, it would be wrong to duct-tape Leo's mouth shut. Did Anya think I was a barbarian? Because I wasn't. *Was I?*

I watched in disbelief as Anya grabbed two rolls of duct tape and started ripping off short pieces. "This should do it," she said, handing me a strip of tape.

"Um," I said. Because I really couldn't picture what I was supposed to do with it. Leo was still in the bathroom. Did she think we were going to go in there to tape him? Because entering the boys' bathroom to launch a tape assault was definitely outside my comfort zone, no matter how much I disliked a person.

Then Anya did something that caught me off guard. She wrapped the tape around her own hand, sticky side out, and began patting me all over.

"How many cats do you own?" she asked. "Five?"

"Just Mitten Man," I said, turning slightly so Anya could reach my backside.

"He's a total shedder," she added, grabbing a fresh piece of tape and continuing her pat job. "Didn't you notice you were covered in cat hair before you left the house? I mean, black is very unforgiving. It shows everything."

I pressed my own piece of tape to an obvious hair patch near my knee. "I guess I was in a hurry." But really, I couldn't believe my parents hadn't said something. I mean, so far the tape had pulled off what looked like a pound of cat fur.

"This is really nice of you," I said, focusing on removing some hair from my stomach area.

"It's nothing," Anya said. "I like you."

And seriously, when she said that, my skin goose-pimpled, because deep down, even though I struggled with Anya's ego and bossiness, I admired her and her talent. And deep down I think I really wanted her to like me, too. So while things weren't going so hot with Venice in Yearbook today, at least things were going well with Anya.

"Okay," Anya said. "What do you bet that Venice and Leo are in the hallway talking right now?"

It was like Anya was reading my mind. Because that was exactly what I was thinking. "Well, I doubt they're both in the boys' bathroom."

Anya lightly swatted the back of my thighs with her taped hand and laughed.

"I'm surprised she likes him," Anya said. "I don't really picture them together."

Again, it was like Anya was literally inside my brain, thinking what I thought and feeling what I felt.

"I totally agree," I said, wadding up my tape, because even

if I still had some cat hair on me, I really didn't care anymore. I wanted to focus on talking to Anya.

"Prediction," Anya said, glancing at the door. "We're going to agree on a lot this year. And we're going to make the most awesome yearbook ever."

I smiled when she said this. And I didn't worry about where Venice fit into this statement. Because I was really irritated by how she was acting.

"Can you be discreet?" Anya asked, glancing at the door again.

Nobody had ever asked me this before. It felt like there was really only one answer. "I think so," I said.

"I'm being serious. You can't tell Venice we're having this conversation," Anya said.

It felt like a total betrayal of my friendship to agree to this. And part of me really wanted to make a run for it and abandon the craft corner. Because I didn't want to betray Venice. But another part of me, the logical part, knew that bolting from the craft corner would only create a different problem. I really didn't understand how I'd gotten here. I never would've predicted that in sixth grade Venice would sneak out of class to hang out with a jerk while an eighth grader defurred me in the craft corner. I thought sixth grade was going to be about feeling like I was almost in high school, and learning crazy math formulas, and studying dramatic novels, and possibly doing push-ups while being timed. I wasn't expecting this. I mean, I was really surprised when I heard myself saying, "You can count on me. I won't tell Venice."

"I need you to keep an eye on Leo," Anya said.

Ugh. This was terrible news. He was the last person in the world I wanted to have to look for on purpose.

"Are you sure?" I asked.

"Okay," Anya said, releasing an exasperated breath. "I wasn't planning on showing this to anybody, but I feel like I don't have a choice."

Anya led me to the back of the room and pulled me into a big closet filled with rows of shelves that towered over us. I saw stacks of old yearbooks, extra glue bottles, blue plastic bins, wicker baskets, and several boxes labeled KEEP ME. She led me to the back wall and grabbed a file. "You can't tell anybody I'm showing you these," she said. "It's completely unethical."

"Right," I said. I was pretty sure that I'd never done anything unethical in a closet before, so this situation felt very serious. I was so anxious to see what was inside that folder I partially closed my eyes.

"Look," she said. "Tell me these aren't the worst."

I opened my eyes and saw a stack of poorly taken photos. There was an enormous swan that was cropped so badly it was missing half its beak. And a person who was sitting outside at what looked like a picnic table, but it was pretty blurry. And a river and possibly a raft filled with people that had terrible shadows.

"What kind of animal is that?" I asked, pointing to a huge beast at the top corner of the raft picture.

"That's either a mosquito or a crane fly," Anya explained. "Apparently, it was on the lens."

"Yeah," I said. "These are pretty bad. Who took them?"

And her response totally blew me away.

"These are Leo's photos. He applied for a position as junior photographer last year and didn't get it. I gave the spot to you and Venice. And now he's out to get me," Anya said.

This all made so much sense. Leo was jealous of me. That was why he was trying to create a toxic triangle with me and Venice. He'd probably been plotting this all summer. He was a bigger jerk than I had realized. Because it was one thing to be jealous of me. But it was a whole other issue to use my best friend to launch a sneak attack and try to ruin my spot in Yearbook. She was going to die when I told her, and also possibly hate Leo more than I did.

"Remember," Anya said. "You promised not to tell anybody."

"Are you sure?" I asked. "Because Venice should probably know that Leo is using her."

"No," Anya said, grabbing my arm and tugging me a little closer to her. "We can't tell anybody I showed you these. Only Ms. Kenny and her editor in chief are allowed to review application materials. It's strict Yearbook policy."

A part of me didn't totally agree with Anya. Because it wasn't like I had asked her to violate Yearbook policy. She had done that on her own. But another part of me felt I was obligated to honor my word. This was a terrible dilemma. Because I really felt like the whole school should know immediately that Leo Banks was a creep and a user who took awful photos.

"Here's the plan," Anya said, sliding Leo's photos back into their folder. "First, you need to act like none of this happened. Second, stick close to Le—"

I interrupted her. "I don't think that second thing should be part of the plan."

"Perry," Anya said, grabbing on to both my shoulders. "In life it's important to keep your friends close and your enemies closer."

"But—" I tried to launch an argument about avoiding your enemies at school.

"If we don't keep him under close watch, he's going to sabotage us. I can feel it in my gut." Anya released her grip on me and pointed to her stomach. "Trust me."

I looked at Anya's stomach. I'd never trusted another person's gut before. Should I start now? Would Venice do this? I wasn't sure she would. And it felt like I should try to be as good a friend to her as she was to me.

"I bet he's telling Venice right now that she should submit all her ideas to Ms. Kenny and bypass me. He's wicked invested in undermining my authority."

That sounded exactly like the advice Leo had already given us. Anya's gut was really good.

Leo was trying to ruin everything. "Why is he so evil?" I asked Anya. I'd never really met a villain before.

"Because I rejected him. And to get back at me, he wants our photos to suck. You heard his ideas. He wants us to travel to farms and photograph potato-sorting equipment."

Everything Anya said was really starting to sink in. "How close do I need to stick?" I asked. I mean, she didn't expect me to eat lunch with him, did she?

"Eat lunch with him if you can. That's when you'll learn the most."

I couldn't even imagine eating lunch with Leo and not puking.

"Venice wants to have him give us advice over the phone," I said. "So I guess I should do that, too."

Anya looked hurt that Leo and Venice had already been talking about Yearbook.

"He's a saboteur. Take as many three-way calls as you can with him. And then call me and report anything I should know."

"So now I'm a spy?" I asked. Because it was one thing to stick close to Leo, but it was a whole different ball game to put him on blast to Anya for everything I saw.

"You're my ally," Anya said. "And next to me you're the most important member of Yearbook."

This was so much pressure. But I kind of liked it.

"I can't let Leo ruin the yearbook," Anya said. "And neither can you. You owe it to our school."

As I stared at a dusty box of dry-erase markers and a broken pencil sharpener, a part of me felt Anya should just take all this information to Ms. Kenny and get Leo kicked out of class, because it was serious stuff. But then I worried that Venice would get kicked out of class too, because she was basically working with Leo to destroy our yearbook even though she didn't know that was what she was doing. My mind couldn't wrap itself around a problem of this size.

"Can I count on you?" Anya asked.

Back in the classroom, I could hear Venice calling my name. I felt so anxious about seeing her now that I'd agreed to keep secrets from her.

"You can count on me," I said. Piper was going to die when I gave her this crazy update. Good thing I had a sister with a background in psychology.

"You won't regret it," Anya said. Then she gave me a quick hug. "Let's get in there and vote for a What's Hot section. Plus, I need you to write some captions."

And so I hurried back into the classroom and sat down next to Venice. It was amazing how different things felt for me from a day ago. Was my life perfect? No. Was Yearbook perfect? Not even close. But sometimes in life you've got to accept what you cannot change.

6

Shopping for Sixth-Grade Portraits

Walking home from school, I got the worst text ever.

> **Piper**
> Bobby's hurt. No dinner tonight.
> SORRY!! 😞

I was sort of stunned that Piper had sent me such a short and terrible text. Even her emoji didn't feel apologetic enough. She should've sent me a hundred crying faces. I wrote her back as fast as I could, because I thought maybe I could change her mind.

> **Me**
> Is he in the hospital? 💀

> **Piper**
> No. His back is out. Needs me to rub Tiger Balm on it and walk his dog. 🐾 🐶 🔔

It bugged me to see that tongue. Because nothing about what was happening was funny.

Me

> When you cancel on me you make my life feel worse.
> SO MUCH IS HAPPENING!!! 💀💀💀💀💀

I stared at my phone, hoping she'd text me an apology and cancel on Bobby and come to dinner.

Piper

> Dinner this weekend. Can't wait for an update.
> I'll bring falafel. Namaste!

I read the texts again to make sure Piper was really canceling on me to feed a dog and rub some balm. She was. Then I just stopped moving and stared at the sidewalk. This meant I was going to have to endure the Venice-and-Leo situation without any help until the weekend. I wasn't sure I could do that. I mean, in addition to Yearbook, Venice and I also had English, Science, and Idaho History together. And it was really hard to act like everything was normal. Today when Ms. Stott made us create a food chain and explain the difference between a producer, a consumer, and a decomposer, and I drew grass, a rabbit, and mold, it took a ton of restraint for me not to label my mold Leo. Because I wasn't an idiot. If Leo started hanging out with Venice, there would be less time for me. And that wasn't how my friendship with Venice worked. We both gave each other all our time. We were total besties.

Before Venice and I started sixth grade, we'd had the most amazing summer ever. I'd traveled with her family to Yellowstone National Park, where we ate s'mores twice a day and watched Old Faithful erupt. Plus, in addition to viewing the geysers, I'd also watched Victor do push-ups in the campground dirt, and that was pretty thrilling, because just like Anya had pointed out when she saw his photo, Victor was hot. And Venice had traveled with my family on a trip to Lake Powell, where we ate apple fritters for breakfast and rode a water weenie every afternoon. Even though nobody told us to, we took turns riding in the last and bumpiest position on the weenie so neither one of our butts would get sore. We looked out for each other like sisters, even when nobody was paying attention. My life felt so far away from those moments with Venice. My world felt like it was shifting, and I didn't feel ready to end up in a new place.

At the sight of a car swerving toward me and honking, I jumped off the sidewalk and fell onto a random lawn. Then I realized the crazy driver was my mom and she was only pulling up alongside me.

"Didn't mean to scare you," she said, popping open the passenger-door lock.

Luckily, I was wearing all black, so I didn't get any visible grass stains.

"Aren't you hot?" my mom asked.

And even though I felt pretty hot, I didn't want to admit that. Because it seemed like my mom was criticizing my outfit. It was like she just couldn't accept that some days, even when the sun was out, a person needed to wear all black. I wished she could trust me more. I wished she could understand that I had an agenda that required power outfits.

"Aren't you supposed to be at work?" I asked. Because it seemed like leaving my dad's office early two days in a row was a bad idea. I mean, I knew he wouldn't fire her. But she always talked about all the data she input and folders she filed. Who was doing that now?

"Maryann, the new office assistant, inputs data like a beast," my mom explained. "Looks like I might be getting a lot of afternoons off." She smiled really huge when she said this.

"Wow," I said. Because I didn't even know my dad had hired a new office assistant, let alone that she was a beast.

"Hop in," she said. "Help me run some errands."

"Um," I said. Because eating muffins and watching television sounded better.

"Come on," she said. "I need to go to the mall. Maybe we can get you a new shirt for your sixth-grade portrait."

I didn't want to turn down a new shirt. I really loved getting new clothes, especially from the mall. I climbed into the car and before I could even buckle my seat belt, my phone rang.

"That sounds like Venice," my mom said, turning off the radio.

"Hello," I said. I probably should have told Venice that I was in the car with my mom. But Venice didn't give me time to work that into the conversation naturally.

"So I have an idea," Venice gushed. "And Leo thinks it's pretty good."

I pictured the two of them riding the bus home together. Talking. Laughing. Sharing ideas. How had he wormed his way into my life so quickly? He really was a decomposer.

"Ask Venice if she wants us to pick her up," my mom said. "I can make a U-turn right here."

I hated it when my mom made U-turns, because sometimes other drivers honked at us. I shook my head. "Let's just go to the mall."

"What are you talking about? I can't go to the mall," Venice said. "I'm still on the bus."

"I actually wasn't talking to you," I said.

"Okay," Venice said. "Anyway, here's my idea."

It really hurt my feelings that Venice didn't ask me who I was talking to if I wasn't talking to her. Did she just automatically assume it was my mom? She should have assumed it might have been a new friend I was considering replacing her with. Because at the rate we were going, that was definitely a possibility.

"Here it is. We need to find our own person to include for What's Hot," Venice said. "We'll pick an awesome sixth grader who's doing amazing things. And not some super-popular, wears-all-the-right-clothes sixth grader. We'll pick one who deserves it."

That seemed like it was in line with what Anya wanted anyway. So that was okay.

"Do you mind if I stop by the bank first?" my mom asked.

I nodded and stuck a finger in my nonphone ear. Didn't my mother understand that I needed to concentrate?

"Okay," I said. "I bet Anya will go for that." I was sort of happy that Venice had come up with a decent idea, even if she had shared it with Leo first.

"Ugh," Venice said. "Stop kissing up to Anya. Who cares what Miss Bossy McBoss-Boss-Pants wants?"

"Whoa," I said. Because when did we start calling Anya Miss Bossy McBoss-Boss-Pants? I wasn't on board with that. And before I could object to this new nickname for Anya, I heard Leo laughing in the background.

"That's a good one," Leo said.

My mother steered the car underneath the shade of a giant pine tree. Then she rolled down all the car windows. "I'll be right back, okay?" she said, hopping out of the car.

"Yeah," I said.

"I'm so relieved to hear you agree with me," Venice said. "I was actually worried that you and Anya were becoming friends or something."

"Well—" I said, but then Venice cut me off.

"The best thing about this plan is we'll pick somebody who needs to be recognized. And that way we can make the stupid new section fair. It won't just be about Anya's friends."

I was pretty sure Anya wasn't going to just include her friends in What's Hot. She had a lot of friends. And one of the topics was fro-yo. Anya wasn't friends with fro-yo.

"Who were you thinking?" I asked.

"I'm not sure. I thought you and I could figure it out together," she said. "Pick somebody really cool and deserving."

That sounded like a fun idea. I liked hanging out with Venice. And if we could decide on our What's Hot ideas together, then Leo wouldn't influence her thinking. He could stick to the business side, where he was actually wanted. And over time, when Anya felt comfortable with it, I could reveal to Venice that Leo-the-saboteur had been using her. And while that might hurt when she first learned about it, in the end that news would help everything return to normal. Because wasn't it better to be told you had a jerk in your life rather than misunderstand what was happening and wrongfully think the jerk was your friend?

"Bye, Leo," I heard Venice say in a distracted way. "Text me later."

It was really hard for me to hear Venice say that. Because I didn't like picturing her texting Leo. I wanted to picture her texting me.

"So maybe you should come over this weekend?" I asked.

But nobody said anything.

"Hello?" I said. Had Venice hung up on me? Were we finished talking? I stared at my phone. Normally we said goodbye. Were we not going to do that anymore? Because that seemed rude.

That was when I got a call I wasn't expecting. Anya!

"Hello?" I said, sounding a little nervous.

"Is this a bad time?" she asked.

To be totally honest, it was sort of a bad time, because I was really disappointed that my best friend had decided hanging up on me and not saying goodbye was going to be the new way we said goodbye, but I figured that wasn't what Anya wanted to hear about.

"It's a good time," I said. I didn't think I should share all my feelings with her right now.

"So do you have any news?" Anya asked.

"Um," I said. "I'm in a parking lot waiting for my mom."

"I mean, did anything happen with Leo today?" she asked.

I thought I was supposed to report to her in Yearbook. I didn't know I was supposed to be checking in with her in the afternoons, too.

"I don't have any classes with Leo. I only see him in Yearbook," I explained.

"He's up to something," she said.

"I think he's still on the bus," I said.

"Daphne Tanner told me that Leo and Venice are coming up with a list of three crazy plans," she said.

"I think they only have one plan," I said.

"What do you mean? You know about their plans and you're not telling me?" she said.

"I just found out," I said. "I haven't even been home yet. My mom swerved and picked me up."

"Okay," Anya said. "Here's the thing. You need to keep me in the loop. I can't get blindsided."

She sounded really paranoid.

"What's the plan?" she demanded. "Tell me exactly what he said."

"Well, I only heard him in the background. Venice did all the talking," I explained.

"I knew it," Anya said. "They're both saboteurs, aren't they?"

It definitely felt like a bad idea to label Venice a saboteur, so I tried to label her something else.

"She's definitely not a saboteur. She really likes you. She said a whole bunch of nice stuff today about your pants," I lied. But really it was only a partial lie. Because Venice *had* mentioned Anya and pants today. Just not in a flattering way.

"I don't totally buy that, but whatever. Tell me about their slimy plan," Anya said.

"Well, Venice wants to pick out a sixth grader to include in the What's Hot section," I said, conveniently leaving out that I was going to help find the person.

"That's bogus," Anya said.

"I don't know," I said. "It seems like a good idea. I mean, the sixth graders matter too."

"Oh yeah," Anya said, sounding really sympathetic. "I agree. But I'm saying that plan is bogus. I know Leo. He's craftier than this."

"You think that Venice called me and told me a fake plan?"

"She might not know it's a fake plan, but I'm pretty sure it's a fake plan."

My mom startled me when she opened her door. "Sorry that took so long," she said, climbing back inside the car. "The person in front of me couldn't remember his PIN."

I nodded.

"Tell Venice that if she still wants to come with us, it's easy for me to swing by," my mom said, pulling out of her stall and aiming the car toward the mall.

I shook my head and whispered to her, "I'm talking to Anya now."

"Who's with you?" Anya asked. She sounded even more paranoid than she had the first time she'd sounded paranoid.

"I'm with my mom," I said.

"Oh," she said, sounding instantly pleasant. "Put me on speaker so I can say hello."

I glanced over at my mom. I didn't really want to do that. "She's driving," I said.

"It'll be quick," Anya said.

I looked at my mom again. "Can I put my phone on speaker so Anya can say hello to you?"

No friend in the history of people I'd been friends with had ever made this request and so it seemed totally weird to me and oddly like a power move.

"Absolutely," my mom said.

"Hi, Mrs. Hall," Anya gushed. "I'm the editor in chief for the yearbook. I just want you to know that I adore having Perry on our team. She's so talented. And such a hard worker."

My mother beamed as she took a right turn into the Grand Teton Mall.

"Thank you, Anya," my mother said. "I'm a big fan of Perry's as well."

This was so embarrassing. I didn't need my mom to tell people she was my fan. I was pretty sure people already knew that. "We're at the mall now," I said. "Gotta go!"

And I meant to just take the phone off speaker and say goodbye to Anya like a civilized person. But I accidentally hung up.

"That was a little rude," my mother said, applying a fresh coat of lipstick.

"Yeah," I said. Because I sort of agreed with her.

I climbed out of the car and saw that Anya was texting me. At first I was worried that it would be an angry text for hanging up on her. But it wasn't. She was just acting paranoid again.

Anya

Stay on him. I'm trying to prevent an ambush.

Luckily, I was pretty good at texting and walking.

Me

Venice doesn't ambush.

Anya

I'm worried about her boyfriend.

Me

Don't call him that!!!!!!!!!!!!!!!!

"Perry, I brought you shopping," my mom said, pointing toward my favorite store, Scoop. "Can you text later?"

"Totally," I said. "Just let me say goodbye."

Me

At mall. Must go.

Anya

OK. Me too. At gym. With Victor. Bye!

I stared at that last text. Victor? Did she mean Venice's brother? He worked as a trainer at the gym. Did Anya train? Why hadn't she mentioned that she knew Victor? Then I thought maybe there was a second Victor. Idaho Falls felt big enough to have two Victors with muscles.

"Why does it look like you're studying your phone?" my mom asked.

And even though I was tempted to ask her how many Victors with muscles she knew, and conduct an unofficial poll about our city's buff Victor population, instead I turned off my phone and hooked my arm around her waist.

"Can we try a different store?" I said. Because while I loved every single thing that Scoop sold, even their seed-bead hair ties, I was pretty sure I needed to buy more than a shirt for my sixth-grade portrait. I needed to buy another power outfit.

"Sure," my mom said. "Lead me there."

I led my mother to the newest store in the mall, Dark Chalk. To make the store look mysterious, black paper covered the glass panel next to the entrance. My mom paused and nervously tried to look inside.

"What's that smell?" she asked.

I wasn't sure. It reminded me of something I'd smelled in our rental car two years ago when we visited Canada. "Probably men's cologne," I said, shrugging.

Walking into Dark Chalk sort of intimidated me. Because the first thing we saw was an authentic Yugoslavian army dress jacket made out of communist-socialist Soviet-era khaki wool.

I knew that about the jacket because my mom read the tag and then said, "This just doesn't feel like your kind of store, Perry."

"Let's not judge it too fast," I said. I tried on an Austrian army cadet cap and looked in the mirror. It was not a good look for me.

"Aren't hats banned at your school?" my mom asked, grimacing at my cadet cap.

"Technically," I said. "But every year they have Crazy Hat Day and so you can put anything you want on your head and come to school."

My mother looked a little anxious to learn this. But she shouldn't have been. I wasn't about to waste my shopping chance on a cap.

"I think what I really want is a shirt," I said.

My mom and I wandered to an area stacked with T-shirts.

"Perry, I refuse to buy you anything with Stalin's profile on it," she said, holding up a black-and-red T-shirt with the outline of a guy's face I didn't recognize.

"That's fair," I said. Because I was surprised my mom would think I'd even wear that terrible shirt.

My mom looked really disgusted when she found that same image on toddler-sized pajamas. I hoped that she wasn't disgusted with me. Because I didn't plan to buy anything super offensive or for babies in this store.

"Do you need any help?" a store clerk asked. He was dressed in a blue military jacket with patches. I wished he wore a tag so I would know which country he was representing.

My mother shook her head pretty aggressively. "No."

I really didn't want my mom to have a meltdown in Dark Chalk. But I also really wanted to find something that would make me look tough and also conceal cat hair. Plus, I thought it would be a good message to send to Venice that I now went clothes shopping without her. Because basically I'd never done that. And she needed to learn that if she was going to start wasting time on Leo, I was going to start wasting time at Dark Chalk buying new clothes without her.

"Maybe I should get pants," I said, pointing to the back wall, which was covered in them. "They look interesting."

My mom followed me there and continued to look unhappy. "They're all camouflage. They look like something soldiers wear. Is that the only thing this store sells?"

I shrugged. Because it was my first time here. So I didn't know how often they rotated merchandise or tweaked their apparel themes. Plus, considering the job ahead of me, dressing like a soldier didn't seem like a totally bad thing. I found a pair of camouflage leggings made up of multiple shades of green and gray. I held them up to me. Not only would I look tough wearing them, I thought they'd probably conceal cat hair. And if I ever needed to hide in a tree, I bet they'd work for that too.

"You'd wear those to school?" my mom asked, looking alarmed. "With what?"

I pressed my future leggings against my thighs so I could imagine exactly what they'd look like on me. "Probably my tunics," I said. But I really thought I could wear these with almost all my shirts. I could also wear them underneath most of my skirts.

"Fine," my mother said, yanking the leggings away from me. Then she balled them up and walked them over to the cash register.

"This is the only thing I'm buying you in this store," my mother said.

I glanced at a stack of Swiss army dungarees that looked like something a weird cartoon character would wear.

"Okay," I said.

After the clerk rang up the leggings, my mother huffily handed me the bag. "FYI, they have a zero return policy here, so I hope you don't change your mind."

It didn't surprise me that Dark Chalk had that kind of policy, because I bet a lot of people regretted their purchases here.

"Don't worry. I'm truly in love with these," I said. I might not have learned much in middle school yet, but I had learned that if you want to make somebody feel good in an instant, exaggerating was a good strategy.

"Perry!" a voice called as I walked into the mall's main hallway.

My mom and I both looked. It was Reece Fontaine. And she was hanging out with Hannah Jones and Fletcher Zamora. They looked exactly how you'd expect popular kids to look at the mall. Trendy, relaxed, and attractive.

"You shop there?" Fletcher asked. "I've never seen anybody shop there."

My mother looked at me like she felt sorry for me. But I didn't feel sorry for me. I hadn't bought anything weird or lame there. Leggings were always a safe purchase.

"Don't pick on her," Reece said. "Is this your mom?"

My mother smiled and said, "Hi, I'm Perry's mom." And I sort of wished my mom could have figured out a way to slink off and let me talk to kids from my school by myself.

"See you later," I said, walking off to avoid anything embarrassing happening.

"Wait," Reece said. "I want to thank you."

"You do?" I asked.

"Yeah," Reece said. "I love the photos you guys took of me at the vending machine."

"Yeah," I said. "Anya took those."

"I know," she said. "But Anya said you cropped it and came up with the caption. I liked it."

I'd only come up with a couple of captions for the photo of Reece doing a backflip next to the vending machine with a bag of M&M's in her mouth. But Anya had really liked them.

REECE FONTAINE SCORES AGAIN.

REECE FONTAINE STICKS THE LANDING.

But it felt great to get this positive feedback.

"I'm glad you like it," I said.

"Our yearbook is going to be so amazing," Hannah said.

"Will you caption my photo too?" Fletcher asked.

But we hadn't even taken any pictures of Fletcher yet. It sort of bothered me that he already knew he was going to be included in a section. But it also flattered me that he thought I did good captions.

"Venice and Anya write good captions too," I said.

But then Fletcher smiled at me and it made my stomach feel wobbly.

"But yours are clev-ah," he said.

Reece flipped her hair and laughed. "Anya showed us a bunch of yours from last week. We loved your stuff the most."

"Wow," I said. Because I thought that kind of stuff stayed in the Yearbook room. I didn't know Anya was showing them to people.

"We're headed to the movies," Reece said. "Find us at lunch."

And she didn't say it in a bossy way. Or a stuck-up way. She said it in a way that made me think she really wanted me to find her tomorrow at lunch.

"You're really blossoming," my mother said, reaching her arm around me.

But I pushed away. Because my mom should have known better than to try to hug me in the mall right after we talked to popular eighth graders.

"Yearbook is really changing things for me," I said. But I didn't elaborate beyond that. Because I was pretty sure my mom would object to me keeping secrets from Venice. But to be honest, I didn't feel totally terrible about that arrangement. Because I knew that in the end good would triumph over awfulness. And I also knew that I wasn't awful. Leo was. I walked down the mall corridor fully aware that I had to keep Leo close until I was triumphant. And based on his terrible ideas so far, I figured that wouldn't take me long at all.

7

Tactical Lunches

Was my life working? I wasn't sure.

My classes were working. I'd come up with a bunch more snappy captions in Yearbook. And in PE, Ms. Pitman had told the whole class that I was the best listener during the partner walk/jog-and-talk. (But really I'd just let Poppy Lansing complain about her life—mostly her stepdad and little brother—while I thought about my own problems as we hoofed it around the track.) And I'd kept up on all my Depression-era reading for English. Science was science, and we'd mostly been studying the anatomy of starfish. (They aren't actually fish and they have tube feet.) Idaho History had gotten somewhat interesting because Mr. Falconer had shown us pictures he'd taken at the Idaho Historical Museum, which included a two-headed calf named Déjà Moo. And Math had gotten fun because Mr. Pickering was assigning worksheets filled with math games, so I was getting As on everything.

Lunch was the place where I questioned everything. Lunch was the place where I caught myself glancing at other tables, looking for friends I'd had before Venice. Kendra Dover, a pretty terrible trumpeter, sat with the kids from band. She always had to stop herself from laughing before she drank her milk. And Tula Mori. She ran track like a demon and hung out with other tough athletes. Even though she brought a lunch that usually had depressing food in it like hard-boiled eggs and lettuce leaves, she seemed happy too. Why wasn't I better friends with them? It was like we drifted apart and became totally different people.

I mean, did that have to happen? I still liked them. Wasn't it possible they still liked me? Seriously. Did they ever think about me? Tula was the first person I ever texted. And for her eighth birthday I gave her a turtle bank. Did she still have it? Would it be totally weird to bring it up? How would it feel if I suddenly joined her table?

"Earth to Perry," Venice said, snapping her fingers.

And that comment really brought me back to my terrible reality. I ate lunch with Venice and Leo. Just the three of us. We sat together at a small round table by the window. There was space for a person or two to join us. There was totally room for Javier and Luke and Eli. But nobody ever did join us. Probably because we looked miserable. Okay. Maybe Leo and Venice didn't look miserable. But I looked miserable enough for everybody.

"Anybody want fresh apple pie?" Leo asked, holding out a plastic box filled with three amazing-looking pieces of pie.

I took a slice and tried to smile. Ever since we'd started eating lunch with him, he'd been trying to manipulate me into liking him by bringing my favorite desserts. I didn't know how he knew exactly what I liked, but he did. Moon pies. Butterscotch cookies. Banana walnut bread. It was totally delicious and it bugged me beyond belief. Because it was really hard for me to strongly dislike somebody who kept being super nice to me, even when I knew it was all for show.

"It feels like we're wasting time," Leo said. "We need to pick a person and commit."

This was what they'd been saying all week. Maybe it was because we were all so different. Or maybe we wanted different things. Or maybe it was because I wasn't trying very hard, but we'd made zero progress when it came to naming a sixth grader for the What's Hot section. Nobody in the sixth-grade class was as accomplished or as popular or as hot as the people Anya had already chosen from the upperclassmen.

I ate my pie and looked concerned. But deep down I was furious with him for trying to get Venice mixed up in his weird plan. Tragically, for me and Anya, I hadn't gotten any closer to figuring out if this was the real plan or if there were other additional terrible plans. I just couldn't figure out a way to ask Leo, "Hey, are you lying to my face about your plan? And do you have secret additional, barfier plans?"

"Even though Anya says she's on board with adding a sixth grader for What's Hot," Leo said, "I'm pretty sure she'll cut out whoever we pick at the last minute if the person doesn't meet her standards."

Venice nodded. "She's like that. We need to pick somebody uncuttable."

Why was Leo even helping us find anybody? He was the advertising manager and a seventh grader. And how did Venice know what Anya was like? Did she spend every afternoon talking to her and reporting on possible plans of sabotage from her fellow classmates? No. That was me. I was the one who knew Anya. And she wasn't as bad as these two thought she was. She just had superhigh standards when it came to what was hot.

"Maybe we're thinking about this wrong," Leo said.

I just kept fake-nodding at him. Because it was way easier for me to do that than join the conversation.

"What do you think?" Venice asked me.

I set down my pie and cleared my throat. "There's got to be a worthy sixth grader," I offered. And that wasn't even a lie. That was something I believed.

"Okay. Let's all of us say our top three picks again," Venice said. "I'll go first. Winnie Dusenberry. She's cute. She's funny. She's popular. Her mom makes and designs those awesome denim skirts with lace trim that she wears. Plus, she writes a blog about her dog that has over five hundred followers."

Leo winced. "Cute? Funny? Popular? I think the dog is the famous part of that equation."

I wished Leo could have been more supportive of Venice. She was trying really hard to think of somebody. I mean, everybody did know who Winnie Dusenberry was. She was just a little plain. And while Venice thought Winnie's home-made skirts looked cute, not everybody did. (Kids can be cruel. Winnie's middle name was Marci. And that rhymed with *barfy*. Enough said.)

"Dion Frater is the fastest sixth grader," Venice said. "He's just amazing. And people like him."

I nodded. And this time it wasn't even fake.

"Yeah," Leo said. "His older brother Barney is a giant

creep. I polled my history class today about Dion to see if people thought he was cool or popular, and some of the class booed me."

"That's absurd," Venice said. "A person's reputation shouldn't be defined by an older brother."

"Yeah," Leo said. "I know. But Barney threw all those water balloons at puppies in the dog park. People think he's a total jerk. And they're not sure about Dion yet."

I hadn't heard about the water balloon incident. It must've happened over the summer when I was out of town.

"This is so hard," Venice said, throwing her napkin onto her tray. "Why can't more sixth graders live hot and interesting lives?"

"Because we're super busy with Idaho History homework," I said. Because I wasn't exactly a hot and interesting sixth grader either. And Mr. Falconer was killing us with take-home worksheets.

"I just keep thinking we need to pick one of the theater kids," Venice said. "Because Anya hates them so much."

"I don't know if it's fair to say she hates them," I said. "Hate is a strong word."

"I'm pretty sure Anya has told the theater kids to their faces that she hates them," Leo said. "I think she has drama-mama issues. Her mom used to perform in local theater."

"Yikes," I said. Because it felt dangerous to be saying unkind things about Anya's mom. I looked over my shoulder to see if she was listening.

"Who do you have on your list?" Venice asked.

"Well," I said, fiddling with the zipper on my jacket. I felt nervous coming up with names, because at the end of the day I wasn't on Venice and Leo's side of things. But I was still a sixth grader, and I did want somebody decent to represent our class. "Chet Baez could work. The local news featured him on a segment about bird-watching." But actually I thought Chet was way too weird to include. "Or maybe Poppy Lansing. She helped her mom decorate a birthday cake for a senator."

Leo and Venice just stared at me. I think they suspected that I wasn't really trying. But I ignored their reaction and finished my top three.

"My third pick is Penny Moffett. She built an authentic teepee in her backyard and the local news covered it. She braided her hair and everything. She looked totally cute. I mean, she has the shiniest hair ever. It was a long segment. Her whole family cooked beans in an old-fashioned pot. Do you remember that?" I asked, turning to face Venice. "After it aired she said a couple of people asked her for her autograph."

"Yeah. But wasn't that three years ago?" Venice asked. "Do people really know who she is?"

I really hated that Venice didn't support my ideas, even if they were lame. I thought she could at least say one thing positive.

"I just think you're approaching it wrong. It shouldn't be about something somebody did one time. That's not really being hot. It should be about who they are deep down," Leo explained. "That's where we should look for their hotness."

"Exactly," Venice said. "Like how Reece is a future Olympian. It defines who she is. It's bigger than hot. She's a hotshot."

"I know," Leo said. "That's exactly what I'm saying. We need somebody at Reece's level."

But there was nobody at Reece's level. Didn't they know that?

"Who were you thinking?" I asked.

Leo tapped his bottom lip with his pointer finger. "Chet Baez is a good pick. He's a little weird, but girls think he's cute. I'm not sure Anya will go for it."

Girls thought Chet Baez was cute? Wow.

"He needs to stop wearing feathers," Venice said. "Do you think we could tell him to knock that off?"

She actually made a good point. Anytime Chet found a feather he immediately figured out a way to fasten it to either his belt or his shoes.

"It's too late," Leo said. "He's already ruined it for himself."

Leo pointed across the cafeteria to where Chet sat with his friends. An enormous black feather was stuck behind one of his ears.

"That's unsanitary," I said. "I mean, birds are a lot dirtier than people think."

"What if he grows up to be a famous falcon trainer on television? Maybe he has a hot future ahead of him," Venice said. "Maybe we should pick him."

I shrugged. "I don't even think he wants that. I think he wants to grow up to be the falcon."

Both Venice and Leo laughed at this, and it made me feel really funny.

"You're a lot cleverer than you look," Leo said.

But that actually offended me. Because it felt like he was saying I looked dull.

"So who are your three?" I asked again. He was really good at shooting down everybody else. What person did he see in the sixth grade who was Reece-level?

"Girls think Hayes Ellsworth is cute. And his family owns the skating rink. He's got some cool videos that he's put on-line," Leo said. "Is that hot?"

I really wanted to roll my eyes at this suggestion. Because Hayes Ellsworth was not cute. And he always had scabs on his elbows from falling down in the roller rink.

"Girls don't think he's cute," Venice said. "We're afraid of his elbows."

Ooh. I liked it when Venice shot down Leo's ideas.

"Didn't Drea Quan win a hot dog–eating contest at the Eastern Idaho State Fair?" Leo asked. "I've heard a ton of people talking about her."

Venice and I looked at each other in horror.

"What's wrong?" Leo asked. "What did I say?"

I let Venice answer him.

"Somebody filmed that with their phone and uploaded it to the Internet and basically she wins the contest, then spends the next five minutes puking hot dogs," Venice said.

"She was actually disqualified," I said. "You can't throw up when the buzzer sounds. It's called a reversal of fortune."

"Maybe that's why I've heard of her," Leo said.

"Well, that's not getting her into the What's Hot section," I said. "Vomiting shouldn't improve your social status. It's dangerous to send that message."

Leo looked at me and laughed again. "Your one-liners are priceless. No wonder Anya likes your captions."

I glanced at Venice to make sure she was okay that her borderline boyfriend was paying me compliments. She didn't appear to care.

"I wish this wasn't so hard," Venice said.

"It's only difficult because we're doing it right," Leo said. "We're figuring out the perfect hot person."

Then I said something that depressed everyone. Even myself. "What if there is no perfect hot person?"

Ring.

"That's it!" Leo said, jumping to his feet.

"What?" Venice asked. "Do you know the perfect hot person?"

I sure hoped Leo wasn't the person to come up with the perfect hot sixth grader. I wanted it to be either Venice or me.

"Over the summer I read *Frankenstein*," Leo said.

I wasn't sure why he was bragging about his summer reading. I felt like telling him that Venice and I had reread *Are You There God? It's Me, Margaret* and *Blubber*.

"The story is about building a monster," Leo said. "That's our solution. We shouldn't try to *find* the perfect hot sixth grader. We should try to *build* the perfect hot sixth grader."

That actually seemed totally impossible. I wasn't sure you could change a person like that. Because at the snake assembly when I tried to shine the light on some nerdier kids, I'd only succeeded in making them look super awkward. I mean, I didn't mean to be rude, but I was beginning to think there was a reason that people who weren't hot weren't hot.

"How do we build a hot sixth grader?" Venice asked.

"We pick somebody who has the potential to be hot. And then we push them toward their hotness," Leo said.

Venice broke into a smile so big it almost cracked her face.

"That's brilliant," Venice said. "We'll pick somebody who deserves to be hot. We'll probably end up changing their life."

I slowly walked to the cans when we dumped our trays and let this sink in. Leo thought we could build a sixth grader for What's Hot? That was nuts. That meant we'd have to make somebody super popular in the next few weeks. And that wasn't how popularity worked in middle school. Popularity was something that happened to you randomly in second or third grade because you wore the right clothes and were cute and weren't an obvious nerd. Also, it helped if you didn't have any major hang-ups, like a bad odor or a disastrous amount of freckles or a history of being dangerous with scissors. Then, if you were lucky, if you were given the gift of popularity, you clung to it like a life preserver as long as you could, until you made it through high school and things started over again in college.

"Okay," Venice gushed. "In our free time today let's try to come up with the person with the most potential."

"Free time?" I asked. Had Venice forgotten that we were on our way to Idaho History, where we had to replicate (freehand) the state seal? And that after that I had Math in Focus? And that after that I had to walk home and spend time with my cat and my mom?

"Yeah," Venice said. "Like when you're walking home alone. You can think about this."

I didn't really enjoy Venice telling me what to think about when I was walking home. And I also didn't appreciate her reminding me that I walked home alone.

"And we can figure it out on the bus," Leo said, giving Venice an obnoxiously loud high five.

"This is going to be the most amazing thing anyone has ever pulled off in the history of Yearbook," Leo said.

But I didn't think that was true. Because after I told Anya about it, I was sure she'd figure out a way to stop Leo and his terrible sixth-grade-monster-building idea.

8

Anya's Pick

As I walked home from school, I felt lucky and unlucky at the same time. Lucky: Venice was still my friend and she supported my ideas. Unlucky: Leo was a total Venice-clinger. Lucky: Anya had come up with a solid plan for kicking Leo to the curb. Unlucky: Following Anya's plan meant lying to Venice. Lucky: The What's Hot section might be able to make an unpopular sixth grader more popular. Unlucky: Our school didn't have a ton of hot and exciting sixth graders.

The more I walked, the more I realized I needed to call Anya and tell her all about Leo's idea right away. So I did.

"He is such a turd," Anya said.

And I really agreed with that statement.

"He and Venice are on the bus together right now," I said glumly. "Trying to figure out the perfect hot person." I pictured them sitting beside each other, sharing a seat.

"I'm not sure how much this matters," Anya said. "If they pick an atrocious person, I'll just cut whoever it is."

When I heard this I cringed a little bit. Because I didn't

want Leo and Venice to be 100 percent right about Anya's snobby personality and impulse to cut sixth graders. So I tried to figure out what she was thinking by asking gentle questions.

"But if they end up picking somebody who actually becomes super popular, why would you want to cut that person?" I asked. "Because wouldn't they kind of belong in What's Hot?"

There was a short pause and I worried that my gentle questions might not have been gentle enough.

"Hello?" I said. "Are you still there?" Sometimes I accidentally hung up on Venice with my cheek.

"I'm still here," Anya said. "I'm thinking."

I kept walking home, listening to Anya breathe. There was something about the speed and intensity of her breathing that seemed a little scary.

"Okay," Anya said. "You're right. If they pick somebody good, it'll tie my hands."

But that didn't seem like the end of the world, even though her voice seemed angry beyond belief. Because we wanted a solid sixth grader, right?

"But if they pick somebody who deserves it—" I started to explain my own thoughts on this, but Anya cut me off.

"No!" Anya said. "You're missing the big picture."

I stopped walking. This was the first time Anya had yelled at me. And it stung.

"If they pick somebody who actually deserves it, then they wouldn't need to make them hot and popular. That person would already be that. It's a disaster on two levels. First, they're trying to mess with my section. Second, they're tampering with a random sixth grader. Just like a lab rat."

"Maybe I should tell them that," I said. Obviously, I would leave out her first point. But the second one made sense to share. Because I didn't think Venice wanted to treat anybody like a tampered rat. She used to have a pet gerbil.

"Don't tell them anything," Anya said. "We can't tip our hand. We can't let them know that we know."

"But they already know that I know. I was there," I corrected.

"But *they* don't know that *I* know that *you* know," Anya explained. "We need to turn this around on them. We need a better idea than their idea."

Oh boy. Going behind Venice's back and reporting to Anya was making me feel worse than I thought it would. It was turning into a real time suck too. Didn't she know that deep down I had a loyal heart *and* had stuff to do? Mitten Man was probably waiting by the door for me right now, dying for an afternoon scoop of dry food. Didn't she ever think about somebody other than herself? Or possibly that person's cat? I didn't have time to think of a better idea.

"It took them about a week to come up with this idea, right?" Anya asked.

"Uh-huh," I said, climbing up my steps.

"Between the two of us, with our brainpower, we should be able to come up with a better sixth grader by tonight," Anya said.

I thought of my Depression-era reading assignment I'd hauled home in my backpack. I thought about the topographic map I had to make of Treasure Valley for Idaho History. I thought of my math worksheet folded up in my math textbook. My brainpower needed to tackle my homework. But I didn't know how to tell Anya that. Because Anya didn't like being told no. Anya liked being told *totally*.

"Well," I said. "Let's think about this." As soon as I walked into the living room Mitten Man pounced on my shoes. And I accidentally stepped on him.

"What was that?" Anya asked.

I hesitated in telling her as I scooped up Mitten Man to comfort him.

"Nothing," I lied.

"Was that one of your eight cats?" Anya asked. "Do your parents rescue a lot of strays?"

I didn't know why Anya always thought the cat population in my house was on the rise. It sort of offended me. Because I didn't collect them. I just owned Mitten Man. And I took great care of him. Except when I stepped on him.

"Let's talk about Venice and Leo's idea," I said, steering the conversation back to where it belonged. I tossed my backpack on the floor and flopped onto my couch. "I don't think this is going to work. Because they can't even figure out who to pick."

"They've already been floating names?" Anya asked, sounding freakishly alarmed. "They're farther along than I thought."

"I guess," I said, kicking off my shoes and picking up the remote.

"Whoa!" Anya said. "Are you near a television? Do you get cable?"

It was almost like she was watching me on a hidden camera. "Yeah," I said.

"Turn to channel three-thirty-one," Anya gushed. "Am I losing my mind or is this the most amazing thing ever?"

I clicked to channel 331 and watched as Fletcher Zamora sang a song about toothpaste while riding a blue bicycle down a snow-covered road.

"He must be freezing," I said. "Look at his breath."

"Those angles. Those cheekbones," Anya said. "The cameraman must be on a crane. See how they're looking down on him. See how it makes his arms look longer?"

"Yeah," I said.

"No way!" Anya said. "Turn to six-sixty-five."

I did. I watched Fletcher eating a hot dog at a giant, fake family picnic with a very photogenic family.

"I think this cameraman is elevated too," Anya said.

"Huh," I said, clicking to another station to find something I wanted to watch. Because I was tired of Anya telling me exactly what I should do.

"When I take his picture for the What's Hot section, I'm going to do something amazing," Anya said.

"Right," I said. I was wondering how much more talking about Fletcher we actually needed to do. "I should probably get started on my homework."

"But you haven't even talked about the list of sixth graders!" Anya protested.

I tried to remember all the way back to lunch. It felt like a lifetime ago.

"They came up with people like Chet Baez, Drea Quan, and Penny Moffett." I thought mentioning these people who had almost no chance at popularity would ease Anya's mind and help me get off the phone.

"Feather boy and the hot-dog puker?" Anya asked. "That's funny. You're right. Those two will never make it. But who's Penny Moffett?"

"Um," I said nervously. Because I'd remembered that Penny had been my pick, and I didn't want to tell Anya that, because I didn't want to look like a traitorous spy. "She's a sixth grader with shiny hair who made the local news by building a teepee with her family and making beans."

Again, there was a pause. "Hello?" I asked. "Did I lose you?" Because sometimes when I watched TV and sat on the couch, I lost people. "Hello?" I didn't know why talking to Anya made me feel so nervous. I didn't feel that way talking to anybody else.

"I can't even picture Penny Moffett. Are you sure she goes to our school?" Anya asked.

I zoomed through the channels until I got to a nature show about swordfish. I was a sucker for nature shows.

"Absolutely," I said. "We're in Science together. She cried when Ms. Stott brought out a sheet of dead starfish."

A shark drifted onto the screen and bit off the swordfish's silver tail. *Click.* I had a rule when watching a nature show—once the main-character animal died, I turned the channel. But this other program looked like a show about deer. Which didn't thrill me. Because I saw those animals all the time. But these deer had giant teeth that looked like fangs and they lived in China. So I kept watching.

"You're making me feel better," Anya said.

"Good!" I said. Because I liked to think of myself as a lifter.

"And you've helped me come up with an idea," Anya said.

"Great!" I cheered. What a relief that we had an idea. Because after I finished watching the deer with fangs, I could start my homework.

"You know what would be fun?" Anya asked.

She'd never asked me that question before. It was a nice break from all this yearbook scheming.

"I'll pick this sixth grader," Anya said. "And it needs to be a real loser."

I didn't think Venice would go for that. Worse, I didn't want Venice to know I'd been talking to Anya behind her back. Plus, I wasn't sure what made this plan fun.

"You're going to tell them that I told you about this?" I asked. Because I knew Venice would feel betrayed and probably be furious with me. Which seemed unfair, because the whole reason I'd been dishonest was to improve our friendship by getting Leo out of our lives.

"I'm smarter than that," Anya said. "I'm going to tell *you* who to pick. And it's going to be a person with zero potential to be popular. And you'll give them that name. Problem solved."

That actually did seem pretty smart. "We should probably just say Chet Baez," I said. "Because I think I could convince Venice and Leo to pick him."

Anya laughed. "Chet Baez has a chance. Girls think he's cute. And do you know how many rare woodpeckers that kid has spotted? Girls love nature dudes."

"No," I said. Because I didn't even know he was out looking for woodpeckers and I wasn't sure why that made him hot.

"I'm going to pick somebody awful. Just terrible. Somebody who will suck all their time and never become an inch more popular no matter how much effort those two weasels put into this insane projec—"

"Well," I interrupted. "I'm actually going to be spending time on this too."

"Totally," Anya said. "I'll be able to hear about every awful moment of it. It's going to be hilarious."

But then she laughed again. I watched the tufted deer on television gently wind its way down a mountain path. I thought for sure the beast probably ate other tufted deer, but the narrator said they were shy vegetarians.

"I know who I want," she said. "He is such a dweeb!"

It surprised me that she could think of the perfect dweeb this quickly. But Anya was like that. Her mind was always running high-speed toward the thing she wanted most.

"Who?" I asked. I hoped it wasn't somebody I liked. I was pretty sure some of my friends were dweebs.

"It's a theater geek," Anya said.

Click. I couldn't concentrate on Anya's plan and watch the fanged deer eat interesting plants, so I turned off the TV.

"I hate those kids," Anya added.

I started to breathe a little faster. Maybe Leo was telling me the truth about Anya hating the theater kids. Because she just told me that she did.

"*Hate* is a strong word," I said.

"Yeah," Anya said, sounding meaner than I'd ever heard her sound. "But it's accurate. Those kids think they're so special because they act. Basically all acting boils down to is lying. Actors are liars. Trust me. I know. My mom was in local theater and she got totally burned by those people."

The hair on the back of my neck stood up. Maybe Leo was telling the truth about that, too. It bugged me that he might be a partially honest person. Because I really wanted him to be a total jerk all the time. It was easier for me to dislike him that way.

"So which theater kid were you thinking?" I asked. I didn't know any of them that well. I mean, Poppy Lansing was taking drama this year, but I doubted Anya would pick her. She was pretty nice, and cute, and she had a popular older sister. Poppy was the sort of person who had potential.

"Derby Esposito!" Anya blurted out.

The name hit me like a bag of bricks.

"Wow," I said.

Anya laughed so hard I didn't know whether or not she was still breathing. "He's negative famous."

"Oh," I said. Anya was right. There was no way Derby Esposito could become hot enough for the What's Hot section. The fact that Anya, an eighth grader who'd only gone to school with him for a month, knew this meant that his reputation had followed him from elementary school in a big way. All of this was mostly his own fault, but I still felt worried for him.

Every tragic nerd has an equally tragic story about how he or she became a nerd. Here's Derby's:

1. In third grade he dressed like Harry Potter for two months until Principal Wolff changed the official dress code, banning caps and wizard wands.

2. In fourth grade he tried to raise a duck in his locker, and the smell got so bad they had to evacuate an entire wing of the school.

3. In fifth grade he fell asleep during movie Friday in the gym, and when he went to use the bathroom he stumbled half asleep into the *girls'* restroom, and when Drea Quan saw him and screamed, he woke up all the way, bolted, slipped, banged into a sink, and broke his arm.

"So what do you think?" Anya asked me. "Am I brilliant?"

I couldn't imagine Venice or Leo being dumb enough to pick Derby. He was too socially damaged to become popular and everybody knew it.

"Um," I said, trying to find a supportive answer that also pointed out all her plan's flaws, and possibly defend Derby.

"There is no way Venice and Leo can make that kid hot," Anya said. "It might sound cruel, but he's a zero."

And I didn't like Anya referring to Derby that way. Because while it was true that he would never be hot, I didn't think that made him a zero. Because a zero meant nothing. And nobody was nothing. Except, I mean, maybe Leo.

"Why would Venice and Leo even pick Derby?" I said. "They know it wouldn't work."

Anya laughed again. "That's where my infiltrator becomes invaluable."

"Are you talking about me?" I asked. Because I really thought she should just use my name.

"Yes, Perry," Anya said. "I'm talking about you. Here's what's gonna happen. These two think they're doing something honorable. They think they're making things at our school more fair. Would you agree with that?"

I nodded. "I agree with that." Originally, I had thought I could do that too. Until I realized it was impossible.

"So we exploit their motives," Anya said. "You're going to convince them that redeeming Derby Esposito, and turning him into a popular person, somebody worthy of being featured in What's Hot, is the honorable thing to do."

"Maybe," I said. Because it was pretty powerful what she was saying. But I wasn't convinced that was enough to convince Venice and Leo. "I think they know it's just going to be a massive waste of time."

"Perry, do you believe in second chances? Do you believe that people who've experienced misfortune should be given the opportunity to experience something better?"

And I totally believed that. Especially for myself.

"I do," I said.

"That's what will motivate Venice and Leo," Anya explained. "Play to their sense of justice. Trick them into caring about Derby's future. Make them believe they can actually help him be something more than a dweeb."

It seemed like this was going to require a ton of lying and manipulation. And I didn't really feel up for it. Wasn't Anya supposed to be teaching me about shutter speeds and aperture settings and ambient light? And how was Derby going to feel at the end of this? Probably dweebier than ever.

"Do you want to take Leo down and break those two up or what?" Anya asked.

"Yes," I said. Because that was a no-brainer. But I didn't want to take Venice down with him. Or Derby.

"Listen, our deadlines are firm. What's Hot gets submitted for final approval to Ms. Kenny in three weeks. It's part of the second signature. Leo and Venice will end up getting so frustrated by all this that they'll end up hating each other's guts. Group work does that to people."

That sounded fantastic. But then I remembered that I'd be helping them. Did that mean they'd hate my guts too? Or I'd hate theirs? Or by the end of this would I hate my own guts? And what about Derby and his guts? My mind spun thinking of all the hater options.

"I don't want to make Derby feel worse than he does about being Derby," I said.

"Don't look at it that way," Anya said. "He's a theater kid. He'll probably love the attention."

That was a better way to look at it. "Okay. I'll float Derby's name," I said. "But I'm not sure Venice and Leo will bite." Really, Venice and Leo were smart people. They might sense a setup right away. Because choosing Derby for What's Hot was crazy. Nobody could make him popular.

"I think you're underestimating them," Anya said. "Leo's ego is totally big enough to take on an impossible project."

"I can't stand Leo's ego," I said.

"Cool," Anya said. "You should float Derby's name tomorrow, for sure."

Anya was so aggressive. We'd just come up with the plan.

Couldn't she give me a couple of days to figure out how to make this work?

"My advice would be to tell them when they're together," Anya said.

Crash.

"What was that?" Anya asked.

I didn't even know. The biggest boom I'd ever heard in my life had just come from the kitchen.

"Something in my kitchen crashed," I said. "But I'm in the living room so I don't know what it is."

"Maybe your cats knocked over something big," Anya suggested. "I hear they can sometimes work as a team, like lions."

I didn't know why Anya kept thinking I owned a cat team. I just had Mitten Man. And he was way too independent to work with other cats.

"So I'm at the gym again, and Victor is here now, so I have to go," Anya said. "But after you find out what crashed, text me about it so I know that you're okay. I don't want anything to happen to my spy."

"Okay," I said. Then I hung up and stared nervously at the kitchen.

"They're ruined!" cried a familiar voice.

But it actually relieved me to hear that voice, because it meant that a destructive stranger wasn't in my house. When I turned the corner, I didn't expect to see Piper standing in front of the stove, wearing two oven mitts. First, she didn't cook much. Second, ever since she stole all our bread my mom had asked her to call before she came.

"I blew up the dolmades," she said. She covered her face with the oven mitts and shook her head back and forth. "Isn't Pyrex supposed to be indestructible?"

I shrugged, because I didn't know anything about Pyrex. I walked around the kitchen island so I could see exactly what had happened. "Is that glass?" I asked. Because there were a million shards of something that looked like glass scattered inside the oven and on the floor.

"Not exactly. It's a Pyrex baking dish," she said.

I remembered that baking dish. But the last time I'd seen it, it had looked much better, probably because it had peach cobbler in it. "What are those green things?" I asked. They looked like weird miniature enchiladas.

"Dolmades," she said. "I was making you an after-school snack."

It was sort of a relief to see that they were covered in Pyrex shards and inedible. "What makes them so green?" I asked.

"They're stuffed grape leaves," she explained. "I wanted to do something special for you to make up for missing dinner last week."

I hated the fact that Piper had flaked on me twice. First, for a monster-truck rally. Then for Bobby. But I didn't think that unexpectedly showing up and making me weird food really made up for anything. She slid the oven mitts off her hands and walked over and gave me a quick hug.

"Do you think Mom is going to kill me?" she asked.

I leaned over and looked inside the oven again. Some of the dolmades had exploded, shooting their stuffing everywhere. "What's all that white stuff?" I mean, I knew blown-up food should look bad, but this dish looked really disgusting.

"Rice," Piper said. "It's part of the filling. Along with onions, cooked raisins, and nuts. It's one of my roommates' recipes."

I could not believe this was an actual food that people chose to eat, and that Piper thought she should make it for me. Cooked raisins were evil and ruined everything. Even cookies. Didn't she know that?

"It's hard to know where to start," Piper said, pulling the kitchen trash can closer to the stove. "Can you hand me the paper towels?"

It was pretty obvious she'd never cleaned up following an explosion. "Maybe we should call a professional," I suggested. Because this job looked overwhelming and I actually had important stuff to do.

Slam.

"Do you think that's Mom?" Piper asked when we heard the front door bang shut.

I nodded. Because other than my dad, Piper, and me, my mom was the only person who owned a key to that door.

"Hello?" my mother called as she rounded the corner into the kitchen.

Piper cringed when she saw my mother's face.

"What happened?" she asked.

"I'm not totally sure," Piper said. "I think it was a defective baking dish." She pointed toward the open oven door.

My mother slowly approached the oven and looked inside, a horrified expression on her face. "What were you thinking? How does one person make this big a mess?"

"I was trying to do something nice for Perry," Piper said.

My mother looked at me in an angry way, like I had something to do with this.

"I had zero idea she was even here," I said. Because I was super innocent and I wanted my mother to know it.

"Perry, go to your room while we sort this out," she said.

"But I didn't do anything!" I said. Because it didn't seem fair to send me anywhere. I should have been allowed to travel freely anywhere I wanted in my own home. I hadn't blown up the dolmades.

"There's glass everywhere," my mother said. "Go to your room. Take Mitten Man with you. If he steps in this, it will cut his paws."

I hadn't thought of that. "Okay," I said. But before I walked out, I took a quick picture of the disaster with my phone.

I left the blast zone and went to my bedroom. Mitten Man was crashed out on his rug-bed next to my closet. I closed the door to my room in case he decided to bolt. Through the wall I could hear Piper and my mom arguing about temperature and glass and thermal shock. It seemed that my mom was mad about a lot more than the dolmades.

"Can you take a little more responsibility for this?" my mother yelled.

"I can't control what Pyrex does!" Piper responded.

"This is why you got fired from the Snow Cone Hut!" my mom shouted. "You don't take responsibility."

"I got fired from the Snow Cone Hut because my manager had a personality disorder and I didn't kiss her butt," Piper countered.

Once Piper brought up the Snow Cone Hut manager's butt, I was pretty sure this fight was going to last until my dad got home. I pulled out my phone and texted Anya. Because she'd said I should do that. And I also sent the picture of the explosion. Because it seemed relevant.

> My sister Piper exploded a weird snack.

I stared at my phone. I thought maybe Venice would call me. She should've been off the bus by now. I texted her the same message and photo too. And added an important detail.

> Piper exploded a weird snack. The oven is full of glass and cooked raisins.

I waited for either one of them to respond. My mom and Piper were still yelling but I also heard banging sounds, so I assumed they were cleaning. And that was going to take hours.

> Good to know. Stay safe, infiltrator.

When I saw that word spelled out, I realized I wasn't totally sure what it meant. So I looked it up.

infiltrator (noun)
a person who secretly becomes part of a group in order to get information or to influence the way the group thinks or behaves. *The infiltrator was identified and killed.*

I did not enjoy seeing that word used in a sentence. Next time I saw Anya, I was going to ask her to stop calling me that. Because I really didn't like thinking of myself as an infiltrator. I thought back to the first day of school and Anya's hit list and the words next to their names. As much as I tried, I still couldn't figure out a word for me. Then I saw Venice was texting me and so I stopped thinking about my word.

Venice

Cooked raisins are evil.

I laughed when I saw that. Because it was like Venice was the perfect friend for me. She totally understood how I felt. So I texted her again. And sent her a picture of me making her favorite goofy face. She was going to laugh so hard.

Me

Call me!

Tragically, she sent me a bummer text right away.

Venice

Can't! Talking to Leo ;)

I stared at that message until my eyeballs felt hot. I couldn't believe it. She didn't even send a return pic. She always sent those. And she'd rather talk to Leo instead of me? Even when I'd sent her photographic proof that things were literally exploding in my life? I felt really mad, but mostly hurt. A tear rolled down my cheek. Because it was one thing for Venice to be friends with Leo, but it was another thing for Leo to become more important than me. I debated what to text back to her, or if I should even text back at all.

But that was a huge lie. I wasn't okay with her choosing Leo over me. And if the only way to fix this situation was to follow Anya's plan, I was willing to do that. I didn't care what I was becoming. Leo had to go. And if Derby had to suffer a little bit more embarrassment, he'd survive just fine. I had to do what I had to do. Whatever it took was whatever it took.

9

Photos Approved

I'd never rehearsed a lie before, and it made me feel weird. Because I couldn't show up to Yearbook and act like my normal self. I had to show up to Yearbook and *pretend* to act like my normal self while delivering a sympathetic and lie-filled plea for Derby. It was pretty hard for me to picture myself doing all that. I didn't consider myself to be good at deception *or* public speaking. But I couldn't focus on that. I dressed in a power outfit, ate my breakfast, and headed to school.

As I gathered everything I needed for Yearbook from my locker, I caught a glimpse of myself in my mini-mirror. I looked nervous. And foggy. I was breathing so fast that my breath had clouded the glass. I wiped off the fog with my hand and shut the door. I kept having doubts about this entire operation. I mean, should I really have been focusing on Derby? Shouldn't I have been focusing on my grades? And improving my friendship with Venice?

But all my doubts flooded out of me the instant I walked

into Yearbook. Venice and Leo were giggling in the craft corner, looking at each other's hands. I approached them with extreme caution, because I was afraid to uncover why they were looking at each other's hands. I feared they'd decided to start going out. And maybe they'd agreed it was time to hold hands in public. That explanation seemed both likely and terrible. But once I got closer, what I found was much worse.

"Look at what Leo let me do to his pinky," Venice said, pointing to Leo's awful hand.

I blinked and blinked again.

"Is that a war horn?" I asked. I looked at my own pinky, which still had most of the polish intact from when Venice had painted it. Leo's pinky looked exactly like mine.

"It is a war horn!" Leo said. "Venice dared me to get it last night and I totally did."

He got it last night? That didn't make sense to me. "You painted your own war horn?" I asked. I was a little bit impressed that Leo was so good at using nail polish. I wouldn't have been able to paint my own war horn. Venice was the only person I knew with those kinds of skills.

"No," Venice said, laughing. "I went over to Leo's to do math homework last night. And I dared him. And he let me. Can you believe it?"

I could not believe it. "You went to Leo's last night?" I asked. "Your mom lets you do that?"

That seemed nuts. My mother would never let me do homework at the house of a horrible seventh grader I barely knew. But Venice seemed so happy and oblivious about everything. It was hard for me to talk to her without yelling. Because if she knew who Leo really was, she would not be at his house on a school night painting his pinky with a war horn. She would freeze him out and never speak to him again.

"Our moms work in the same crew," Leo said.

This was truly a shocking development. I had no idea that Leo's mom worked for the same catering company as Venice's mom. Why hadn't Venice told me that? "Since when?" I asked in a disgusted way.

Venice shrugged. "Probably years. But I didn't know that until I was telling my mom about Leo and she figured it out."

I could not believe that Venice had talked to her mom about Leo. Furthermore, I couldn't believe that on a night when I was home stuck in my room—literally forced to stay in there with my cat because of a dangerous Pyrex explosion that had left shards of glass in our kitchen area—that instead of calling me and seeing if I was okay, she was painting a gross boy's pinky at his house. And I was also a little surprised that Leo didn't mind going around school with his nail painted. What kind of jerk was this kid? Taking in all this new information made the room spin. Whiteboards. Chairs. Tables. Fluorescent lights. I sat down next to Venice and glared at Leo's pinky. I was stunned. I wasn't even sure how life would go on after this point. Everything felt ruined. My friendship. My future. Yearbook. And then, in the middle of my dizzy spell, I found myself saying these persuasive words. Where had they come from? I didn't know. They just started tumbling out.

"Last night I had probably the best idea I've ever had in my life," I said.

Venice sat up a little bit straighter and smiled. "Is this

about your topographic map? Did you find a way to label your rivers?"

Venice's words bounced off me. I totally ignored her. I was on a roll.

"We need to pick somebody who deserves a little bit more popularity. Somebody who will appreciate it," I said. "I thought of somebody who needs to be recognized right now, or he might remain invisible forever."

"Sounds like you're leaning toward Chet Baez," Leo said. "I can see that."

I shook my head. "We need to give somebody a second chance."

"The hot-dog puker?" Leo asked, sounding very surprised.

I couldn't believe how annoyingly impatient he was. I cleared my throat and leaned forward. And then I said the name in a slow and solemn way. "Derby Esposito."

I could tell by the way Venice flinched that I'd really stunned her with this announcement.

"The drama geek who hyperventilated at the python assembly?" Leo asked.

I slowly let out a breath. "Let's stop calling him a geek," I said. "I think that's part of his problem. He's forced to wear all these labels."

Leo looked confused. "He calls himself a drama geek. He wears a T-shirt every Tuesday that says WORLD'S BIGGEST DRAMA GEEK."

I really wished I could push a button and send Leo to live on a different planet. He really didn't belong on Earth with us.

"Perry," Venice scolded. "It was insane when he tried to raise that duck in his locker. Duck poop contains bacteria that's harmful to people. He should have known that."

This was going to be harder than I had realized. "I know it's easy to blame Derby for being Derby. But isn't Derby only behaving like Derby because he doesn't know how else to be?"

Leo looked at Venice. "He really tried to raise a duck in his locker?"

And that was when I pulled out the big guns. "Don't you think the reason Derby tried to do that is because he felt his life was missing something?"

Venice looked unconvinced. "Probably a duck," she said, folding her arms across her chest.

And when she did that, when she folded her arms, I got really offended for Derby. Because it was like these two felt he didn't deserve to be popular.

"If we're being serious about picking somebody who deserves a spot, then we'd be ridiculously cruel to choose anybody besides Derby." Then I slammed my hand on the table and stood up. "And being in What's Hot wouldn't be a temporary solution. It would be permanent, because that picture will last forever. We have one chance to turn Derby's life into something awesome. And I think we should take it."

Once I finished, Venice and Leo remained totally quiet. Maybe slamming the table was a bit too dramatic for them. Then I noticed that Venice looked like she was on the verge of tears.

"What you just said was amazing," Venice said.

Leo nodded and I watched his stupid bangs fall over his eyes.

"So you agree with me?" I asked. Because it seemed totally unbelievable that she would.

"You're right. If anybody deserves this chance it's Derby," Venice said.

I had to smile when Venice said this. Because Anya was going to die when she heard it. But in a good way.

"Our first step should be hanging out with him and getting to know what makes him tick," Leo said. "Find out what hidden talents he has."

"The section has to be delivered to Ms. Kenny in three weeks," Venice said. "That means we need pictures and captions. And a reason to include Derby at all."

Venice and Leo looked toward me to see what I had to contribute.

"We should spend a ton of time with him," I said. "I say we start by eating lunch with him." I almost laughed when I said that, because I totally couldn't imagine eating with Derby. But ever since Leo had started joining us, lunches had become a painful patch of time for me anyway, so I didn't care if we invited the school's biggest goofball to join us.

Leo flipped his bangs out of his face. "And he's in PE with me and Math with both of us." He jerked his thumb at Venice when he said that.

"Lunch?" Venice asked.

I kept pushing my argument. "Derby will only change if we lead him toward that change. Lunches are critical."

Leo started laughing and I felt myself getting hot. I

couldn't believe he would laugh at me right in my face like that.

"You are so awesome," Leo said. "I didn't see this coming at all."

I thought it was pretty rude for Leo to say he couldn't see my awesomeness coming. It had been there the whole time.

"Let's do this," Leo said. "Let's take Derby Esposito and make him popular. And let's show Anya that her section belongs to everybody."

I think Leo stuck his hand out like he wanted to do a cheer or something, but that felt unnecessary.

"Glad we settled that," I said, ignoring his hand. "I'm sure you've got some business things to do. Venice and I need to see if Ms. Kenny has approved the assembly photos yet." Ms. Kenny was supposed to email the handful she'd approved, but we still hadn't gotten them. We were hoping she had sent them this morning.

Leo smiled. "Okay. I guess I'll go back to my table." He winked at Venice twice. And she tried to wink back at him, but Venice was actually a terrible winker, so she just squinted her eyes shut at him, her left one more than her right.

"He is totally amaze-balls," Venice said, staring at Leo's backside as he walked to his table. "And so are you. I'm so lucky to have you guys."

As soon as we opened our account, we saw the photos. Ms. Kenny had picked four.

"They look awesome!" Venice said. "We are going to write the best captions for them."

The first photo was of Mr. Mortimer standing with his

arms outstretched and the python winding itself around his neck and shoulders.

The second was a crowd reaction shot. "Rocky DeBoom looks like he's freaking out. It's so cool."

The third one was a photo I'd taken of Venice standing next to Ms. Kenny and the blue box before the snake was let out.

"When did you even take that one?" Venice asked. "I look like I'm disgusted. My face is so puckered."

"You look cute," I said. "That's why I took it."

And the fourth was of Anya, Sailor, and Sabrina standing next to Mr. Mortimer. The other people in the shot weren't in focus. It wasn't an amazing picture. But it was the only one of everybody holding the snake.

"It sucks that the ones with Derby near the head didn't turn out," Venice said.

I tried not to think about Derby and that day too much. Back then, I had still believed I could help people and change the system. Now I didn't feel that way. I needed to wait until next year, until I had more power. And I guess that meant Derby and the rest of the school nerds had to wait too.

"Look!" Venice said, pointing to the photo of Rocky De-Boom. "You got a great picture of Leo. He's totally photo-bombing Rocky."

"Huh?" I said. Because I specifically remembered not taking his picture. That little sneak. He'd lowered himself a full row to fall in line with my jock photo. And Ms. Kenny had picked it.

"Thank you so much for taking such a good picture of him," Venice said. "You're the best."

I looked at Venice and smiled. I almost felt sorry for her. Because if she only knew that Leo was using her and was actually amaze-awful, she would probably start crying. It was crazy how much he'd been able to deceive her in such a small amount of time. It was like he was an expert at it. Like instead of watching TV or going to the mall, he spent all his free time practicing deception techniques. It made me sick to my stomach. Because Venice deserved to be with somebody who was way better than that. Somebody who had her best interests in mind. She actually was lucky that I was in her life. Because she needed a friend like me to get things back on track for her.

10

Walking Tacos

It took three days before Derby Esposito agreed to eat lunch with the three of us. During this time, Anya nearly lost her mind. She was thrilled that I'd been able to convince Venice and Leo to take on Derby as a project. But she worried that she didn't have more influence over the ongoing operation.

"I just wish I knew what Leo was telling Derby in PE," Anya said. "I feel so helpless. What if something goes wrong?"

I shrugged. Because at this point she really just had to trust her own plan. And Derby's instincts to act strange all the time. Things were really up to him. "We'll know a lot more after today," I said.

Anya frowned. "Is there any way you could get out of class after lunch and come talk to me?" she asked. "It's going to kill me to wait until after school."

I pointed at her so she'd know I meant business. "I can't. I have Idaho History, and Mr. Falconer doesn't let people make up missed classes. He's strict," I said. I mean, seriously. What was she thinking?

"You're totally right. Forget that I asked," she said, handing me a pile of photos. "Can you caption these for me?"

"What are these for?" I asked. Because I didn't even know which section they belonged in, and that was important as far as coming up with the right tone.

"These are bonus photos. They're shots I love and I'm not sure where they go yet," Anya said.

When I heard that, I worried that she'd assigned me a bunch of extra work that might not go anywhere.

"So they might not even make it into the yearbook?" I asked.

"I'm ninety percent sure that eighty percent of those photos will make it in," Anya said.

I knew how to do math. That meant there was a 10 percent chance I was wasting all my time. And a 90 percent chance I was wasting 20 percent of my captions.

"When do we shoot group photos again?" I asked, because the dates kept shifting. Ms. Kenny had asked us to take the photos this week. But Anya wanted to make everybody attend another month of meetings, to make sure they were really committed to their clubs. Because she didn't want to take a bunch of pictures of club members who were going to drop out as soon as pictures were taken. "Quitters don't deserve to be in the yearbook photos," she'd argued.

But I was really excited to do group photos, because Anya had said that I got to take them due to what she'd called my "innate gift for posed shots."

"There's no rush on group photos," Anya said.

"But that means we'll be shooting the first football games at the same time we're shooting the clubs," I said. "That's a lot of work." Because that meant we had to attend all the club meetings after school. As well as all the football games after school and on weekends. And also some of the practices after school. That basically took all my after-school life.

"That's Yearbook!" Anya said. "It's a tremendous amount of nonstop work."

"Right," I said. Then I drifted off and joined Venice, who was busy arranging the layout for the upcoming sixth-grade portraits. I really missed my old life with her.

"I saw you talking to Anya," Venice said. "She's seemed stressed out all week. She's super alpha about the group photos."

I nodded. But really, I wished Venice had said, "Perry! It's great to see you!" And then not said anything insulting about Anya when she was standing ten feet away.

"Did Leo tell you he brought cannoli for Derby?" Venice said.

I glanced at her. Leo was really going to try to make this Derby thing work. It was almost impressive. Except I still hated Leo, so it wasn't. Also, I'd never heard of cannoli before. "What are they?" I asked.

Venice smiled in a weird way, like she was excited to tell me about cannoli. "They're tubes of fried pastry filled with sweetened ricotta cheese. And Leo put chocolate chips on the ends."

"Oh," I said. Except for the cheese, those sounded decent.

"They're Italian," Venice said.

"Okay," I said. But really I didn't care where my food came from as long as jalapeños and/or sauerkraut hadn't touched it.

"He called me last night when he was making them. I'm the one who told him to add the chocolate chips. I had them that way at a restaurant once," Venice said.

She still had that goofy smile on her face. It was sort of distracting to sit next to her, so I focused on labeling the photo files. But then I thought of something I really needed to ask her.

"Do you and Leo ever take photos together?" I asked.

Venice smiled big when I said that. And I got worried they were out there secretly doing that. And that she didn't care that he sucked at it. Which started to make me feel awful. Because that was something that up to this moment I thought only Venice and I did together. And I didn't want to lose that, too.

"Leo doesn't take pictures," Venice said. "He cracked the lens on his phone last year, and he doesn't own a camera."

I almost gasped. What a liar. I'd seen his terrible pictures. He definitely owned a camera! I mean, why would he lie about that? It was just one big manipulation. The same way the cannoli were meant to manipulate Derby into liking and possibly trusting Leo. What a faker! It was so obvious to me now. The more Venice liked Leo, the more he could influence Venice and her behavior around Anya. It wasn't a coincidence that Venice kept disliking Anya the more she liked Leo. And that Venice kept bucking all of Anya's ideas. Leo was playing Venice big-time. And my hands were tied and I couldn't say anything about it yet because I'd made a promise to Anya in that stupid closet. This was rotten.

"Hey there," Leo said, breezing by us on his way to the

pencil sharpener. "Just so you know, Derby wants to eat at a table that gets sunlight. So look for us on the south wall."

I glared at him. How was I supposed to know which wall was south? Did he think I brought a compass to school?

"That's the wall farthest from the dump cans," Leo said.

I kept glaring at him. He was so good at lying. It was like he didn't even notice he was doing it.

"Are you okay?" Leo asked, reaching out and touching my shoulder.

It took every piece of willpower I had not to knock his hand right off me. "I've just got a lot on my mind."

He squeezed my shoulder one last time before letting go. "Yeah," he said. "It looks like it."

Then he walked off and I shot eyeball daggers into the back of him. Because he'd basically told me that I had a stressful face.

"How much should we tell Derby about why we want to start hanging out with him?" Venice asked. "I mean, it's rude to tell somebody that we basically think he's the most unpopular person ever and we want to help him improve his life."

I agreed. That approach did seem pretty rude. "Maybe we just pretend like we think he's interesting," I said. Because I really hadn't thought that far ahead. I just kept hoping we'd get to the part where the stress of group work drove Venice and Leo apart, so they could start hating each other's guts as soon as possible.

"That's a smart idea," Venice said. "Leo was thinking he'd kick off the conversation. You know. Because they're both guys."

"Right," I said. But I was pretty sure Leo would fall on his face. I mean, this was a pretty delicate operation that stood a high chance of failure. I couldn't imagine Leo connecting with Derby.

"Leo is great at connecting with people," Venice said.

And I totally rolled my eyes at that comment. Because the only person Leo was great at connecting with was Venice. And that was because their whole relationship was built on lies. As far as I was concerned, lunch couldn't start soon enough.

Finding Derby at a south table was pretty easy, because he was dressed head to toe in stripes like a referee. Plus, he was wearing sneakers with coat-hanger laces.

"Hi, Derby," Venice said as she set her tray down across from him.

I set my tray down too and then I waved. "Fun outfit," I said.

Derby took a fork and gently pried open his milk carton with it. "I'm playing a diabetic referee in a scene today for Drama."

We watched as he placed three napkins inside his collar and draped them over his chest area.

"Walking tacos are pretty messy," Venice said, imitating the gesture and tucking a napkin in her own shirt.

Since there were also cheese sandwiches on the line that day, I was surprised anybody at our table had bought a walking taco. But Venice, Leo, and Derby had. I actually didn't like those tacos for several reasons. First, you had to eat your taco out of a corn-chip bag. Second, the chili inside the bag made the corn chips soggy. Third, the sour cream got steamy and didn't taste awesome. Fourth, I was pretty sure the chips were made with genetically modified corn (Piper had told me that).

"I just want to make sure that my stripes stay white," Derby said. "When I act, I channel a lot of energy from my clothes."

"That makes sense," Leo said, scooping out a big bite of taco.

And then it was sort of like we all froze. I froze because I was waiting for Leo to take charge of the conversation. I suspected that was why Venice froze too. And I didn't know why Leo froze. Probably because he was just as awful at connecting with Derby as I thought he would be.

"Is this about the python?" Derby asked.

And that really surprised me. Because why would we even want to discuss that publicly? It had been a low moment for all of us.

"No," Venice said. "What would make you think that?"

Derby shrugged. "Because that's the only interaction I've had with you guys. When you tried to force me to hold a deadly reptile's head."

Wow. This was going pretty terribly. I thought I should probably jump in. Because I was probably the only one who could explain that disaster. "That was totally my fault. I was trying to get a good picture of the python and I thought your height worked well with the handler and the snake's length and girth. I just got caught up in framing the shot," I lied, trying to make it sound totally reasonable.

"Yeah," Leo said with way too much enthusiasm. "She was framing the shot."

"Oh," Derby said.

Then there were two whole minutes of complete and total and awkward silence.

"This feels awkward," Derby said, chomping on his soggy chips. "If this isn't about the python, I'm not sure why I'm here. I mean, none of you have ever talked to me before."

"That's not true," Venice said. "You trick-or-treat at my house every year and I always compliment your costume. Two years ago when you came as a tide pool, I absolutely loved those fake sea urchins you wore for shoes."

Derby wiped his mouth with three paper napkins, one after the other, like he was super worried he had walking taco stuck to his face.

"Those were sea anemones," he corrected, glancing around the table.

"Oh," Venice said, sounding super disappointed. But she shouldn't have sounded like that at all. I was impressed she'd been able to remember Derby's Halloween shoes from two years ago. Because I didn't even remember all my own shoes that were in my closet.

"I thought you said you were bringing cannoli," Derby said.

Leo popped the lid off the plastic container and handed it to him.

"Are they all for me?" Derby asked.

And then Leo did something majorly shocking. "Sure," he said, giving away all our cannoli.

We just sat there and watched Derby eat. It was gross. He kept sticking his tongue into the fried pastry tube, like he was afraid to eat that part. I think he noticed us staring because he stopped and said, "After I eat hard foods like corn chips, sometimes my teeth feel sore. It's my braces."

Derby smiled at us and revealed a mouth filled with braces and walking taco and cannoli filling. It was disgusting.

"So why am I here?" Derby asked, picking off the chocolate chips from his second cannoli. "What's the deal?"

And I wasn't sure if he meant my deal, or Venice's deal, or Leo's deal, or if he thought we had a collective deal.

"Well," Leo said. "I'm glad you asked."

But as soon as Leo started talking, Derby did something totally weird. He reached into the front pocket of his referee shirt and pulled out finger pinches of dirt.

"Is that dirt?" Venice asked as Derby dropped it into his mouth.

"Do you really think I'm putting dirt in my mouth?" Derby asked. "Do I look like an animal?"

I shook my head. "You look like a referee." I felt like I had to say something. Because everything just felt too awkward otherwise.

"Ms. Stott took away my flower," he said, gesturing to his front pocket. "She said it was a class disturbance."

But I wasn't sure what that had to do with anything.

"I filled my front pocket with chocolate cookie crumbs. And I stuck a plastic daisy in it," he explained. "So I don't have my daisy, but I've got my dirt. I thought it was a cool look for the scene I'm doing fifth period. I'm a referee who goes into diabetic shock. But I'm brought back around with my own cookie crumbs."

"What play is that from? And is it part of your grade to dress like that?" I asked. Because I was considering taking Drama next semester. But now I was worried I'd have to wear costumes and pretend I had a medical condition even when I wasn't in class.

"It's a monologue I wrote," Derby said. "I'm wearing this because it helps me identify with my character. It doesn't have anything to do with my grade."

That was pretty shocking. Because I'd only wear an outfit like that if it guaranteed me an A.

Derby squirmed a little bit in his chair and looked in the direction of his drama-geek friends at the next table. I wasn't sure why Leo was doing such a terrible job of talking to Derby. If Leo didn't make his move soon, Derby might bolt. I mean, Leo really shouldn't have given away all the cannoli until he'd presented Derby with the plan. It was like when my parents took me to Hogle Zoo and I got to feed the giraffes. I made sure to pet the giraffe *before* I fed it my cracker. Otherwise, it would have taken the cracker and run off.

"So, um, I think it's really great that you joined us for lunch today," Leo said. "Are you having fun?"

Derby shook his head. "Not really."

"Well," Leo said. "Um, that's too bad, because I'm really glad you're at our table. I'm having a lot of fun."

"You're acting really weird," Derby said. "You're scaring me."

And it sort of felt like Derby might have been a better judge of character than any of us had realized.

"Don't be scared," Venice said, jumping in to rescue Leo. "We're actually very nice people."

But that statement didn't really lighten the mood.

"This still feels weird," Derby said, reaching deep into his pocket and pulling out more of his cookie crumbs.

"We actually want to talk to you about your status," Leo said.

But I thought that was the wrong thing to say. Because Derby's status was awful. Was Leo going to tell Derby that to his face?

"Oh," Derby said. "So you've heard."

Then we all looked at one another. We'd heard he was a geek years ago. Probably everybody in the state of Idaho knew that.

Derby smiled again and I really hoped he had a toothbrush in his locker. Because it was going to take some serious circular brushing to defood those things. "Ms. Harlow made me student director for the school play."

"Wow!" Venice said, sounding both sincere and impressed. "That's so amazing. A sixth grader never gets that."

Derby nodded. "It's nice that Ms. Harlow believes in me. Not everybody does."

"And that's why we're here," Leo said, jumping in at what he probably thought was the perfect opening. "We believe in you too."

That sounded so corny that I rolled my eyes.

"What—what Leo is—is trying to say," Venice stammered, trying to help again, "is that we think you're cool and interesting. And we want other people to think that too."

Derby slowly shook his head and took off his triple-napkin bib. "Stop it. Okay. Just stop it," he said. "I know what's going on. And I'm tempted to get up and leave right now. Because I'm not a clown. You can't buy me with cannoli."

Wow. This was going way worse than I thought it would go. And I was expecting it to be a small disaster.

"We don't think you're a clown. And we totally didn't mean to upset you," Venice said. "We meant to do the opposite."

"You're not the first people to come to me with this kind of offer," Derby said, pushing his tray away.

"We're not?" I asked. Because it seemed totally bizarre that another group of people were also interested in making Derby popular.

"Reece Fontaine called me last night. So did Fletcher Zamora. And I'm pretty sure the Ringer twins left a note in my locker," Derby said.

It was unbelievable that all these people would even want to talk to Derby.

"How did Reece get your phone number?" I asked. Because that, to me, felt like possibly a lie.

Derby smirked at me. "She's Reece. She has her ways."

At this point, Leo's mouth dropped open and Venice looked at me really panicked, and I realized that if this plan had basically any chance of going forward, I had to take control.

"And what exactly did these people want?" I asked. Because there was no way in the world that this many people were invested in Derby's future.

"The same thing everybody else wants. Special consideration," Derby said, leaning back in his chair.

"And this is for what again?" I asked. Because it just felt like we still weren't on the same page.

"*The Wizard of Oz*," Derby said. "Our play is gonna be the bomb and everybody knows it. Shazam!" He snapped his fingers, but for some reason they didn't make a sound.

Okay. This made more sense. People were sucking up to Derby because they thought he had casting power.

"That is *not* why we are here," Leo said. "None of us are actors. And none of us want to be. We're here for *you*."

And I don't know if everybody else thought that sounded creepy, but it made me feel uncomfortable. Especially when Leo pointed his finger in Derby's face.

"Thanks for the cannoli," Derby said. "But I'm going to go join my people." He nodded at the drama-geek table.

Venice seemed heartbroken. Which made me feel bad. I was her friend. I didn't want her to feel that way. I wanted her to feel happy. And while I was busy thinking about how bad I felt that my friend felt sad, Venice did something awful. She reached over and gently clutched Leo's hand. I was stunned! Because whenever Venice had been upset before, she'd turn to me and I'd give her a fist bump or cross my eyes. But I guess that was all changing now. I guess she was going to turn to Leo. I had to rework this situation immediately.

"Derby, I'm going to be totally honest with you," I lied. "We invited you here because we're on Yearbook. And we think you're somebody who should be remembered. And the best way for that to happen is to be featured in a special section. So we were hoping to get some good pictures of a few trailblazing sixth graders and make the best section ever. And we picked you."

"Who are the other sixth graders?" Derby asked.

I wasn't prepared to advance my lie that far ahead. My mind raced trying to think of other worthy candidates.

"It's just you for now," Leo said, practically ruining my entire plan.

"We're starting with you," I corrected. "But we're adding other people very soon. So maybe if you gave us your class schedule, we could figure out a time to find you this week and take a few shots."

"Hmm," Derby said, looking pretty doubtfully at me.

I faked some confidence and pressed forward with my plan. "Where are you first period?" I asked. "Maybe we could swing by and get a couple of pictures tomorrow."

"No way. I have Idaho History first period," Derby said. "Mr. Falconer doesn't allow flash photography in that room because of his historic letter and collection of authentic Nez Percé moccasins."

I didn't know why Mr. Falconer had so many crazy rules. Or why he hung that framed letter from Thomas Jefferson on the wall. If he wanted it to last forever, I felt he should've laminated it.

"Maybe we could do it during lunch?" I asked. "Or after school?"

"You want to hang out after school with me?" Derby asked.

I nodded enthusiastically.

"Um, I'll need to talk this over with my mom," Derby said, arranging all his lunch trash onto his tray.

"Really?" I asked.

"I need to split," Derby said. "I want to read through my monologue a couple more times."

"Don't forget to clean your braces," I added.

Derby blushed and looked totally embarrassed.

"I can't help it," I explained. "My dad's a dentist. I always look at people's teeth."

Derby got up to leave and stepped on Penny Moffett's heel as he rushed off, almost taking them both down to the floor.

"Ciao," Leo said.

"Ciao," Derby mumbled back.

"Did you guys just meow at each other?" I asked. Because that was what it sounded like to me.

"*Ciao* means 'goodbye' in Italian," Venice said.

I wasn't sure why everybody had suddenly fallen in love with Italian. I sure hadn't.

As Derby approached the drama-geek table he tripped again on a rogue orange peel.

"He's lucky he only broke one arm in the girls' bathroom," Leo said. "That kid lacks coordination."

"Let's not say mean things about Derby," I said. "We want him to trust us."

"I didn't say it loud enough for him to hear me," Leo argued.

But I didn't even think that was the point. I thought we all needed to be on team Derby now for this to work.

"I don't know why he complained about the cannoli. Those were exactly what he'd asked for," Leo said.

I shrugged. "At least we have a chance to get some good pictures. If his mom tells him it's okay."

"Is Derby's mom normal?" Leo asked.

Leo and I both looked at Venice. "How should I know?" she said.

"You had the inside scoop on his Halloween costumes," I said.

"Let's just assume that his mom is going to say it's cool," Leo said.

But I wasn't sure we should assume that.

"The bigger issue we have is that taking pictures of Derby doesn't automatically and suddenly make him popular," Leo said.

And it was like Leo needed everything spelled out.

"Duh," I said in a snarky way. "That's why we need to instruct him on what to wear. If we can change how he dresses, even for a week, that can have some real impact."

"You're right," Venice said. "If we change what he looks like right away, it will be a lot easier to help him."

"Okay. I should call him and tell him to wear different clothes for the picture," Leo said.

But Leo was terrible at talking to Derby.

"Perry should do it," Venice said. "She's better at it."

And I wanted to laugh in Leo's face when Venice said that, because what she was really saying was that Leo sucked at talking to Derby.

I watched Leo pull his hand away from Venice. Wow. Anya was right. Group work did have the potential to cause relationship-ending stress.

"I'll call him tonight," I said. "And I'll see if I can get a read on his mom."

"Where will you get his number?" Leo asked.

"Reece," I said.

"You have her number?" Venice asked.

"Anya does," I said.

"You're so connected," Venice said.

And she didn't even know the half of it.

11

Mom Threat

Anya O'Shea had zero patience. On the way home from school, she called me three times. I was still three blocks away from my house when I stood in the shade of an elm tree and finally answered. She sounded upset.

"It's really important for you to keep me informed," Anya said. "I don't want my yearbook to have any hiccups."

And I thought it was pretty telling that Anya referred to it as *her* yearbook, because really it was the entire school's yearbook. But I didn't correct her.

"I'm walking home and standing on a random corner," I explained. I watched as two small birds hopped along the power lines above me.

"Sorry," Anya said. "You probably think I'm being really pushy. I'm just super scared."

She was right. I did think she was being super pushy. And it really surprised me to learn that she was super scared. Also, the small birds on the wire had multiplied and there were, like, a dozen of them.

"So I watched you guys like a hawk all lunch," Anya said. "But it was impossible to tell how things were going. By the way, news alert, I saw Venice and Leo hold hands under the table."

But that wasn't even news. Because I was there when it happened and also when it stopped happening.

"I need to keep walking," I told her. "I think a bunch of birds are getting ready to attack me." I quickly hurried past the whole growing flock of them.

"It's probably because you smell like twenty cats," Anya said. "They've got really specific pheromones. Birds can sense them big-time."

I didn't think her logic made any sense. Because if that was true, I should've been attacked by birds pretty regularly. And that wasn't the case.

I was so relieved when I rounded the corner to my street and zero wildlife followed me.

"Just tell me what you know for sure," Anya said.

"I don't know anything for sure yet," I started.

"What?" Anya said, totally freaking out prematurely. "You're killing me."

"Listen," I said, using my stern voice. "Derby suspects that we're up to something, so we have to take it slow. He's going to check with his mom and get back to us."

"What a mess," Anya said. "FYI, it's always good to keep moms out of your schemes."

"I know that," I said. "It's not like I invited his mom to be part of this. Derby did." I'd made it two more streets when I got the feeling I was being followed. I looked behind me for the flock of birds. But I didn't see any.

"Okay," Anya said, taking a deep breath. "Let's not get mad at each other. We're on the same team."

But I didn't even know if that was true anymore. I flipped around again and noticed Hayes Ellsworth half a block away. Was Hayes following me?

"So where do things stand now?" Anya asked.

I turned back around and kept walking. "I'm going to call Derby tonight and see if we can set up a time to take pictures," I explained. "If his mom is cool with that."

"I loved what you were saying until you mentioned his mom," Anya said. "You should cut her out of things ASAP. I mean, moms can totally get in the way."

"Yeah," I said. And it was like Anya wasn't even listening to me. Because I didn't have any power over what Derby told his mom. And I tried to think of a way to tell her this again, but she kept talking.

"Okay. Here's the plan. Call me after you talk to Derby. If you can't reach me, call Sabrina. I'll be with her and her phone has way better reception."

Anya was sounding extra bossy today.

"Can I text you?" I asked. "I've got a lot of homework tonight." I'd made it to my house, but I didn't want to go inside until I was done talking to her. My mom's car was there and I didn't want her to hear any of this.

"That is the rudest thing you've ever said to me," Anya spat back. "This totally deserves more than a text."

I nodded. But really I was starting to feel super bullied by Anya's requests.

"Okay," I said. "If I end up talking to him, I'll totally call. Otherwise, I'll text."

"Cool," Anya said, clearly happy that she was getting exactly what she wanted. "Is it weird that this feels fun to me?"

But then she didn't even give me a chance to answer. She just hung up.

"Perry!" a voice called. "Perry!"

Instead of climbing my steps I turned around and faced a breathless and slightly sweaty Hayes.

"I've been trying to catch up with you for blocks," he said, letting his backpack slide off his arm and land on my lawn.

"Why?" I asked. Because nobody had ever followed me for several blocks before. That I knew of . . .

"I've got some extra passes to go skating," he said. "I thought you might want them."

He reached his arm out to me and I saw his scabby elbows. I wasn't sure what to do. If I took the free passes, did that mean I had to go skating with him? If I took Venice skating, would she want Leo to come? Looking at the four free passes fluttering in the breeze caused me to feel many things, and most of them were negative.

Hayes didn't stop trying to hand them to me, even though I didn't react. He actually reached and put them inside my hand, and then closed his fingers around mine and gave me a quick and powerful squeeze. Then he winked at me. "Don't let them blow away," he said. "I don't give these out to just anybody."

"Oh," I said. And then I had no idea what to say. I couldn't stop looking at his elbows. "Thanks!" Then I flipped around and went inside. When I saw Mitten Man slink into the living room, I started to feel more relaxed. "You are so lucky you don't have to go to school," I told him, scooping him up in my arms. "It can be a terrible place."

But then my mom rounded the corner and I regretted saying that.

"What's wrong?" she asked. "Did something happen at school?"

Flashing back on Anya's advice, I really had no desire to add my mom to my scheme.

"I just have a lot of homework," I fibbed.

"About that," my mom said. "Dad called me this afternoon and he's concerned."

"About my homework?" I asked. Because that sounded weird. Because he hadn't mentioned that to me. And really, I was lying about having a lot of it.

"He went on TRAC and saw that you've got an assignment due next week in Idaho History that's worth ten percent of your grade," she said.

"Oh yeah," I said. "It's nothing big. It's a map."

"Ten percent of your grade seems like a lot. How big is your map supposed to be?"

I put my hands out in front of me and made a square. "It's a topographic map. I have to glue cardboard to show the elevation of the Treasure Valley."

"Where is it?" my mom asked.

"Near Boise. It's where a bunch of waterways drain into the Snake River," I explained.

"I know where Treasure Valley is," she said. "I meant your map."

But that question seemed crazy, because my map didn't exist yet. And I think my mom could tell I felt this way, because she said, "This isn't fifth grade, Perry. You can't throw it together at the last minute and hope it all works out. Your teacher is expecting you to have put some real effort into it."

"How do you know that?" I asked. Because it seemed that maybe my mom was talking to Mr. Falconer behind my back. And that was strange.

"If it's worth ten percent of your grade, he's expecting a serious map," my mom said.

She was actually starting to frighten me. Because I'd seen other maps from the year before displayed at the back of the classroom. And I hadn't realized they took that much effort.

"How much cardboard do you need?" she asked. "Should I have Dad buy some on the way home?"

"I figured we had some," I said.

"Craft cardboard?" my mother asked with a voice filled with a ton of surprise. "Do you have your assignment with you?"

But I really hated how my mom was treating me like a child. I still had three whole days to work on it. I dug through my backpack until I found the assignment sheet. "Here," I said.

She took it and began studying it. After a minute, she turned the page. I hadn't even realized there was a second page.

"Have you read the whole thing?" she asked.

I shook my head. "Just the front page."

"Okay," my mom said. "I don't want to upset you, because I know you're putting a lot of your time into Yearbook, but you can't let your other classes slide."

"Nothing is sliding," I said. "I still have a few days."

"But you don't even have the proper materials," my mom said.

But I knew that wasn't true. I grabbed some paper and a pencil out of my backpack. "This is all I need. Plus, the cardboard."

My mother wrinkled her face in disappointment. "Perry, you need C-flute or B-flute corrugated cardboard. And your rivers must be labeled in blue. He suggests using a brush pen for that. And your mountains and valleys need to be labeled in black pen. No pencil marking allowed. And for scissors he recommends something with a partially serrated stainless steel blade with blunt tips."

I returned my ridiculously inadequate pencil to my backpack. The way my mom talked about my map did make it sound like I should be working on it right away.

"You're lucky Dad checked on this," she said.

"You're making me feel bad," I said, collapsing onto the couch. "I'm doing my best here."

And I felt very overwhelmed all of a sudden by my unmade topographic map and my dad's daily habit of checking all my classes on TRAC.

"I don't want to make you upset," my mom said. "I just don't want you to neglect your classes."

"Six is too many," I said. Because really, my day would be so much easier if I could stop attending Idaho History altogether.

"I totally understand how you feel," my mom said. "I still have nightmares that I forgot to study for an important exam. I spend my whole dream cramming for it, racing around, and looking for the classroom. It's just awful. And sometimes I'm not wearing pants."

The idea that I'd grow up and be my mom's age and still have dreams about my Idaho History homework really terrified me.

"Is Venice working on her map?" she asked. "Maybe you could work on it together."

I shook my head. "Our teacher gave us independent assignments. Each of us got something different. I got assigned a topographic map and she got assigned a diorama of the Idaho portion of the Oregon Trail."

"He sounds tough," my mom said.

"Mr. Falconer is in love with Idaho," I said. "He collects ancient memorabilia and hangs it on his walls and then forbids flash photos because he doesn't want anything to fade."

"Wow," my mom said. "That's intense. I'm surprised you haven't mentioned any of that before."

But that felt like a complaint about me. And that wasn't really what I wanted to hear from my mom. I just wanted her to agree that Mr. Falconer and his assignment were pretty terrible. Then my phone started ringing. And it was a number I didn't recognize.

"Is that Venice?" my mom asked.

And I shrugged. "I have no idea who it is."

My mom looked a little concerned. "Can I answer it?"

And while I didn't love the idea of my mom answering my phone, I also thought that if it was Anya calling me on a different number, maybe my mom answering it was a good thing.

"Okay," I said. "But I'm not in the mood to talk to anybody. I've got too much homework."

"Hello?" she said. "Yes, this is Perry's phone. Who's this?"

And I tried to listen to see if I could recognize Anya's voice, but it sort of sounded like a boy.

"Derby Esposito," my mom said. "Perry's not around right now."

I started flapping my hands in front of her face to let her know that she should hang up and stop talking to Derby right now.

"What? You were calling to get our home phone number because your mother wants to talk to me?" my mom said.

And this was like the worst thing that had ever happened in my living room. "No," I mouthed. "Hang up!" I swung for my phone to try to grab it away, but my mom stood up and turned away from me.

"Sure," she said. "I'm happy to talk with her. Hi, I'm Perry's mom." She started walking toward the kitchen.

"Mom, hang up," I said. "Hang up my phone."

But she kept talking.

"Yes," my mom said. "Perry is a junior photographer on Yearbook."

It was like my whole plan and life and everything was crashing down around me. Why had I let my mother answer my phone? And why had Derby Esposito called me to get my home phone number? Why?

"I'll have to talk to Perry about that," she said. "But it shouldn't be a problem to set that up. We're free tonight."

Oh no! My mother was setting something up with Derby's

mom. And had said we were free tonight. What was happening?

"No. Don't do it, Mom," I said. "Hang up! You're not being
rude if you do that. You're being helpful! We are not free! We
are not free!"

But my mother frowned at me and wagged her finger. I'd
only seen her do that one other time before, and that was to
a dog.

"Oh, Derby's in the middle of gluing a school project?"
she said. "Is this for Idaho History? I think Perry is making
that same map."

I couldn't believe that my mom was telling Derby's mom
details about our personal lives. Why did they need to know
that stuff?

"Oh, he is?" my mom said. "Sounds like Derby's having
the same experience as Perry."

Did my mother secretly hate me? Why was she jeopardiz-
ing everything in my life I'd tried to build?

"Okay," she said. "When Perry surfaces, I'll run that by
her. Bye."

And then my mom handed me back my phone and I held
it to my chest and started breathing very hard.

"Calm down," she said. "That was your friend Derby's
mom."

And I just ignored the fact that she'd called Derby my
friend and got to what mattered. "What did she say? What
did Derby say? What are you setting up?" I asked.

"Don't hyperventilate," my mom said. "She wants to
meet you."

And this was way worse than I'd expected. "Huh?" I said.

"Did you tell her no way?" Because I really didn't want to get Derby's mom any further involved in this. What would Anya say if I told her I'd met Derby's mom? I couldn't let that happen.

"She seems a little protective," my mom said. "And she said you're going to take some special pictures of him. And she's a little leery about that because of what happened with the python. And she wanted to talk to you about that."

"Mom," I said. "I am not going to talk to Derby's mom about this. Or the python. Or anything."

"Why are you acting like this?" she asked. "She wants to drop by tomorrow night."

"No!" I said. "I don't want to meet his mom."

"Well, I already told her she could come by. And she's bringing some of Derby's leftover cardboard, because apparently some sixth graders don't wait until the last minute to do their assignments."

I could not believe that my mother had just compared me to Derby in a negative way. Was she trying to damage my self-esteem?

"Derby can keep his cardboard," I said. "Could you please call Mrs. Esposito right now and un-tell her everything you just told her? Because this could ruin my life. Derby is a giant goof. The whole school thinks he's a joke. I mean, I'm trying to help him, but having this meeting could really jeopardize my reputation."

And then my mom looked at me with a ton of disappointment on her face and I really regretted telling her all that.

"You need to lower your voice and stop talking to me that way and accept the fact that Derby is coming over tomorrow night and giving you his cardboard. And you will talk to Mrs. Esposito. And you will be nice to them. And you will never again put somebody's feelings below your reputation. Because that's mean."

"Mom," I said, trying to calm her down.

"No more talking," my mom said. "Go to your room."

And that really stunned me. Because I hadn't realized she was that mad.

"Fine," I said, in a grumpy whisper-huff.

"And leave your phone with me," she said.

Leave my phone? It felt like somebody had hit me in the face with a basketball. (That actually happened to me in third grade. It was the worst pain ever, especially around my nose.) I surrendered my phone to my mother and stumbled back to my room and collapsed onto my bed. How had things gotten this bad this fast? I replayed the day in my mind. Things had started going bad the second Leo messed up at lunch. In fact, if Leo had been able to talk to Derby like a normal person, I wouldn't have had to talk to Derby much at all. And then I bet Derby wouldn't have tried to call me. I put all the pieces together. My life was falling apart because Leo Banks was still in it. And he was so absorbed with his own great life and new relationship with Venice that he didn't even notice he was ruining mine.

Never had my life felt this out of control. My mind spun. There was so much pressure on me to find a solution. I stared at my ceiling waiting for the perfect idea to hit me. But all I saw was my dusty ceiling light and a dozen pale-green glow-in-the-dark stars that had stopped glowing months ago. Venice and I had stuck those stars up there last year. We thought they'd make my room look like outer space when we turned off the lights. But their glow was too wimpy. When I flicked off the light and learned this, I was pretty disappointed. Because I'd ordered them online and they'd had a thousand over-the-top amazing reviews.

"Either all those people were liars or we got a defective batch," I'd told Venice as we lay side by side staring at the dim fake stars.

And Venice, who was the most amazing friend in the world, said, "They kind of work. When I close my eyes I see the Big Dipper."

And that had made me laugh so hard. And her too. We just lay there laughing at how terrible my stars looked. I could feel tears wanting to fall out of my eyes when I thought about this. But I didn't want to cry. That wasn't going to help me. I squeezed my eyes shut as tight as I could. But instead of seeing the Big Dipper, all I saw was darkness. And for a second I worried that this was a sign. Maybe there was no solution to this. Maybe Leo was going to successfully steal Venice away from me and I was just going to have to live with it.

12

Volleyball Shots

Yearbook felt electric the moment I entered the classroom. And then the best thing happened. Venice raced to greet me at the door and asked, "Are you okay? When I texted you last night, your mom texted back 'This is Perry's mom and she's grounded.' "

And that sort of surprised me. Because I didn't realize my mom thought that.

Because sending me to my room and grounding me were two different things.

"It wasn't that dramatic. I got behind on my topographic map," I explained. I decided to leave out the part about Derby calling my phone. And my mom talking to Derby. And my mom setting up a meeting at my house tonight with Derby and his mom and me.

Venice's face looked pink, like she was super excited or incredibly happy or maybe had a temperature. And I could tell right away that she didn't want to talk about my map.

"What's wrong in here?" I asked. Because everybody was already in their assigned seats working. Even Anya. And the bell hadn't even rung.

"Ms. Kenny blew up," Venice said. Her eyes were as big as paper plates.

"Is she okay?" I asked. Because immediately my mind leaped to the Pyrex explosion at my house.

"Yeah. But she's so upset with Anya," Venice said with a tiny smile.

It relieved me to learn my first-period teacher had not actually blown up. At least my life hadn't spun into that much tragedy.

Venice started speaking in a whisper. "Anya was supposed to shoot the clubs this week."

I followed Venice's lead and whispered back to her. "I thought that got moved to next month."

Venice shook her head. "Ms. Kenny never approved that."

I glanced at Anya, who was furiously writing something down on a yellow legal pad.

Venice tugged on my arm to get my attention back. "We have to finish shooting all clubs by next week. Ms. Kenny said we're photographically behind. And she also said that Anya needs to learn how to delegate."

Ring.

I felt a hand on my shoulder and flipped around.

"Hi, Perry," Ms. Kenny said. "Did Venice tell you that we've adjusted the shooting schedule?"

I nodded. I was really surprised that Ms. Kenny had made

Anya change her plans. She seemed really set on how she wanted to do it.

"You can grab your lanyard and head out," Ms. Kenny said. "Anya's got the updated list."

Venice leaned into me and quietly squealed. "She's in so much trouble."

I watched as Anya started cramming equipment into the gear bag. She seemed very upset. But at least she wasn't asking me a million questions about Derby and how that was going. At this rate, as long as she stayed mad, I could easily avoid telling her about Derby's mom coming to my house tonight.

"Here," Venice said, enthusiastically handing me my lanyard.

But I was so shocked by everything that I just stood there and let Venice slip it over my neck.

"You know this means you'll be taking the pictures today, right?" Venice asked.

I was so upset from all the bad stuff happening that it seemed unbelievable that good stuff could be happening at the same time.

"I'm going to love that," I said.

Then Venice flung her arm through mine and hugged me a little. But I wasn't expecting it and it sort of knocked me off balance. "I can't wait to hear how the call with Derby went," she whispered. "School is getting so exciting."

I stared at Venice when she said this. Was this what school felt like to her? Because I felt totally burdened by my lies and pretty exhausted with all the planning and phone calls. Was

I doing something wrong? Because suddenly her life in sixth grade seemed way better than mine.

Once Anya had all her stuff, she didn't even ask us to follow her; she just walked out of the room and we tagged along behind her.

"So which club are we shooting first?" Venice asked as she practically skipped. "Maybe we should do languages first. Spanish. French. German."

But Anya didn't answer. She just kept huffily walking toward the gymnasium.

"Are you going to shoot them in the gym?" Venice asked. "I thought we'd do it in the library. Isn't that where they shot them last year?"

Anya still didn't answer. And when she reached the gym door, she pulled on it so hard that I thought I heard her elbow pop.

"We actually can't do clubs right now," Anya said in a voice so angry that it quivered. "Because none of the clubs know we've adjusted the schedule. I'm going to have to email their presidents. The soonest we can shoot any of them is Friday."

"Oh," Venice said, sounding super bummed out.

"So why are we at the gym?" I asked. Because if we weren't going to take pictures, why did we grab all the equipment?

Anya didn't even answer me and walked through the door.

"Is there a reason she's mad at me?" I whispered to Venice. Because I started getting really paranoid that I'd done something wrong that I'd forgotten about.

But before Venice could answer me, Anya flipped around

and faced me. "Please stop whispering. I have excellent hearing."

And that made Venice and me both jump a little. Because Anya said that so loudly and with such force that a little bit of her spit landed on us.

"Today's schedule stays the same," Anya snapped.

But then I realized I didn't even know today's schedule. So I raised my hand.

"You're not in class," Anya barked at me. "You don't need to do that."

"Um," I said, super surprised by her level of hostility. "What is the schedule?"

And then Anya sort of lost it and threw her bag down on the floor and started digging through it. Venice and I looked at each other. And when Anya continued to dig through her bag I felt a little bit bad. Like maybe I was making her waste valuable time.

"It's cool if you can't find the schedule," I said.

Anya looked up at me and frowned. Some of her blond hair stuck to her pink glossy lips. "Can you give me a minute?"

And then Venice and I just stood there again. Inside the gym I heard a bunch of sneaker squeaks and ball slaps.

"Who has gym first period?" I asked. Because it sounded really aggressive in there.

"That's actually the volleyball team," Anya said. "We're going in there to take some photos of practice."

"Cool," I said. But Anya totally ignored me.

Finally, Anya found what she wanted in the bag. She handed me a list written on yellow paper.

SHOOT SCHEDULE WEDNESDAY

~ BOYS' VOLLEYBALL PRACTICE SHOTS

~ FLETCHER ZAMORA (LADDER)

~ GIRLS' VOLLEYBALL PRACTICE SHOTS

~ MAKE VENICE AND PARTY WRITE CAPTIONS

The list made a lot of sense until I got to the part where she'd misspelled my name. A typo I could understand. But this list was handwritten.

"Um," I said. "You wrote Party instead of Perry."

Venice squinted and looked at that line a little closer. "Oh yeah. She did."

Anya snatched the list back from me. "I meant to do that. It's your nickname. It's what the design squad calls you."

"I have a nickname?" I asked. "And it's Party?" That seemed like a positive development, because it meant that people thought I was fun. But I wasn't sure why they were using it behind my back and not to my face.

"Let's go," Anya said, totally ignoring my questions. "I want to get these done before they develop head sweat."

As we walked through the gym, the boys kept practicing. I only recognized a couple of them. I didn't really run with the school athletes.

"Let's set up the tripod here," Anya said.

And then she just stood there, because I guess she expected Venice and me to do that.

"Um," I said. "I didn't bring the tripod."

"It's in the bag," Anya said.

Venice and I pulled out the tripod and locked the legs into place.

"Shouldn't the team be wearing their uniforms?" I asked. Because if they weren't, I thought the photos would look unprofessional.

"They're wearing their uniforms," Anya said.

And then I took a closer look and realized that was true.

"Okay," Anya said. "Which one of you has the loudest mouth?"

And I thought that was a pretty harsh question. "Um," I said. "We're both pretty good at keeping secrets."

Venice nodded.

"What are you talking about?" Anya said. "I need for one of you to yell at these guys to stop playing so we can let them know we're shooting."

"Oh," I said. That actually made more sense than what I thought. "Venice does."

But Venice looked a little hurt when I said that. "I think you do," she responded.

"No way," I said. "When you yell it makes the posters in my bedroom shake."

"I never yell in your bedroom," Venice said. "What are you talking about?"

"Okay," Anya interrupted. "Can you guys fight on your own time?"

But I thought that was pretty harsh. Because I didn't even think we were fighting. We were having a small disagreement about whether or not Venice had ever yelled in my room. Which she had.

"Okay," Anya said, in a really disgusted voice. "We don't have time to do this right now. We're supposed to be at the janitor's closet."

"We are?" I asked. I didn't see that on the shoot list.

"We're picking up a ladder," Anya said.

I watched Anya stick her fingers in her mouth and unleash a whistle that would stop any dog. She yelled, "We're going to come back to take some shots in ten minutes. So can you guys dial down the activity so you don't develop head sweat?"

I was really surprised Anya was so hung up about that. I mean, they were athletes. I felt sweat would make them look extremely authentic.

Coach Battle jogged over to us to see what was wrong. "I forgot something," Anya said. "But we'll be right back."

"No problem," Coach said. "We'll be here."

But I was surprised we were leaving without taking our pictures. It seemed like a waste of time. I reached for the tripod to fold it back up, but Anya stopped me. "Leave it," she said. "Let's move."

And then Anya basically started running and so did Venice and I.

"I hate making Fletcher wait," Anya said. "He's used to working with professionals."

After a long burst of running, and two tight turns, we'd made it to the janitor's closet. But Fletcher wasn't there. I think Anya could read my mind, because she saw me looking around and said, "He's meeting us behind the building. Better light."

And then I watched as Anya opened the closet door, which I'd assumed would be locked, and walked inside it.

"I'll need help carrying it," Anya said.

Bang. Bang.

"Do you need help right now?" I asked.

I watched as Anya tried to steer the top of the ladder through the door.

"Grab it," she said.

Venice and I both grabbed the ladder and helped lead Anya out of the closet.

"Now hurry to the west exit," she said.

Even though we were wearing lanyards, I had this un-shakable feeling I was doing something wrong. As we hustled down the hallway, every few doorways I sneaked a look in-side. I timed it so that I caught a glimpse of Derby while he was taking his Idaho History quiz. I worried that he'd wave at me. Because I wasn't really in a position where I could wave back. But he didn't.

When we got to the west exit, I saw Fletcher standing out-side in a long blue coat. He opened the door for us, and I sort of hoped he'd help with the ladder. But he didn't.

"Cool prop," Fletcher said as he finger-brushed his hair.

"It'll look better if you're on the ground and I shoot from above you," Anya said. "Like your toothpaste commercial. I loved those angles."

Fletcher didn't seem to mind this idea at all. I watched as Anya climbed up to the very top of the ladder. It didn't seem totally safe to do that, because the ladder wobbled.

"Can you two hold this thing so I don't die?" Anya said.

Venice and I rushed to grab a leg.

"Spread out the coat underneath you," Anya instructed.

Fletcher laid the coat on the concrete and then sat on top of it.

"Look up at me," Anya instructed.

Click. Click. Click.

"Do something more interesting with your legs," Anya suggested.

Fletcher bent his knees and leaned back.

"Way too much crotch," Anya said. "Do something else."

Fletcher rolled onto his side and shot Anya a sly grin.

"Nice," Anya said.

"He's totally ruining that jacket," Venice whispered to me.

But I sort of worried that Anya would hear her whispering and that would throw her off. She seemed to be in a flow.

"Take your shoes off," Anya said.

Fletcher dramatically kicked off his sneakers.

"Love the socks!" Anya cheered.

"I wonder if Ms. Kenny knows we're out here taking Fletcher Zamora's picture with the janitor's ladder," Venice whispered.

"Shhh," I said. Because I really didn't want Anya to hear us complaining about her.

"Leo told on her," Venice said.

"Shhh!" I said louder.

"He thinks she gets away with murder," Venice continued, still whispering.

"Shhh! Shhh!" I said. Sadly, because I was shushing Venice so aggressively, I moved the ladder a little too.

"Argh!" Anya cried.

I braced the ladder with my whole body as it rocked back and forth. Fletcher jumped up and tried to help. I was surprised by how good he smelled. Also, his chest felt warm in a really amazing way.

"You okay?" Fletcher asked Anya.

Anya had a firm grip on the ladder with both hands and was glaring down at me.

"I actually need to get back to Trig," Fletcher said. "If you want to take more, maybe we can set something up by the greenbelt. Maybe the rock gardens at Taylor's Crossing. Or the waterfalls."

After seeing Anya on a ladder, I didn't think it was smart for her to try to take Fletcher's picture near waterfalls.

"We'll see how these turn out," Anya said. "I've got to run and shoot the volleyball team."

"I really wish she'd say 'we,'" Venice whispered. "Because we're all doing it together."

"I can totally hear you," Anya said.

And that worried me. Because that meant she'd also heard that Leo had ratted on her. But to be honest, Anya had probably already guessed that.

"Let's go," Anya said.

I didn't realize she'd climbed down from the ladder.

"Let's hurry," Anya said. "I promised Ms. Kenny I'd turn in practice shots today."

We all took our original ladder-carrying positions and weaved our way back to the janitor's closet. Luckily, it was still unlocked.

"I can't believe they don't lock this," Venice said. "They keep a ton of chemicals in here."

"They do lock it," Anya said. "After first period."

And I don't know why I decided to store that information, but I did.

The second I slammed the closet door shut, Anya was ready to split. "Let's move."

"I need a bathroom," Venice said.

Anya looked furious to hear that. "Meet us in the gym."

All three of us walk-jogged down the hallway, but Venice dove into the bathroom while Anya and I continued to the gym. It totally surprised me that we'd managed to get the ladder, shoot Fletcher, return the ladder, and get back to the gym in less than fifteen minutes. We worked as a team much better than we should have.

"I'm not even going to waste time complaining about Leo the snitch," Anya said. "That kid is going down."

"Okay," I said. Because that was pretty good news.

Anya glanced around, moving her gaze from one player to the next. She looked disappointed.

"Do you think it's rude if I tell them to take off their jackets?" Anya asked.

Even though they were lobbing serves to one another and popping the volleyball over the net, most of the team hadn't taken their warm-up jackets off yet. I think it was because the gym still felt refrigerator cold.

"They look okay on," I said.

But Anya shot me a very annoyed look. "We can't see their muscles. Volleyball players have some of the best deltoids. It's a shame not to showcase that."

I shrugged. I never really thought about deltoids when

I took people's pictures. I usually worried about whether or not their hair looked good and their eyes were open. "They probably won't mind taking them off," I said. Because that was what Anya wanted to hear.

She ran over to talk to Coach Battle. A second later he blew his whistle. Then all the volleyball players peeled themselves out of their jackets.

Anya rushed back to the tripod. "Check out Henry's biceps. And triceps. They're hot. I mean, even his elbows are exciting."

"Huh," I said. Because it had never occurred to me that an elbow could be exciting.

Then Hayes dove to the floor to scoop a ball and I saw his scabs again and I realized that healthy elbows were super important in determining a person's hotness level. Really, any big scabs were a problem.

"I've got to get back and label the photo files we did last week. Ms. Kenny thinks we're getting sloppy. I mean, she's totally overreacting," Anya said.

But I thought that was a little rude to say. Because I wasn't getting sloppy at all. Anya had never let me label or download anything.

"I want action shots. Passing. Digging. Tipping. All of it," Anya said.

But I didn't really play volleyball. So I wasn't sure what some of those things were.

"Are you following any of this?" Anya asked me. "Does Venice understand volleyball?"

And before I could answer, Anya was already backing up.

"Of course she understands volleyball. With a brother like Victor she probably knows everything about everything when it comes to sports."

And if Anya hadn't been backing up to leave, I might have asked her how well she knew Venice's brother. But it just didn't feel like the right time.

"Tell Venice I want the best pike. The best campfire. The best attack block. The best pancake. The best power alley. And the best dink," Anya said. "And if you get a good butt shot, take it."

"Okay," I said. But I really couldn't remember any of the moves she'd just rattled off, and I also couldn't imagine putting butt shots in our yearbook.

"I'm gone," she said as she hit the door. "Don't expect me to come back and help you. After I label files, I'm sending emails to club presidents. If Ms. Kenny comes to check on me, tell her that exactly. You and your traitor friend should send me all the shots when you're done. Cool?"

I wanted to tell Anya not to call Venice a traitor in public places like the gym, because it felt mean to damage her reputation like that. But she wasn't exactly being loyal to Anya. So I just said, "Cool." Because that was easier than starting a serious conversation while she was backing up and leaving me to take pictures of cute guys.

And then she slipped out and I felt so relieved. It was like Anya had forgotten we were even mixed up with Derby. The stress of plotting his popularity behind his back melted out of me.

Then the gym door flew back open and Anya popped her

head through it. "And can you call me later about Derby? I mean, I need to stay on top of that."

"Okay," I said. I could feel the melted stress unmelting and becoming real again. I felt somewhat happy that she wasn't going to hound me. She did say that I could call her. But that nagging feeling that something might go wrong returned. As long as things went okay with Mrs. Esposito tonight, I really didn't have any major-major-serious problems. I mean, today was turning out to be a good day.

Venice burst through the door the second after Anya finally left. Venice was so excited that we were taking pictures together that she did a cartwheel toward me. I smiled huge when she did this. Because Venice hadn't done a cartwheel toward me in weeks.

"Perry!" a voice called. "Perry!"

I looked over and saw Hayes. He had a volleyball and was tossing it up.

"Want a picture of me serving?" he asked.

"Um," I said, switching lenses. "Venice and I still need to set things up."

Then Hayes winked at me. When he began the wink, I thought maybe he just had something in his eye. But by the time he finished it, I was totally sure it was a wink. Which freaked me out. Because following me for blocks, giving me free skate passes, and winking at me in the gym meant that Hayes liked me. And I didn't want that. My life felt complicated enough.

Venice gave me a quick hug and I handed her the camera to set up on the tripod. I helped her a little, but I felt so distracted. Why did the design squad think I was a Party? Was I more fun than I realized? Maybe Hayes saw that too. Maybe people were noticing things about me that I didn't even think I was showing them.

Party. It felt like a total compliment. But it also felt a little dangerous.

13

Quiz Time

My morning got better. I left Yearbook happy. And I stayed happy all day long. (Taking pictures with Venice did that for me.) PE was excellent, even though I had to learn how to play shuffleboard, because I made a great joke while pushing a tang to hit a biscuit. Poppy Lansing pushed a disc toward me and fell and I said, "Sometimes you've got to risk it to get the biscuit." And people laughed so hard I heard snorts. And I had a pretty good time in English, even though I had to write a letter from the perspective of a starving person fleeing the dust bowl for California. Sure, my letter was depressing and I talked about how hungry I was, but I ended on an upbeat note where I discussed possibly visiting the ocean and seeing whales.

And I also had a pretty good time in Science, even though Ms. Stott made us watch a video on the anatomy of an eyeball. Because I just closed my eyes during the gross parts where they showed us actual eyeballs. Leo didn't even bug me too much at lunch, because he helped Venice and me study for our Idaho History quiz. I mean, after I lied to them and told them, "Derby couldn't talk last night so we're catching up tonight," they basically suspended all Derby planning. We just focused on important Nez Percé stuff, like Chief Joseph and the Wallowa Valley. It wasn't until Idaho History started that my day took a nosedive. Seriously. All the Party vibes got sucked out of me.

Venice and I sat at our desks waiting for class to start. Luckily, we'd been assigned seats across from each other. Which was convenient on the days I forgot a pen. Which had happened a few times. Because it was hard for me to dress as cute as possible, remember to have my debit card loaded with lunch money, keep all my lies straight, plot my next move, and pack all my school supplies.

As soon as we had gotten to class, Venice said something so annoying that I nearly lost my mind. Which was weird, because she hadn't been annoying all day.

"Remember that Leo said Mr. Falconer marks you down if you misspell the answer," Venice said. "And try to stay calm. Because Leo says it's not the quizzes that will kill you, it's the midterm. Leo actually joined a study group for it last year."

I really didn't care what Leo did in his spare time. And it offended me that Venice would assume the midterm might kill me. Because I thought she should have assumed that I might kill the midterm. But over the past few days I'd gotten good at not telling Venice what I really felt.

"Thanks," I said, fake smiling. "We should definitely study together for it."

"That's a good idea. We should invite Leo," Venice said. "I

bet he still remembers some of the questions. He's basically a genius. You know, I think he makes this year, like, three times as much fun as last year."

And that was it. She'd crossed a line. Because Leo hadn't made this year three times more fun. He'd made it eighty-seven times more awful. And it was one thing to pretend to like him when he was helping me study. But it was quite another thing to pretend to like him when he wasn't around and Venice was still gushing about him. I tried not to look upset and I kept fake smiling at her. "I don't know. Last year was pretty fun."

But behind my smile I was seething. Leo wasn't improving anything for anyone. And the only reason Venice thought otherwise was because she didn't know about Leo's awful true motives. That kid was pure dishonest yuck.

Ring.

"Good luck on your quiz," Venice said. "Remember, *Nez Percé* has an accent over the last *e.*"

I nodded.

"Remember, Leo said Mr. Falconer won't give you credit without it."

I nodded again. How could Venice not detect that I really didn't care what Leo said about anything, even accent marks? Even though I knew I was great at being fake around Leo, I was sort of disappointed that Venice hadn't picked up on it. Because I thought a best friend should know the difference between when you're being real and when you're posing.

"I'm going to die if I don't tell you something," Venice whispered.

I glanced at her. "Okay," I whispered back.

"The reason I was in such a good mood this morning is because something happened on the bus."

And that made me feel bad, because it meant that maybe when she cartwheeled toward me it was because she was happy about something other than taking pictures with me. Which seemed totally rude to be bringing up now.

"Leo wants to kiss me," Venice whispered.

My mind exploded. *What? Venice? Kiss? Leo?* This made her happy? Venice shouldn't kiss Leo. Was she being serious?

I looked at her and raised my eyebrows. My first impulse was to stand up in the middle of Idaho History and demand that Venice promise me that she would not ever kiss Leo Banks. But I knew that was tactically the wrong thing to do. Because it would shut down the flow of information. And probably Mr. Falconer would give me an F on my quiz. Plus, it might just drive Venice further into Leo's awful arms. Mr. Falconer stood in front of the class ready to distribute our quizzes. But it felt like such a bad time to take a quiz. Because my best friend had just confessed to me that she wanted to kiss a jerk.

"On the mouth?" I asked in disbelief.

Venice blushed and nodded.

"I'm handing out quizzes," Mr. Falconer said. "No talking."

But that was pretty much an impossible request. Because when your best friend told you she thought Leo Banks wanted to kiss her on the mouth, you had to keep talking about it.

"When did he tell you this?" I asked.

I imagined them having a barfy late-night call when he confessed all his feelings about her.

"No talking," Mr. Falconer said. "Or you get a zero on the quiz."

I imagined my dad checking TRAC and seeing the zero where my score should be. I bit my lips together. It felt like I was dying.

Why did Venice need to kiss Leo? She didn't. She had her whole life to kiss an idiot. The quiz landed on my desk, still warm from the copier.

"You have all class to finish," Mr. Falconer said. "So pace yourself."

But I found it really hard to concentrate on this quiz when Venice was possibly going to kiss a jerk and ruin both our lives.

"Don't do it," I whispered.

"What?" Venice mouthed.

"No," I mouthed back.

"Nez Percé," Venice whispered.

She must have thought I'd mouthed the word *one* and so she'd given me the answer to the first question. But I didn't care about that. I cared about us.

"Who said that?" Mr. Falconer asked. "I just heard an answer. I will fail whoever is talking."

And that actually frightened me. Because I feared that a few people in that class might actually snitch. So I stopped looking at Venice and focused on my quiz. There were forty questions. Leo never told us there would be that many. This didn't feel like a quiz. It felt like a major test. And there were way too many hard questions. He wanted to know how many river miles were in Idaho. And which president established the Caribou National Forest in 1907. And the name for Idaho residents.

3,100 river miles
Theodore Roosevelt
Idahoans

I kept scribbling answers and looking at the clock. I had to come up with one correct answer at least every minute or I wouldn't have time to answer the terrible short-essay question and review my answers before the bell rang. Geez. Suddenly this class felt very flunkable.

By the time I finished the quiz, my hand was shaking. And I had a total of six scratch-outs. And I'd gotten so paranoid that Mr. Falconer was going to realize all my scratch-outs said *Leo* that I scratched hard enough on four of them to make holes in the paper and get ink on the desk.

Venice noticed. "When you write the wrong answer, you really freak out."

And I was too upset to think of a good explanation to give her. Also, I sort of blamed her. Because she was the person who was dragging Leo into my life. And I felt like if these two kissed, Leo would be sticking around longer than ever. Because once two people did that, it meant they were super serious. And even if you broke up or moved, you always remembered that stupid person. Because even my mom and dad remembered their first kisses. Even though they both happened forever ago. Back when nobody wore bicycle helmets and the world didn't have any cell towers.

I left that class in a total daze.

"Have fun in Math in Focus," Venice said, hurrying down the hall.

But I didn't tell Venice to have fun in Geometry. Because she was in there with Leo. And Derby. Then I realized I really didn't want Venice talking to Derby and figuring out that I was lying about yesterday and today.

I ran down the hall after Venice. "Wait! Wait!" And then something terrible happened. Venice stopped and turned around at the same time that Derby showed up.

"Hi," Derby said, sliding between us to enter his classroom.

And I was so paranoid that Venice would find out that Derby and his mom were coming over to my house and I hadn't told her. And I was so paranoid that this would lead to her finding out that my mom had talked to Derby on the phone yesterday. And I was so worried that this would lead her to doubt my truthfulness in other things (which was totally fair, because I had accidentally become a huge liar-face) that I tried to fix everything by telling a public partial truth.

"Talk to you tonight, Derby," I said.

And Derby looked at me like I was crazy. He looked at me like he couldn't believe I'd run all the way down here just to say that. And Venice looked at me that way too.

Derby slowly turned back around and walked to his seat. I stood next to Venice, breathing very heavy from all my hallway running.

"Are you okay?" Venice asked. "You're going to be late for class if you keep standing here."

I nodded. "I just want to make sure nothing gets screwed

up," I said to Venice. "So don't talk to Derby or let Leo talk to him. Okay?"

Venice sort of glared at me like she was upset. And it didn't feel pleasant.

"Okay?" I asked again.

"First, that's not a problem," Venice said. "We have a test today." But then Venice frowned at me in a really hurtful way. "Second, it's rude to think that my boyfriend or I would screw anything up for us. We're being really careful."

That word hit me like a giant bag of rocks. *Boyfriend. Boyfriend. Boyfriend.* I covered my ears and opened my mouth in horror. But no sound came out.

"Perry?" Venice asked, grabbing my arm and shaking it a little bit. "What's wrong?"

I closed my mouth. But I didn't even know how to answer that question. Because there were so many things wrong.

"Let go of your ears and go to class," Venice said. "I need to review for my test."

And even though I was still standing in her doorway, Venice walked off. I watched her take a seat next to Leo. And then Leo looked up and waved at me. I waved back. Then I grabbed all my stuff and headed toward my math class.

I wasn't too surprised when I arrived right as the bell rang. And I wasn't too surprised that I couldn't focus all during class and found myself drawing stick figures with lopsided heads without mouths that looked depressed. I had to do something (besides math) so I didn't go crazy.

When the bell rang at the end of class and I went to my locker, I really thought Venice would find me. But she didn't. As I panned the crowd I saw her and Leo walking to their bus together holding hands. I was starting to fear that the Derby project, no matter how stressful, might not break these two up at all. I mean, they looked tight. Plus, I knew this meant they were official now. I watched them board their bus and find a seat. Venice sat near the window. I watched her laugh and laugh. What was so funny? How could she be *that* happy on a school bus? It was pretty heartbreaking and unbelievable. So I finally just turned away.

14

Moms

The walk home felt incredibly long. I kept asking myself terrible questions. Would Venice kiss Leo on the bus? If Venice and Leo were girlfriend and boyfriend, what did that make me? If I had six scratch-outs and three wrong answers (I knew I'd missed three for sure), did that mean I couldn't get an A on the quiz? Did I know anybody who could replace Venice as my best friend? How long was I going to have to stay an infiltrator? What was I going to say to Derby? Why did his mom want to talk to me? Do moms really ruin schemes? When had I become a schemer? And was Hayes Ellsworth following me again? I flipped around to check. He wasn't. But was sixth grade always going to feel this hard?

I don't know how it happened, but Derby and his mother beat me to my house. I mean, I walked straight home at a fairly fast pace, but their giant green minivan was already in the driveway. I knew it was their minivan due to the bumper stickers.

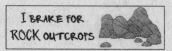

My family didn't know anybody who would have those bumper stickers. Also, when I peeked into the passenger window, I saw a backpack that had DERBY and a wizard's cap embroidered on it. I walked up the front steps feeling incredibly nervous. I hoped my mom hadn't said anything crazy or embarrassing. Actually, considering the real nature of the Derby project, I sort of hoped that my mom hadn't said anything at all. I carefully opened the front door and looked into my living room.

It felt really weird seeing Derby sitting on my couch. And it felt even weirder seeing Mitten Man curled up right next to his sneakered feet.

"Look who's here," my mom said. "It's your friend Derby and his mom."

And I looked at Derby and smiled. And I smiled at his mom too. And then I looked at my own mom and I shot her a worried face. Because she really shouldn't have been labeling people my friends until we'd both agreed that they actually were.

"Do you want any lemonade?" my mom asked.

Then I noticed that Derby and his mom already had lemonade. Geez. How long had they been here? What had they been talking about?

"Okay," I said.

And my mom handed me a glass.

"Did you have a good day?" my mom asked. "How was your quiz?"

And it sort of felt weird to talk about my day in front of Derby, but I did it anyway.

"It was actually really hard," I said. "It had forty short-answer questions and one essay."

"Sounds like a beast," my mom said.

And then something weird happened. Derby started talking to my mom.

"The teacher found out that students from last year were sharing old quiz questions, so he made it a lot harder," Derby explained.

"Really?" I asked. Because that was exactly what Leo had done, which meant that it was Leo's fault that the quiz had kicked my butt.

"So what obstacle did you pick for the essay question?" Derby asked.

It took me a second to realize that Derby was talking to me. Because it just felt so strange having him in my living room.

"Um, Lewis and Clark crossing the Bitterroot Range," I said.

Derby drank some of his lemonade and nodded. "Me too. Which crossing?"

But I didn't even understand Derby's question. "The one where they almost starved and had to eat a horse," I said. Because that was exactly what Mr. Falconer had told us had happened when Lewis and Clark crossed the Bitterroot Range.

Derby nodded again. "So you picked the first crossing. I picked their return trip and how they got stuck in the spring snow."

I just blinked. I didn't even remember their return trip. It felt like Derby had just pointed out that I might have failed my essay question by not stating which crossing I'd chosen. Was that what had just happened?

"Um," I said. "Now I'm worried I failed that question."

Derby drank more lemonade and looked super apologetic. "Yeah. He's a brutal grader."

"I'm sure you didn't fail," my mom said. "You had an answer."

But that didn't make me feel any better, because my mom didn't even know about Mr. Falconer's terrible scratch-out policy. Or how he graded down for misspellings and grammar mistakes.

"But I didn't state which crossing," I explained. Then I sat down with a big plunk right on the ottoman.

"Well, let's not worry about that now," my mom said.

But it was easy for her to say that. Because it wasn't her grade.

"I saw you carrying a ladder today," Derby said. "What was that for?"

He seemed so comfortable on my couch. And I thought that was weird. Because I sure wouldn't have felt comfortable on his couch. Especially with my mom there. My mom looked at me in a concerned way. Like maybe she didn't approve of me carrying a ladder around school.

"Was it for Yearbook?" Derby asked. "Were you doing some cool aerial photography?"

I couldn't figure out a reason to lie to Derby. "We were taking pictures of Fletcher Zamora," I told him. "Anya wanted a different angle."

Derby nodded. "Will you use a ladder to take my pictures?"

And that seemed pretty aggressive to request a ladder, but it also seemed like he was agreeing to let me take his picture. So I agreed to his demands pretty quickly.

"We could totally do that," I said.

"Where did you get the ladder from?" my mom asked. "Do you mean a step stool?"

My mom needed to stop worrying about the ladder and let me talk to Derby. But before I could think of a reason to make her leave the room, Derby got really excited and jumped up so he could demonstrate how big the ladder had been.

"It was a giant nine-foot ladder," Derby said. "You could paint a building with it. And Anya sat on the very top and took Fletcher's pictures. And he posed on top of a fur coat."

He was right about everything except the fur coat part. I wasn't sure how he knew this.

"It was a cheap coat," I explained to everybody. "It wasn't fur. Venice would never allow that."

Because Venice really loved animals. And she thought fur coats were cruel.

"You could break your neck on a nine-foot ladder," my mother huffed. "Where did you get it?"

"They took it from the janitor's closet," Derby said.

I couldn't believe what a blabbermouth Derby was. He needed to stop talking right away.

"It's cool, Mom," I assured her. "We totally had faculty permission." And I didn't even know if that was true, but it sounded good. "Plus, Venice and I held the ladder so Anya wouldn't fall. And I didn't climb it. My neck was never in any danger."

"But there was this one moment when you let go and the ladder started wobbling," Derby said. And then Derby imitated a wobbling ladder. "And then you grabbed it again and everything was fine."

My mother gasped. Which made sense. Because it was shocking that Derby was spying on me like this.

"How do you know this?" I asked. Because it felt creepy that Derby knew all these details.

"Everybody in first-period Idaho History saw you guys out the window," Derby explained.

"Huh," I said. Because I hadn't thought about people watching us through the windows.

"It sounds incredibly dangerous," my mother said. "Promise me you won't ever do that again."

"Okay," I said. Then there was a little bit of awkward silence in the room. I guess because nobody knew what to say. And also because Derby was awkward.

"Derby," Mrs. Esposito said as she dug around in her purse. "I forgot the cardboard in the car. Maybe you and Mrs. Hall could get it. Here are the keys."

"Okay," Derby said, snatching the keys up and leaping for the door.

"Be right back," my mom said.

And this totally felt like a setup. Like my mom had

planned to leave me alone with Derby's mom. Which felt very awful. Because my mom shouldn't have been setting me up. We should have been on the same team.

"Perry," Mrs. Esposito said. "The reason I'm here is I want to understand why the yearbook wants to take Derby's picture."

And it felt really awful lying to somebody else's mom. So I tried to be as honest as possible.

"Um," I said, trying to find the perfect words. "Yearbook has a new section this year. For interesting people. And we want Derby to be in that."

I was just so sick of lying and trying to remember my lies that I just said mostly the truth.

"Interesting?" Mrs. Esposito echoed. She raised her eyebrows and leaned forward. "What does that mean exactly?"

"Um," I said. Derby's mom was sort of intimidating. She had really bright green eyes that seemed to look right through me. And her hair was curly. And that was distracting too. Because basically all my friends and family had straight or wavy hair. Plus, she smelled like mint gum, which I wasn't used to smelling. Because my dad didn't let me chew gum, even when it was sugar-free. "We, uh, what are you asking me?"

Because it felt like Mrs. Esposito was getting at something.

"I'd like to see any pictures before they're printed or distributed in any way," she said.

"Okay," I said. Because they probably weren't going to get that far.

"It's important that I have your word. I'm still bothered

by what happened to Rose last year," Mrs. Esposito said, leaning forward and sounding a little hostile. "Middle school seems far more vicious than I remember."

"Who's Rose?" I asked. Because last year I was still in elementary school.

"Derby's sister. Her yearbook photo was edited so she was missing her front teeth." She said this in a very bitter way. Which made sense. "She was devastated when she saw that picture." Mrs. Esposito kept looking at me like I'd done that awful thing.

"Yeah," I said. "That's terrible. We have a really strict image-edit policy so that never happens again."

"Based on what happened at the snake assembly and Derby's subsequent panic attack, I'm worried this year's photographers are as bad as last year's," Mrs. Esposito said.

"Um, I can explain that," I said. I felt really uncomfortable talking about the python assembly, because I considered that event one of the major failures of my life. But I wanted to make sure Derby's mom knew I wasn't an awful person. "I'm not trying to do anything rotten to Derby. I wanted him to stand by the snake's head because that was the most in-focus part of the picture. I was trying really hard to make that photo turn out. For Derby."

Mrs. Esposito kept staring really hard at me. It was almost like she knew I was up to something.

"Derby has a kind heart. And I don't want to see anything unkind happen to him," Mrs. Esposito said.

And I sort of felt like I should explain to her how middle school worked. And tell her that maybe she should pay more attention to how Derby dressed. Because sometimes he wore T-shirts that stated he was a geek and so it was very likely unkind things would happen to him on a pretty regular basis.

"Right," I said, looking out the window to see where everybody had gone. Because it felt really weird to talk to somebody's mom by myself for this long.

"Once, somebody told him that for every day he dressed like Harry Potter he'd give Derby a dollar," she said. "And do you know what happened?"

And I tried to act like I didn't know about this story. Because suddenly I felt very guilty for laughing at him when he'd done this.

"He hid clothes in a backpack and changed into Harry Potter clothes before school every day for two months, trying to earn enough money to buy a bike."

When she put it that way, it made the situation sound very tragic.

"I had no idea he was doing this. And he never got any money. The principal called him into his office and told him he had to dress normally," she said.

"He should have gotten the money," I said. Because knowing the full story, I felt Derby had been totally robbed.

Mrs. Esposito leaned forward even more. She was basically teetering on the edge of our wingback chair. "I don't want anybody making my son look like a clown."

And I sort of felt like telling her about the outfit Derby had worn a couple of days ago and the coma-fighting cookie crumbs in his pocket. Because maybe he'd hidden that in a backpack too. Because, drama assignment or not, that definitely felt like a clowny outfit. But I couldn't figure out how to bring that up without sounding mean. So I tried to ease her worries.

"Nobody is going to make Derby look like a clown," I said. "I like Derby. I really do think he's interesting. And I want other kids to see that too."

And then things got really awkward, because her chin trembled and her eyes looked extra wet and I thought she was going to cry. "Do you need a tissue?" I asked, looking around for my mom. Because she really, really, really should have been back by now.

Then I felt something I didn't expect. I felt myself getting hugged. It was so weird getting hugged by another person's mom. It really caught me off guard. One moment I was standing in front of her. The next moment I could smell her deodorant and mint gum and then her buttons bumped into my face. But that wasn't even the craziest thing that happened. As unbelievable as it sounds, something even more shocking happened. My hug reflexes kicked in and I embraced her back. It was nuts. Mrs. Esposito and I were hugging in my living room. She was happy that I was being kind to her son. Except that wasn't the exact truth.

And as she hugged me I was hit by an awful realization. The exact truth was that I had been using Derby to break up Venice and Leo. The exact truth was that I wasn't being a very good person, even though Mrs. Esposito thought I was. The exact truth was that I was faking roughly 60 percent of my life. And realizing the exact truth made me feel like a rotten person. I mean, in that moment, I felt totally unlike myself.

But how could I fix any of this now? Was there even a solution? I thought about all the stuff I'd done. Wasn't it technically still in the planning phase? Wasn't it possible to actually do what Venice and Leo thought we were doing? Maybe all I needed to do was talk to Anya. If I could convince her to include Derby in the What's Hot section, wouldn't that solve most of my problems? I mean, I still had to put up with Leo and figure out what was going on with Hayes. But maybe Piper could give me advice with that stuff. My life had one giant obstacle. And I needed to do whatever it took to make Anya say yes to putting Derby in that section seriously. It was time for him to be popular.

My mom and Derby walked through the front door laughing. I quickly moved away from Mrs. Esposito.

"He's letting you borrow his brush pen and his special scissors," my mom said.

I was sort of relieved that I didn't have to try to use regular scissors, because I'd heard that somebody last year got vicious blisters trying to make this map.

"If you've got any questions, you can call me," Derby said. "Just make sure you stack everything and line up your canyon before you start gluing."

"Right," I said.

"It was really great to meet you," Mrs. Esposito said as she stood up.

"You don't need to hurry off," my mom said.

But really, they did. Because I had a bunch of stuff I needed to do. I had to get in touch with Anya and make her change her mind about Derby. And I realized what would really help was if Derby was starting to become popular already. So I needed to talk to Venice and figure out a way to take Derby's picture that would improve his life. I knew if we did something cool and dramatic and other people saw us through the windows, it could improve his social standing immediately. And we needed to secure some backup clothes in case he brought terrible clothes. And we probably needed some cool props. My mind was racing with ideas on how to make Derby hot enough for Anya and her precious What's Hot section. And he needed to get out of my house immediately so I could act on them.

"Bye!" I said. "Thanks for the craft supplies!"

And I waved at them with a bunch of energy, hoping that would make them leave quicker.

My mom frowned at me a little bit. But I didn't let that bother me. Because she didn't understand how much everything had shifted at this exact moment in my life. Piper was wrong. I didn't have to wait a year to fix the yearbook. Derby was the ticket. I had a huge project on my hands, but this could work. Derby Esposito deserved a spot. And I could make it happen.

15

The Gym

Anya never texted me back when I told her we needed to talk. Even when I used a fire emoji three times followed by exclamation points. It wasn't until Saturday that she finally bothered to respond.

Anya:

> At gym. Deltoid day.

I didn't even know what that was supposed to mean. Was it a joke?

Me

> Need to talk super bad. About Derby.

And I didn't want to say too much more, because I didn't want her to shoot down my idea. I wanted her to hear me out. Because I knew deep down that she had a heart and that I could convince her that putting Derby in What's Hot, even though he wasn't hot, was the right thing to do.

> Is this an emergency?

And I didn't even hesitate when I answered.

> YES!

> With Victor. Come find me.

> Where?

> Gym. Duh.

My mom wasn't thrilled when I asked her to drop me off at the gym. But she had to go to the post office anyway, so it didn't take too much to convince her to let me hitch a ride.

"If you're interested in working out, we can buy you a DVD," my mom said. "At your age, gyms are a rip-off."

And before I got out of the car I explained to her one more time that I wasn't interested in sweating to dance music in public. "Yeah, I'm only here to talk with Anya."

"Your relationship with her has really blossomed," my mom said.

And I didn't bother to correct her, because in Science Ms. Stott had taught us that bacteria can blossom and cloud water and destroy fish and plants and basically everything it touches. So I thought that word sort of worked in describing my relationship with Anya.

"It has," I said as I slammed the door.

"I'll be back in a half hour," my mom said.

And I said, "Okay," and ran inside. Because I was hoping a half hour was enough time to change Anya's mind.

I'd only been to a gym one time in my life. Venice and I had dropped off a ham sandwich for Victor. I'd only made it to the front desk, but I remembered the feeling of humidity and intensity. And I remembered the clinking sound the weights made when people set them down on the metal racks. When I entered the gym this time, looking for Anya, I arrived at the same front desk and felt the same humidity and intensity and heard the same clinking sounds. Looking around, taking it in, all the sameness and spandex felt haunting.

"Can I help you?" the girl behind the counter asked. She had fluffy blond hair and was wearing a sweat bandana. I must've looked totally lost because she said, "Are you looking for your mom?"

"No," I said. "She's at the post office. I'm looking for my friend."

"Do you want me to page her?" she asked, picking up a phone.

And that did seem like the quickest way to find Anya. So I said, "Sure. Her name is Anya O'Shea."

Then the gym music stopped playing and there was a soft beeping sound and then the blond woman said in a voice so loud it felt like the beginning stages of an earthquake, "Anya O'Shea. You've got a friend at the front desk." And then there was a terrible pause where everybody looked at me. "I repeat. Anya O'Shea. Your friend is at the front desk."

"Thanks," I said. But really I was worried that maybe I should've just walked around and looked for her in the weight room. Because maybe she didn't want her name blasted through the gym's speaker system.

It didn't take long before Anya and Victor emerged from a giant mirrored room filled with stair-stepping machines. I was actually glad I'd paged her, because I didn't think I would've checked that room. Because the door leading into it was dripping with water and it felt unsanitary to touch a door handle that had unidentifiable moisture on it.

"You didn't need to page me," Anya said, looking a little upset.

"Hey, Perry," Victor said, smiling at me while looking smoking hot in black shorts and a gray T-shirt.

"Are you Anya's trainer?" I asked. Because I really felt like I needed to make sure their relationship was only professional. Because if it was more than that, I thought Venice should know.

"Every Saturday," Victor said. "We're getting her into fighting shape."

And that was pretty alarming news. Because who was Anya preparing to fight?

"Let's not talk about me," Anya said. "Victor, could you go grab us some water?"

"Sure," Victor said. "What about you, Party? Do you want any?" he asked, smiling and winking at me.

"Um," I said. "I'm okay." Because I was totally thrown by him calling me Party.

Victor walked off and Anya punched my arm a little. "You're acting like a total nutzoid. What's going on?"

"Did Victor just call me Party?" I asked. "I thought that's what the design squad called me."

"Nicknames spread," Anya said. "So be quick. Tell me. What's happening with Derby? I need to get back to my cardio."

Looking at Anya in her white-and-black spandex work-out clothes, I felt suddenly nervous. I really hoped I could convince her that Derby belonged in the What's Hot section.

"I think we should put him in it," I said, looking Anya directly in the pink and somewhat sweaty face.

"In what?" Anya asked.

I couldn't believe that she didn't understand what I was saying. "In the section."

"In the What's Hot section?" Anya asked, opening her eyes super wide.

I nodded. I felt relieved that she could picture it.

"You want to feature Derby Esposito in the What's Hot section in *my* yearbook?" Anya asked. She looked away from me and glanced at the clock. "You seriously tracked me down at the gym to ask me this?"

Then I started getting super nervous that things were going worse than I'd imagined.

"Listen," I explained. "His mom came to my house yesterday."

She held her hand out in front of my face. "Stop," she said. "I told you to keep his mom out of this."

"But that was impossible, because of what happened to Rose's front teeth last year," I tried to explain.

Anya rolled her eyes. "That happened forever ago. That's ancient history. I can't believe you're bringing that up."

I could see Victor coming toward us. I'd forgotten how sculpted he looked. I mean, I could see all the muscles that made up his quadriceps flex when he walked.

"I just need you to say that you'll think about it," I offered.

Anya looked at me like she hated me. Which seemed really unfair, because I'd sacrificed a ton of my free time to help her.

"This isn't how life works, Perry," Anya said pretty quickly and quietly as Victor approached. "An unpopular sixth grader doesn't show up and start making crazy demands during a popular eighth grader's fitness session. I mean, I'm paying by the minute for this experience."

"Right, I'm sorry," I said. It was weird to me that Anya had forgotten that she'd asked me to find her here. "But Derby is a nice kid and it would be a nice thing to do. Please?" I begged. "Just consider it."

Victor tossed a clean towel to Anya and she draped it over her shoulders. "I can't consider that," Anya said. "Not ever."

"Are you guys talking about Yearbook?" Victor asked. "Venice is so stoked about shooting the football game against Sugar City next week."

I was surprised to hear this, because this game wasn't on the shoot calendar. We were scheduled to shoot the game against North Fremont in two weeks. Had Anya changed the calendar?

"She's great at action shots," Anya said, sounding really sincere.

But really, that was what Anya had said about me. She'd said she liked Venice's black-and-white shots best.

"All right," Victor said. "When you're finished, come back to the treadmill. Twenty minutes left. And bye, Party."

Anya didn't waste much more time with me.

"We're done," Anya said as she began to walk away. Then

she stopped and turned around and pointed her water bottle at me and wagged it. "No, we're not." It felt hostile and I wasn't prepared for it. "Why are you doing this?" she asked.

I didn't even know what she wanted to hear. "You told me to come to the gym and find you. And so—"

"No," Anya said, shaking her head. "Why are you trying to ruin the What's Hot section? Was this your whole plan all along? To trick me into trusting you so you could just shove any no-name nerd into one of the most important features? Were you only pretending to be my friend? Was that part of your plan too? Seriously. How fake are you?"

I felt stunned by what was happening. Because I hadn't planned anything. I was probably more surprised than Anya that I was standing here in this situation. "Um, I'm not fake anymore," I tried to explain. "It's just that I think people are way too mean to Derby. I want to do something nice for him."

Anya looked madder than I'd ever seen her before. She tightened her fingers into fists and then released them. "Well, I'm not going to ruin the What's Hot section because you feel like doing a favor for a dweeb," she said. Then it was like she was so disgusted with me she couldn't even look at me anymore. She turned her head to stare at the clock. "Baylor Kitts is going to be picked for the What's Hot section for sixth grade. It makes total sense. She's got about a gazillion signatures on her cast. People love her. Sabrina and Sailor and I decided on her last week."

I felt like I'd been punched in the face. Baylor Kitts was a rich girl who rode horses. I mean, I think she owned three.

And she wasn't very interesting. I didn't think she was hot. She was kind of a snob who sometimes hung around Sabrina.

"I'll see you Monday," Anya said.

"But I don't want Baylor," I said. "She doesn't represent the sixth grade. She's way too into horses. And dressage. And—"

Anya flipped around and her face had an expression I'd never seen before. It wasn't angry and pinched and stressed. It was eye-rolly and annoyed and dunzo. That was right, I could see it in her face: Anya O'Shea was done with me.

"That's it. I've never done this before, but I'm taking away your nickname."

"Huh?" I said. Everything was happening so fast now that I felt disoriented.

"You are no longer Party. Every year, the eighth graders name one member of the Yearbook staff Party, and as a surprise when we turn in the first signature we throw her a personal party and get her a cake and give her gifts. This year it was you. But I'm taking it back."

"You guys were going to throw me a party?" I asked. Because that revelation totally blew my mind. I mean, I understood the nickname Party now. And I didn't want to lose it.

"Javier is the new Party," she said. "Now I've really got to go."

I watched her stomp off and swing open the sweaty door. This wasn't how I expected things to go. I mean, I had really thought Anya would be more reasonable. Did she really hate nerds? Why was she so interested in keeping them down? Was she insecure? Or at her core did she have a snob heart?

Was she really done with me? I didn't know. And I wasn't sure how to figure out all the answers.

Walking out to the gym parking lot, looking for my mom's car, I made myself a promise. I would stop caring about what Anya thought. Seriously. It didn't matter anymore. I mean, middle school no longer made any sense to me. Popular kids were getting more popular, and there wasn't any reason for this to be happening. Why couldn't Drea Quan get a boost? Why did all the girls think Rocky DeBoom was cute? Why hadn't anybody ever stuffed annoying Leo into a trash can? It was crazy. None of it made sense anymore. Baylor Kitts didn't deserve any more popularity. It was time for Derby to get his turn.

16

The Derby Shoot

On Sunday night, I felt like I knew what I needed to do. I decided to pretend like the gym never happened and to press forward with the make-Derby-popular plan. Venice and I were totally on the same page when it came to Derby. Except when I told her we needed a fake fur coat.

"That might make him look like a dweeb," Venice said.

But I didn't have a ton of time to fight with her. I had to go to bed in thirty minutes. Plus, my parents thought I was in my bedroom dutifully constructing my topographic map. If they found me on my phone, they might take it away. They could be cruel like that.

"We need to think about what Derby wants," I explained.

"He wants to look like a dweeb?" she said.

And then I realized it was time for me to get bossy with Venice. And also make Venice get bossy with Leo. I had to stop pretending everything was cool between us. It was time I got real. "Listen, I'm going to email you the exact list of everything we need tomorrow. You need to call Leo and make him bring all this stuff."

Venice didn't answer me.

"Listen," I repeated in a very serious voice. "I wasn't going to tell you this, but I feel I have to now. Derby and I have done more than talk on the phone. He came to my house last week."

"What?" Venice asked.

I thought that would shock her to her senses.

"He basically demanded that we take his picture from the top of a ladder and use a coat just like we did with Fletcher," I said.

"How did he know we did that?"

"He could see out the windows in Idaho History," I told her. "That's why we have to set the ladder up in the exact same spot. And do the exact same thing. So everybody in the classroom thinks Derby is as cool as Fletcher. We need to treat them totally as equals. So people get confused and think Derby is popular."

"Wait," Venice said. "You're skipping stuff. Why was Derby at your house?"

And then I decided I needed to stop lying to Venice too. "Because his mom was paranoid that we were trying to trick him and she was worried that we were secretly mean kids who were going to image-edit his face and remove his teeth."

Venice gasped. "We're not like that at all."

Then I heard her phone beep. And I knew it was Leo. And that really bugged me. Because he was interrupting a superserious conversation. I couldn't believe he didn't have more patience.

"Okay," I said. "I need to work on my topographic map. I'm going to send you the email and I'm just gonna hope that you and Leo deliver."

"We'll do our best," Venice said.

But I wasn't sure that was enough. Because that meant she might leave stuff off the list.

"I need everything on this list or we might fail and Derby will remain Derby and Anya will still be Miss Bossy McBoss-Boss-Pants and nothing will change," I said. "Except maybe Anya will get bossier."

There was silence again. And I was really afraid she'd accepted Leo's call and was talking to him.

"Okay," Venice said. "We'll deliver."

And that totally thrilled me. "Awesome!" I yelled.

Then I heard a knock on my door. "Everything okay in there?"

And even though I'd promised myself that I would stop lying, I felt like under these exact circumstances, it was okay to fib to my parents.

"Treasure Valley has never looked so good!" I said.

"What?" Venice asked.

"Nothing," I said. "My parents think I'm making my map."

"Mr. Falconer is nuts," Venice said. "Those projects are so hard. My fingers are stained green from making the pasture for my diorama."

But I didn't have time to worry about Venice's finger stains. I had to hang up before my parents caught me on the phone. So I recapped our situation quickly. "Me do homework. You and Leo deliver. Cool?"

"Cool. Leo totally knows how to deliver," Venice said. "His brother works for a pizza place."

But I didn't care about Leo or his brother. Didn't Venice know that?

I went to the living room and pretended that I was looking up some important map-building information.

"How's it going?" my dad asked.

"Better and better," I said. Because that was a safer answer than telling him I hadn't started yet.

"Do you need any help?" he asked.

"Maybe later," I said. "When I get to the glue stage."

"I'm all yours," he said.

But I wasn't going to get to the glue stage until tomorrow. Because I was still on the dress-Derby-normal stage.

Venice and Leo:

Here is a list of everything we need. If you can't get something, please text me. I will try to get it myself. Even though I am super busy and don't have time to do that.

Essential Items:

- Sneakers with laces that aren't neon or weird looking or made out of coat hangers

- 1 pair jeans with thrashed knees that don't flare at the bottom

- 1 pair gray pants (in case his knees look terrible exposed)

- 3 different shirts (No dweeby sayings. No stripes. No patterns. No collars. Stuff Leo wears would work. Avoid harsh colors like black and white)

- 2 pairs socks that are neutral color (No terrible ankle socks. Must go to mid-calf at least)

- 1 large chain (essential for backdrop)

- brush/comb

- hair spray

- colorless lip balm (in case his are chapped)

- water bottle (in case we need to restyle hair from scratch)

- hair gel

- leaves (live green ones or dead brown ones)

- a red or green or yellow hoodie (In case hair is total failure and we need to cover it. These colors look good in black-and-whites.)

- fake fur coat (Derby needs this!)

Thanks for your help.
Bye!
Perry

I looked over the list. It seemed totally reasonable.

"Are you sending emails?" my dad asked.

And then I realized I had forgotten that I'd lied to him about why I was on the computer. I really needed to stop doing that.

"I needed to give some information to Venice," I said.

He seemed to think that was okay. "It's pretty much time for bed."

"Yeah," I said. Because I felt totally exhausted.

"Here's some good news. After you turn your map in you don't have any major assignments for a week," he said.

But I already knew that. Because I was responsible and checked TRAC twice a day. I mean, it felt like my homework was never going to end.

"You have to write a report on a nineteenth-century biologist," my dad said.

"Right," I said. But really, I thought that sounded crazy. Because writing an essay for Science felt weird. We should have only been dissecting dead things and watching gross movies for that class. I hurried back to my room and got ready for bed. I felt so excited to turn Derby's life around. I mean, after talking to his mom it did really feel like if anybody on the planet deserved a shot at being popular, it was Derby Esposito.

I stared at the totally faded stars on my ceiling. I wondered if Venice ever regretted giving them all to me. As I drifted off to sleep, I told myself that I should ask her about that. Because maybe I could give her some of mine. That way she wouldn't have to fall asleep under a totally empty ceiling.

* * *

It took Venice and Leo several days to deliver. And the day they did, it sort of blew my mind. Because it meant Derby's photo shoot was really going to happen. I ate my breakfast as fast as I could and got all my stuff together.

"You sure are eager," my mom said as I zoomed out of the house.

I called to her over my shoulder, "It's going to be an amazing day."

I walked to school faster than I'd ever walked before, even though I knew that once I got there I'd probably have to face Anya. But even when that happened, I told myself that it would be okay. Because we'd be seeing each other in a public space. And it wasn't like she could yell at me in front of Ms. Kenny. And why should all her ideas win and mine lose? It shouldn't have been that way. I wasn't going to let her destroy my chance to help Derby escape his dweebiness.

I didn't race to the Yearbook room. Instead, I raced to the janitor's closet to make sure it was unlocked. I grabbed the silver knob and turned it. Bingo. It opened. This was really going to work. On a normal day, where Anya hadn't declared I was awful at the local gym and stripped me of my fabulous nickname, I would have checked with her to make sure it was cool for me to borrow the ladder. But I didn't need to do that anymore. Because if she was done with me, I was done with her. All I needed to do was get Ms. Kenny's permission to leave and take Venice and Leo with me and perfectly recreate Fletcher's photo shoot. I mean, every stinking detail needed to be the same. Except for Fletcher.

Before I had a chance to approach Ms. Kenny, Sabrina came bopping over to my desk wearing boots with tiny bells on the sides. She looked super calm as she jingled over. Then she smiled. "Anya sent me over here."

"Oh," I said in a depressed voice. That wasn't awesome news. I liked Sabrina. And I didn't want her to start delivering mean messages to me from Anya. I mean, if Anya and I were done, I didn't think she should be communicating to me through the design squad.

"Don't freak out," Sabrina said, giving my side a playful nudge with her elbow. "She wants to ask you something."

I glanced over at Anya. She was talking to Javier and Eli by the master calendar. And they were laughing. I bet she was giving Javier my nickname. I mean, he looked super happy about something. It was really painful to watch that happen, even if I wasn't sure that was even what was going on by the whiteboard.

"Does she want me to come over there?" I asked. Because maybe I'd misunderstood what it meant to be *done*.

"No!" Sabrina said, grabbing hold of my wrist. "Don't go over there."

She looked really scared that I might do that. "Okay."

"I'm going to ask you something for her," Sabrina said.

And that was interesting to learn, because I wasn't sure what it could be.

"Remember last week?" she asked.

And that question seemed sort of big. "All of it?" Because I certainly remembered some parts of it better than others.

"Okay," Sabrina said in a whisper, looking over her shoulder. "Anya needs me to ask you something and you can't tell anybody that I'm asking."

This made me feel uncomfortable for several reasons. "Um," I said. "I guess."

Sabrina looked back at Anya and smiled. "Do you think Fletcher was flirting with Anya when you guys took his picture?"

I blinked. "Um," I said again. Because I didn't really think that. Unless I had missed something, he did zero flirting with Anya and maybe a tiny bit of flirting with the coat.

"It's just," Sabrina said, drumming her pen on the desk, "Anya says she felt a vibe. And she wants to know if anybody else felt it."

This was so stupid. If Anya and I were done, then she shouldn't have sent Sabrina over to quiz me about vibes. It was like Anya didn't even know the definition of the word *done.* It was like I needed to have Piper call her and tell her.

"Oh my heck," Sabrina said. "I can totally read your mind right now."

"Huh?" I said. Because that was a creepy thing to tell somebody. And I really hoped it wasn't true. Because I didn't want Sabrina to be done with me. Even though she was a follower, there was something sweet about her that I liked.

"You can't read my mind," I said, shaking my head.

She nodded. "I totally can."

How do you politely make mean people leave you alone forever? That was what I wanted in this moment. I wanted Anya to vanish, like a greasy fingerprint that gets wiped off a window. Squeak. Poof. Gone.

"Tell me what you saw," Sabrina said, grabbing on to my hands. "Anya is going to flip out."

What had I seen? A pushy eighth grader kissing up to a photogenic seventh grader who had starred in a toothpaste commercial?

"Did you notice anything about his face?" Sabrina asked.

I couldn't believe she was still pressing me for details. Anya must've had a mega-crush on Fletcher.

"He did blink a lot," I said.

"Really?" Sabrina said, getting a little giddy. "Anya said that too. And she swears he puckered his lips like this." Sabrina made fish lips several times in a row. "Did you see him do that?"

I had not seen that. And I sort of doubted it had happened. "I missed that." I looked over at Anya again. She'd pulled out a small mirror and was finger-combing her bob.

"Anya said he was sly about it," Sabrina said. "But I totally think he might like her."

"Huh," I said. Because I really was super eager to ask Ms. Kenny for permission to leave and get far, far away from this conversation.

"They'd make a hot couple," Sabrina gushed. "They'd be fierce."

"That's true," I said. "Hey, I need to ask Ms. Kenny about something really quick."

And I didn't even wait for Sabrina to react to that. I just hurried over to Ms. Kenny's desk.

Ring.

I jumped a little when I heard the warning bells. They always caught me off guard. Ms. Kenny stapled an advertisement contract together as I approached. I wasn't sure exactly how to catch her attention, so I just blurted out what I needed to say.

"Can Venice and I borrow the staff lanyards so we can take a few pictures this morning for the What's Hot section?" I asked. "And maybe take Leo with us?"

"Does Anya know?" Ms. Kenny asked.

And that was the perfect question to ask me. Because while Anya might have been furious with what I was doing, I didn't have to tell Ms. Kenny that. "Anya knows," I said.

"That's fine," Ms. Kenny said, handing me three staff lanyards. "Don't forget after school you're taking the girls' basketball photos. I wish you'd already taken the club photos. I keep feeling like you're behind."

I understood why she felt that way. But that was really all Anya's fault. "We'll make it happen," I said. Because I really wanted to be taking more pictures. And now that Ms. Kenny was letting me take my first photos on my own, maybe she'd let me take others on my own. I smiled at her.

"Do you know if Anya sent an email reminding the team?" Ms. Kenny asked.

I shrugged. "I emailed Poppy Lansing." Not only had I reminded her about the shoot, I'd sent her an article that listed the most flattering hairstyles for group shots.

"Okay," she said. "I'll double-check with Anya."

I tried to ignore the fact that Anya was glaring at me something fierce when Ms. Kenny handed me the staff lanyards and I walked back to my desk. I just kind of sat there and tried to stay calm. I focused on thinking about happy things. Like muffins.

As soon as Venice and Leo arrived, things got pretty exciting pretty fast. They had two big backpacks full of stuff. I rushed over to them.

"I think it's a little weird that you wanted a chain," Leo said.

But I ignored that comment and focused on what was important. "Where is it?"

He carefully set the second backpack down on the floor. It jangled a little bit when he did that.

"The hair gel has a watermelon scent," Venice said. "Is that okay?"

I nodded. Because it didn't matter what anything smelled like. It only mattered what it looked like.

Ring.

When the bell rang I was super excited to get going.

"Leo," I said. "We need you to help us carry the ladder."

"Whoa," Venice said. "We're using the ladder again."

I pointed at her. "Derby requested it. The ladder is happening."

"Should we drop the backpacks off at the shoot site first?" Leo asked.

But I worried that somebody would steal them. I mean, just because we were in middle school didn't mean we weren't totally surrounded by thieves.

"We wear them," I said.

Anya gave me a death stare as I slinked out of the room with Leo and Venice. Luckily, Leo wore the heavy backpack and Venice volunteered to wear the other one. I was super relieved when we got to the janitor's closet and it was still open.

"We're allowed to do this?" Leo asked as we walked past the mop bucket and grabbed the ladder by its metal legs.

"Totally," I said.

It was actually a good thing we had Leo with us, because

he was excellent at aiming the ladder out of the closet and guiding it down the hallway. Plus, he took the heaviest end.

"Where are we going again?" Leo asked.

I couldn't believe he'd already forgotten. "The west exit," I reminded him.

"Can you guys handle this if I go and get Derby?" I asked.

I wasn't sure if Venice had the arm strength to get the ladder out of the building.

"I'm fine," Leo said.

"It's cool," Venice said.

I was so thrilled by how things were going, I ran down the hallway to get to Derby's class.

Knock. Knock. Knock.

I felt so nervous as Mr. Falconer opened the door. Because it was one thing to sit in a classroom while your teacher teaches you. But it was a totally different thing to talk to him in the hallway.

I lifted up my staff lanyard so he could read it. "Is it okay if we borrow Derby for a few minutes?" I asked.

And I was totally expecting Mr. Falconer to demand more details. But he did the craziest thing. He said, "Sure, Perry."

Derby didn't look thrilled when he came to the front of the class to meet me.

"I told you that I didn't want to miss first period," he said.

But he didn't understand what a good plan we had. He didn't understand that we were going to take his picture where everybody could see him and that I'd gotten the ladder and a coat and that things were going to be awesome.

"We need to match the light from yesterday," I explained. Which was the exact truth.

Derby and I hurried down the hallway to the west exit, and when we got there it was super amazing to see everything already spread out. The coat on the ground. The ladder standing up. The chain curled into a mound.

"So we brought different clothes for you," I said.

Venice unzipped a backpack and handed him a pair of jeans with shredded knees and a red T-shirt.

"Isn't what I'm wearing okay?" Derby asked. He stretched his arms out and rotated for us. His pants were yellow corduroys, but maybe a little too faded. And his shirt was light tan, so it didn't really provide any contrast.

I tried to explain this to him as kindly as possible. "Your look is way too monochromatic. You'll look like a noodle." Because he looked exactly like a piece of fettuccini with a hairstyle on top.

"A noodle?" Derby asked, sounding offended.

"What she means is that your top half and bottom half match too much. Jeans will read better in the lens," Venice said. "Trust us."

But Derby still looked offended. He didn't look like he wanted to trust us at all.

"Let's take a look at what I've got," Leo said. "Something will work."

"I'm not changing outside in front of everybody," Derby said.

And I was shocked that Derby thought we wanted that. Because revealing his underwear to Idaho History wasn't going to make him popular. "Of course," I agreed. "Go inside to the bathroom. Here, use my lanyard."

I didn't think he'd run into any problems, but I also

didn't want anybody to look twice at him in the hallway during classtime.

"His hair looks really good today," Venice said. "I think he used gel."

"I thought the same thing," I said.

While Leo was inside with Derby, Venice helped me get the camera ready and attach the right portrait lens.

"I think he'll look better not smiling," Venice said. "So take some serious pictures. He's got a strong jaw."

I was surprised that Venice thought I needed coaching. "Don't worry. I'm probably going to take a million different shots. I'll get his strong jaw for sure."

I loved taking pictures so much. And I'd never done it from on top of a ladder before. When I heard the door squeak open, I was super excited to see how awesome Derby would look. Except I didn't see that. I saw the janitor, Mr. Zeller.

"Is that my ladder?" he asked.

But it seemed pretty obvious that it was, because it had spray painting on the side that read:

Rocky Mountain Middle School
Property of JANITOR

"We're only using it for a second," I explained.

"Students aren't allowed to use janitorial equipment," Mr. Zeller said. "Especially not this. There's liability issues."

He walked over to the ladder and started folding it up.

"But we're on Yearbook staff," I said. "We're taking important student photos."

"Nobody contacted me about that," he said. "I got a message that students were horseplaying with equipment."

"That's wrong," Venice countered. "There's no horseplay going on here. Only photography."

Mr. Zeller stopped folding the ladder and looked at us both very carefully. But he must not have liked what he saw, because he started folding the ladder again. "I'll need to speak to Principal Hunt."

Venice and I looked at each other. This wasn't good.

"Do you have hall passes?" Mr. Zeller asked.

"We have a staff lanyard," Venice said, sliding it off her neck and handing it to him. "We're on Yearbook."

His big hands took the lanyard and inspected it. "And where's yours?"

And I really didn't want to tell him that it was in the boys' bathroom. Because that might have made us look like we were more suspicious than we actually were.

"Where did you get this chain?" Mr. Zeller asked, picking it up. "You can't have this at school."

It really alarmed me that he said that, because I worried he might take it away. And we needed it. I mean, I had really fallen in love with its artistic potential. "It's a prop," I explained.

When I said that I could see some alarm in Mr. Zeller's face. He set it back on the ground with an enormous clank. Then he pulled a walkie-talkie out of his front coverall pocket.

"Principal Hunt," he said. "I've got students acting suspiciously near the west exit. They've got chains and backpacks and janitorial equipment."

When he put it that way we sounded like total criminals.

"This sucks," Venice whispered to me.

I stared at the walkie-talkie, waiting for Principal Hunt to respond.

While we waited, Mr. Zeller bent over and started snooping in our backpacks.

"It's just some clothes and styling products," I explained. It really bothered me that Mr. Zeller didn't understand that we were photographers. Didn't he notice our camera?

"You haven't told me where you got this chain," Mr. Zeller said.

And I looked at Venice because I didn't know where she'd gotten it.

Mr. Zeller's walkie-talkie crackled and a voice started coming through. "Do you recognize the suspicious students?"

I whispered to Venice, "Did the chain come from your garage?"

She shook her head. "I took it from my neighbors."

"You borrowed it with their permission?" I asked. Because I really hoped we weren't in possession of a stolen chain. That just looked bad.

"I just took it," Venice said. "You said we had to have it."

This was totally insane. I couldn't imagine things getting any worse. But then Derby and Leo walked out of the building and joined the drama, and that actually felt a little worse. Oddly, Derby looked pretty cute. Leo's outfit looked totally great on him. And Derby's knees, which I'd feared seeing in broad daylight, didn't look too bad either.

"I've got four students," Mr. Zeller said. "Let me get their names."

He pointed his walkie-talkie at us. "Who are you?"

I spoke first. "I'm Perry Hall," I said. "I'm taking pictures for Yearbook. And this is Venice Garcia. She's another photographer. And this is Leo Banks. He's on Yearbook too. And this is Derby Esposito. He's the reason we're here. We're taking his picture for a special yearbook section."

Mr. Zeller looked pretty upset with us. Then he repeated our names into the walkie-talkie.

"Bring them to the office," the voice replied.

"You heard her," Mr. Zeller said, pointing to the door.

"What about our stuff?" Leo asked.

"Pack it up," Mr. Zeller said.

And in the moment, I did what any good photographer would do. I took my shot. "Derby," I said. "Look at me."

And Derby looked at me. And he didn't smile. Because I hadn't told him to.

Click. Click. Click. Click. Click.

I didn't know if the five pictures looked good or horrible. They happened too quickly.

"What are you doing?" Mr. Zeller said in a stern voice. "I said pack it up."

And it was depressing to hear that, because it probably meant we weren't going to be able to take additional pictures of Derby today.

"Sorry," I mumbled as I screwed the lens cap back on. But I didn't really feel that way. I felt sad. And disappointed. Because I was so close to taking really life-changing pictures. I was sure of it.

We all followed Mr. Zeller down the hall. It felt really stressful to walk past all the doors. Before when I had walked past them it felt cool. But walking toward possible punishment felt very different, like people inside the classrooms were judging me.

"We probably shouldn't mention that we stole the chain," I whispered to Venice.

"Why did you bring a stolen chain?" Derby asked. He looked totally freaked out.

"Props like that can really transform a shot," I explained.

Before I knew it, we were standing in front of Principal Hunt's door. Mr. Zeller knocked on it three times.

"I really don't know why you brought us here," I said to Mr. Zeller, sort of hoping maybe he'd let us return to class. "We're supposed to take pictures. It's the entire purpose of being Yearbook photographers. We were selected to do this from a pool of applicants. I mean, it's our job."

Then the door creaked open and it became pretty clear that we were going to have to talk things over with Principal Hunt.

"Explain that to the principal," Mr. Zeller said.

"I'll speak to them one at a time," Principal Hunt said.

And when she said this, I really hoped that I could get in there first to try to smooth things over. So I squeezed past everybody else until I was the person closest to her door.

But then she said something rotten. "Derby Esposito, come inside."

And when Derby walked into the principal's office I felt really sorry for him. Because all he wanted was to be photographed like Fletcher. But now he was speaking with Principal Hunt. And then while we were waiting, Leo started talking crazy theories again. The conspiracy kind.

"This feels like a setup," he said, glancing around the hallway.

But that sounded pretty stupid to me. Because why would Mr. Zeller be setting us up?

"You think it was Anya?" Venice asked.

And that actually didn't sound totally stupid. It sounded possible.

"She was afraid that we might actually make Derby popular, so she ratted us out and sabotaged the shoot," Leo said. "I can feel it."

"I don't know," I said, trying to process this traumatic development. "She told me a few days ago that she was done with me."

"That doesn't mean anything," Venice snapped. "I've heard her tell Sailor that at least three times."

"Really?" I said. Because it seemed cruel to say that to your friends.

"You trust Anya way too much," Leo said. "We're going to get in serious trouble. We're going to get our lanyards suspended."

I couldn't believe how wrong Leo was. Because Anya and I weren't even speaking. But I didn't bother telling him that. Because what he said about our lanyards really worried me. I didn't even know that could happen. So I asked a pretty important question. "That can happen?"

"It happened last year to Zoe Dunn and Penelope Cooper," Leo said. "They got in trouble for interviewing the boys' volleyball team in the boys' locker room. Their lanyards were suspended immediately."

"When did they get them back?" I asked.

"Never," Leo said.

But I wasn't too freaked out to learn this, because girls interviewing boys in the boys' locker room did sound like trouble.

"Did Anya set up Zoe and Penelope?" Venice asked.

But I really thought we needed to stop talking about Anya and focus on figuring out a way to explain things to Principal Hunt so we looked like great students who were just doing their jobs.

"She got jealous of Zoe because she was friends with a bunch of the volleyball players," Leo said. "Anya sent them to the locker room to do interviews, then she ratted on them."

But I wondered if that was really true. Because that meant Anya was pure evil.

"This makes total sense. How else did Mr. Zeller find us so quickly?" Venice asked.

"He probably missed his ladder," I said. Because I just didn't believe Anya was the worst person in the world. Yet.

"But the ladder could have been anywhere. He walked right to us. And remember he said he was responding to a report of kids playing around," Venice said. "Somebody reported us."

I did remember him saying that.

"Perry Hall," Principal Hunt called.

And I waited for Derby to leave the office so I could enter. But he didn't leave. He stayed in there.

"Perry Hall," Principal Hunt called again. This time it was a little louder.

"Go in, Perry," Venice said, gently pushing on my back.

I walked into Principal Hunt's office and I saw two

terrible things. First, there was a stuffed deer head on her wall, which made the room feel very death-y. Second, Derby had tear marks on his face.

"I want to start by saying that I think this is a very serious matter," Principal Hunt said.

And that sort of knocked me off balance. Because I didn't think that was a good place to start.

"We consider chains weapons at Rocky Mountain Middle School, and bringing a weapon to school in a backpack could result in expulsion."

And I wasn't exactly sure what that word meant. Until Derby said something in a trembling voice.

"I'm directing the school play. Please don't expel me," he said. "I didn't even know about the chain."

Things were worse than I thought. So I did the only thing I could think to do. I tried to talk my way out of this.

"This is a super-big misunderstanding," I said. "Because we were taking pictures of Derby for the yearbook's What's Hot section, and I thought a chain would be a dramatic way to frame him. So we didn't intend to chain anybody, if that's what you were thinking."

Principal Hunt rubbed her eyes. "Let's bring in Venice and Leo."

And then Venice and Leo walked in together and I realized their shirts sort of matched and that they totally looked like a couple and that depressed me even further.

"I'm getting more than one story about what happened here. And I'm also being told that you thought you had permission to be out there," Principal Hunt said. "So here's what we're going to do. I'm going to put each of you in a room by yourself. And I'm going to give you some paper and a pen. And I want you to answer three questions. Who gave you permission to take the ladder? Who brought the chain onto school property? Why were you taking Derby's picture?"

But it seemed like Principal Hunt hadn't heard what I'd already said. So I took a stab at the last question. "This was for What's Hot. It's a new section in the yearbook."

But Principal Hunt put her finger to her lips and then shushed me.

"I want all four of your answers," Principal Hunt said. "Written down. This will help me figure out whom to punish. And what the punishment will be."

And this was basically the worst thing anybody had ever told me.

"Leo, you'll go to the cafeteria. Venice, you'll go to the attendance office. Derby, you'll go to the library. And, Perry, you'll write your response in here."

I looked around her office in horror. I could see a couple of bald patches on the dead deer's neck and that really traumatized me. Because it probably meant all its fur was coming loose. And if she told me to sit at the desk underneath that head, I would probably get dead-deer fur on me.

"Do you have any questions before I separate you?" Principal Hunt asked.

But I decided not to ask about the deer head. Because I thought of a more important question. "Do you have a scratch-out policy?"

"A what?" Principal Hunt asked.

"In Mr. Falconer's class he marks our grade down if we change our mind and scratch out an answer. I'm just wondering if scratch-outs will be held against us," I asked. "In his class it's actually possible to go in the hole."

Principal Hunt seemed surprised to learn about that policy. "You can change anything. This is your official statement. Once you're finished, it will stand as your official record of what happened."

Derby looked like he was in pain. I could see his lip trembling. And I felt terrible for him. Except he shouldn't have been too worried. Because he didn't know too much about the plans. Plus, he got to write his statement in the library and they had comfortable chairs in there.

I watched as everybody left the room. Principal Hunt handed me a stack of paper. I started counting the pages. There were eight pieces. Did she think my answer should take eight pieces of paper? I think she noticed my alarm because she said, "You don't need to use it all. Just answer the three questions as best you can."

I heard the door squeak shut a little, but not all the way. I could totally see the attendance secretary, Ms. Boz, and she could see me.

"Don't you need your office?" I asked Principal Hunt. Because I got worried that she'd come in here and work with me. And that seemed stressful.

"Mr. Hamer has an emergency and we can't find a sub. So I'll be in his classroom," she said. "Don't worry. I'll check on you."

I watched her leave and glanced out the door at Ms. Boz. Then I looked at the blank pages. And I'm not sure exactly what happened or why it happened, but something inside me felt the overwhelming need to confess. All of it. Everything. The whole entire truth. It needed to have a place to go. I decided to put it here. In these pages. This was where I'd write the exact truth.

17

Shut Up!

It took me forever to write the exact truth. Principal Hunt
checked on my progress four times. On the fifth time, she
leaned in and said, "Don't think you have to deliver a novel."
But I didn't think that.

When you write the exact truth, it's hard to know when
to stop. For example, I wasn't sure how much she needed to
know about the ladder. It was a confusing question, because
it assumed that we had only used the ladder one time. But that
wasn't the exact truth. I just wanted to get everything right.

Who gave you permission to take the ladder?

Do you mean the first or second time? Because we used it
two times, but only got in trouble once. Last week Anya used
it to take pictures of Fletcher Zamora for What's Hot. I asked
her if it was okay to do this, and she said that we had faculty
permission. I didn't get her permission this time. Because

we had a big fight at her gym on Saturday and she said, "We're done." Which my sister (who is in college) says means that you are permanently forever done. It's called being dunzo. So because Anya and I were dunzo, I asked Ms. Kenny for permission for staff lanyards. But I never brought up the ladder. But I guess I should have asked Ms. Kenny. I don't know if we even had faculty permission the first time. Also, Mr. Zeller should probably keep that closet locked. Because in addition to the ladder, if we were thieves, we could have taken anything. Even dangerous cleaning chemicals.

Who brought the chain onto school property?

Is a bus considered school property? I never saw the chain until it was set up next to the ladder. I heard it jangle inside a backpack in the Yearbook room. I think Leo carried the backpack with the chain off the bus. Maybe Venice carried it onto the bus. I don't know that for sure. It's quite heavy. It's possible that Leo carried it the whole way for her. I believe it belongs to the Hoffmans. And they are great neighbors for Venice. So I hope they don't get in trouble. Three people in their family are firemen. They are awesome. I am the person who wanted the chain. But I didn't know it would be that big. I thought it might be the size of a big necklace. Also, I didn't realize that a chain was a weapon. Because bikes have chains and kids are allowed to park them on school property. So probably somebody should make a rule about bike chains not being weapons. Or there might be more confusion. Unless bike chains are weapons. Are they?

Let me say right now that I like Derby Esposito. And my goal here was to include him in a special yearbook section called What's Hot. You might not have heard of this section, because it is brand-new. Venice and Leo and I decided to put Derby in it. Okay. I won't lie. At first we were doing this because we thought he was a geek who didn't belong in the section. But then I became an infiltrator. Should I mention that here? Well, Anya needed an infiltrator and so I became one because there is some bad blood between her and Leo because he's a difficult person. And Anya said that Leo was trying to undermine her power. Which makes sense, because I think he has a problem with powerful girls. Except for Venice. Because he likes her.

I actually like Derby now. His mom came to my house to make sure we weren't going to make him look ridiculous or do anything terrible to his photo. She brought up what happened to Rose and her front teeth. (That's rotten.) I just want you to know that I would never do that. I am a serious artist. My photos matter. All I want is for Derby to look like his true self. (But with cuter hair and no weird clothes.) Derby deserves a second chance. He doesn't have to stay a geek forever. I hope he doesn't get punished. He just wanted his picture taken. He's basically innocent.

I was pretty sure I'd reached a stopping point, but I wasn't completely sure. I wanted to read back over it again, but I also needed to use the bathroom. Was that allowed? I wondered.

Knock. Knock. Knock.

"Yes?" Ms. Boz said, turning away from her computer.

"Am I allowed to go to the bathroom?" I asked.

If she said I wasn't, I didn't know what I was going to do.

"Here's a hall pass," Ms. Boz said. "Come right back."

I grabbed the hall pass, which was actually a long wooden ruler, and also took my answers with me. I didn't want Principal Hunt to come across my pages and read them thinking I was done.

I felt nervous walking the empty halls. I thought everybody was looking at me again. I focused on getting to the bathroom and not making eye contact with anybody. I hadn't even made it into the stall when I heard a voice that made me flip around with lightning speed.

"Don't say too much," the voice whispered.

It was Anya! What was she doing here? How did she know I was in the bathroom?

"If you're wondering how I knew you were in here, you walked right by my class," she said.

"Oh," I said. I probably should have guessed that.

"I've already talked to Leo and Venice," Anya said. "Leo is taking full responsibility for the chain. So just say that."

But I knew that Anya hated me. So I didn't really think I could believe anything she said to me in this bathroom. I tried to tell her this in a tactful way. "You are probably being evil and lying to me right now. I know you hate me."

Anya flipped her bob and groaned. "I'm not an idiot. Even though I'm mad at you, I can't let you get in trouble. If you get in trouble, all of Yearbook gets in trouble. I'm trying to save everybody."

I looked down at my papers. What Anya was saying actually sounded pretty reasonable. She glanced down at my papers too and she looked really alarmed. "Stop writing. Seriously. Everybody else wrote three or four sentences and they're back in class. What are you doing? And why did you bring it into the bathroom?"

I looked down at the many pages I'd filled. "I'm writing the exact truth."

Anya covered her mouth in horror. "Stop doing that!"

But I shook my head. Because it felt really freeing to be doing that.

"Here's the deal," Anya said. "The less they know, the smaller the punishment. The more you give them, the worse it gets."

But I didn't even know if I should trust Anya. Because the longer I stood in the bathroom looking at her, the more I'd started thinking that she had ratted on us about the ladder. And that she'd never been my friend. And that she'd been using me ever since she met me. Because all she wanted was to make a yearbook with her friends and people she liked in it. And then it hit me. In addition to writing the exact truth, I started saying the exact truth.

"Anya, I'm beginning to think that a big part of why I'm in this situation is because I listened to you," I said.

Anya looked over her shoulder really nervously. "I can't stay here too long. If I get caught talking to you, I'll get in trouble."

But it really annoyed me to hear that, because I was already in trouble.

"Did you tell Mr. Zeller we had his ladder?" I asked. "Leo said you did."

Anya looked really horrified when I said that. And that was when I realized it was true. Anya had set us up. Leo wasn't a conspiracy theorist. He just understood how terrible Anya could be.

"You are so awful," I said. "I'm going to include that in my answer." I turned and hurried into the stall.

"Wait," Anya said, slipping into the stall behind me and closing the door. "I never confessed that I did. You can't include that."

But I turned my back to her and faced the toilet. "I can include my suspicions."

And then Anya gasped. "How many pages have you written? Have you gone insane?"

But I hadn't gone insane. I was coming clean.

"You should leave," I said. "It's weird that you're in here with me."

"I think *you're* having a weird moment," Anya said. "Seriously. I'm worried about you. Because you think you're fixing things. But actually you're just making a bigger mess. You should really throw everything away and start over. And keep it simpler."

I couldn't believe that Anya O'Shea had tracked me down in the bathroom to lecture me on how to answer my three questions. I could feel her reading over my shoulder.

"Hey," she said. "Is that my name?"

Duh. Of course it was her name. "Yes," I said. "Because you're part of this." I finally turned around to face her. We were standing so close I could feel Anya's breath. And it made me feel really brave to do this. Because Anya wasn't acting totally bossy and mean now. She was acting nervous.

"You're a snitch?" she asked. "Great. That's going to really help us gel in Yearbook."

"Just stop it," I said, moving past her and exiting the stall. "You can't keep bossing me around. I bet Leo was right. You picked sixth graders to work with because you thought we'd be sheep."

"You need to stop listening to Leo and go back to the principal's office and pick up a pen and start crossing out my name."

"No!" I yelled. "That's not what needs to happen. I'm going to tell you what needs to happen."

Then Anya puffed herself up and got huffy and said, "Fine. Tell me."

And then I didn't know what to say. Because I'd never yelled at anybody before.

"I'm waiting," Anya said.

And then I just said how I felt. "Shut up and leave," I said. "I need to pee." And I knew I was being rude. But I was also really sick of being tricked and bullied. It sort of felt like Anya was ruining my life. Also, I really couldn't hold it much longer.

"You're telling me to shut up?" Anya asked. She sounded very surprised.

"Yes," I said. "Because I need to finish here and go back and finish these," I said, waving the papers around. "Also, I'd really appreciate it if I could have my nickname back. I don't think Javier even looks like a Party. I should be Party."

Anya started backing up toward the door. "Okay," Anya said. "I'll grant your wish and I'll shut up and leave. I'll even let you be Party again. But you're making your own punishment way worse. It might feel better now to think you're being honest. But that's not how Principal Hunt is going to feel. You're going to look like a sneaky little backstabber. And she'll see that. People value loyalty. And you haven't been loyal to anyone. Not Venice. Not Derby. Not me. Not even yourself."

I stayed really tense the whole time she was talking so her words would bounce off me. But after Anya left I started to cry. Because even though she was being mean, she was saying somewhat true things. I had backstabbed Venice. And I'd backstabbed Leo, even though he deserved it. And I'd backstabbed Anya a little bit too. But I didn't think I'd backstabbed Derby. Because I told him I was going to get him in What's Hot. And I was doing everything I could to deliver on that promise. Sure, I might have initially picked him because I thought he couldn't make it into the section, but after spending time with him and his mom I'd come to feel differently about Derby. He didn't deserve the life he had. I wanted him to have a better one.

After I was done in the bathroom, I walked back down the hall and grabbed some tissues from a box on Principal Hunt's desk. Was I making a mistake? Had I said too much? I didn't know. But I also didn't care. Sixth grade was killing me. I couldn't keep this up. I needed a normal life again. After I blew my nose I stared at the papers. Tears dripped onto them and started to smear the ink. I folded them in half.

I don't know how long I spent in that room melting down

and pulling myself back together. I just know when Principal Hunt finally came back in she looked totally surprised to see me.

"Have you been in here the whole time?" she asked. "Did you miss lunch?"

And I didn't even try to read back through all the pages I'd written. I just handed her the fresh, inky, tear-stained stack of them. "I did miss lunch. Because I needed to finish."

She took the papers from me and her eyes got really big when she saw that I'd written five and a half pages.

"Is this part of your homework?" she asked.

But I shook my head. I felt so proud of what I'd done.

"I've answered your three questions," I said. "There was a lot of stuff you needed to know."

"I see," she said, reaching for her stapler. "I'll read these as soon as I can. Until then please return to class. We'll meet soon to discuss the outcome."

"Okay," I said. Because that sounded reasonable, because she'd used the word *outcome* and not *punishment.*

And I don't know if I can explain how good I felt leaving Principal Hunt's office. Finally, all that lying and planning was behind me. All I needed to do was go to class, do my homework, hang out with Venice, and enjoy Yearbook. Yes, it was possible that I'd get my lanyard suspended for a little while. But I figured I probably deserved some punishment. I mean, I'd been totally dishonest for weeks.

I finished school that day feeling as light as a puffy cloud. In Science, when I learned about animal vision, my mind didn't wander and start thinking about my problems at all. Because by writing them all down it was like I'd gotten them out of me. I stayed totally focused when I learned about how a horse had one terrible blind spot but amazing peripheral vision. And how Mitten Man probably had red-green color blindness, but could see great in dim light. And the rest of the day continued to feel that way too. I was in a stress-free learning zone. And I stayed in the zone even when I got to Idaho History and Mr. Falconer told us he wasn't through grading our brutal quizzes from last week. Plus, I didn't freak out when he reminded me about my topographic map that I hadn't officially started. I was done feeling panicked and awful all the time. It was time to chill out and learn. That was right. My life had turned a corner. It was time for me to start having a much better time.

18

Stuck

When I got home, I thought my mom was going to know all about what had happened at school. But she didn't seem to know anything. Because she was sitting at the kitchen table totally focused on a box of rice.

"You're never going to guess what happened today," she said.

And rather than try to guess, I tried to keep being honest. "You're right. I can't."

"I dropped my phone," she said.

That was terrible news. Because my dad didn't believe in buying the protection plan, so this was probably going to cost her a ton of money.

"Did your screen break?" I asked. "Because that doesn't make it ruined." And then I was prepared to tell my mom about a lot of kids at school who had broken screens but still used their phones with hardly any problem. As long as it wasn't so broken that you got broken glass on your face.

"I didn't drop it on the ground," she said. "I dropped it in water."

Yikes. That was terrible news. Because everybody knew that doing that was the worst thing you could ever do to it.

"Bummer," I said. "Did it fall in the sink?"

Because my mom was always soaking pots.

"Not exactly," my mom said.

"Did you drop it in your lemon water?" I asked. Because ever since my mom had quit drinking diet soda she'd started drinking giant glasses of fizzy water with lemon, and I could see a phone fitting inside one of those.

She looked sort of embarrassed. She nestled her phone in a plastic container filled with dry rice.

"Where did you drop it?" I asked. Because I started to worry that maybe she'd gone to the public swimming pool without me.

"It fell in the toilet," she said as she popped the lid on the container.

"Gross," I said. Because I couldn't believe my mom had reached into the toilet to get it back. "You should probably throw it away now."

My mother looked shocked when I said this. But she shouldn't have. Once I dropped a five-dollar bill in the toilet and I flushed it. Because my other choice was saving toilet money. And that felt very unsanitary.

"I powered it off and took out the SIM card," my mom said. "So there's still a chance. I'm going to leave it in rice for forty-eight hours and see what happens."

"You better remember to throw that rice away," I said. "Because that's disgusting."

"Don't worry," my mom said.

But that wasn't what I wanted to hear. I wanted to hear her promise to throw out the rice.

"Did this happen in our toilet?" I asked. Because suddenly that felt like important information.

"No," she said. "It happened at the mall."

And then my eyes got really big. Because dropping your phone in a mall toilet seemed a million times worse than dropping it in your personal toilet.

"You should really toss it, Mom," I said. "Seriously. Have you ever stopped and looked closely at a mall toilet?"

My mom sort of glared at me when I said that. "As a matter of fact, I have," she said. "Just this afternoon."

She picked up the plastic container filled with rice and her toilet phone and put it on top of the refrigerator. She seemed totally stressed out and overwhelmed. I felt bad for her. Because I hadn't felt that way in hours.

"Don't you have a map to work on?" she asked.

And I didn't even get offended that she was so snippy with me. Because losing your phone in a mall toilet was a true tragedy. Because even if you saved it, it would never feel the same. It would feel like a phone that had fallen into a public toilet.

When I got to my room I decided that instead of starting my map, I'd rather call Piper. Because I hadn't heard from her in forever. And I really wanted to tell her all about what I'd done today. Because I thought she would be pretty impressed with my spunk and honesty.

Me: I feel like a totally new person.

Piper: Is this Perry?

Me: It is. But it's like I'm new and improved.

Piper: Have you been eating a bunch of sugar? You
sound funny.

Me: It's because I did something amazing today.

Piper: Victor said he saw you at the gym. Did you join
a gym?

Me: No. When did you see Victor?

Piper: We cross at parties and stuff. Hey. So what's
your news? Bobby is coming over to make me waffles.

Piper was so lucky to have a waffle-making boyfriend. I sat
down on my bed and took a deep breath. Because I had so much
to tell my sister. "So what's the last thing I told you about Anya?"

"The girl who wears the crocodile belt?" Piper asked.

"Yes," I said.

"Well, if that's the same girl Victor is training, you need
to totally avoid her. She's psycho."

I was a little surprised to hear that. Because it had taken
me forever to figure that out. And I had class with her every
day. "Did Victor tell you that?" I asked. He was one of those
people who had giant muscles and brains.

"Maybe," she said. "I hate spreading gossip. I'm just trying to keep you safe."

"Um," I said. "She's the photography editor for Yearbook. She's going to be in my life for a long time."

"Yeah," Piper said. "Have you thought about dropping out of Yearbook?"

This conversation was making me feel pretty horrible. "No," I said, very firmly. "Yearbook is important to me."

"Is this what you called to tell me?" Piper asked.

"No," I said. "I wanted to catch you up with what's going on with me. You'll never believe what's happened." And then I spent the next five minutes telling Piper about my week. Leo. Venice. Derby. Derby's mom. The Fletcher photo. The ladder. Mr. Zeller. The chain. Principal Hunt's deer head. My confessions. Anya's rage. Being dunzo. Saying everything as fast as I did in one quick story made the drama seem very intense. Then I waited for Piper's response. And I waited. And I finally said, "Piper? Did you hear what I said?"

"Okay," Piper said. "You never told me Anya was *super* psycho."

"It's like I just figured it out," I said.

"Well, if you're not dropping out of Yearbook, the best thing you can do is avoid being alone with her and ride it out."

"Is that code for something?" I asked.

"No."

"But I need your expert advice. Help me," I said. "After somebody says you're dunzo but then stays in your life, what do you do?"

"Perry," Piper said. "I can't tell you what to do. Only you can solve your problems. That's how life works."

And I gasped when Piper said that. Because she should have told me that weeks ago, before I counted on her guidance to destroy Leo and save myself.

"Okay," Piper said. "You sound totally freaked out."

"I am," I said. "I need you to be more helpful. A super-psycho person has said we're dunzo, but she isn't acting like we're dunzo and it's a total nightmare. And I still need to make Derby popular."

"Okay," Piper said. "Here's what you should do. Sit and be still. Cross-legged. Turn the lights out. Be in a calming dark place. And focus on the outcome you want."

That actually sounded really hard. "How do I turn the lights off while sitting cross-legged?" I asked. I'd already sat on my floor, preparing to try this strategy, but it seemed impossible.

"Stop goofing around," Piper said. "You know, middle school isn't a joke. It's three whole years. You're going to remember them until the day you die. That stuff matters. Your teachers. Your friends. Your psycho classmates. Take it seriously. Maybe you'll end up in detention. Maybe you won't. But take this seriously."

And before I could explain to her that I was taking it seriously, and follow up with her about that terrifying detention comment, I heard Bobby's voice in the background.

"Babe," he said. "I think I forgot the syrup."

"That's okay," Piper cooed. "Perry, I've got to go. Are you going to be okay?" And I really didn't think Piper even cared what my answer was going to be. She probably just wanted to hang out with Bobby and eat waffles.

"I guess," I said. "I've got a map to build."

I couldn't believe how much worse I felt after talking to Piper. I thought she'd have stuff figured out because she was older. But she made life feel like a big mystery. And that was not how I wanted to think about it right now. I wanted to feel like I was on the right path. I wanted to feel like everything was going to turn out pretty good. I mean, I couldn't even picture myself in detention.

I stared at my phone and realized that if I didn't do something drastic I was going to stare at it forever, waiting for a call or text. But did I really want to hear from anybody right now? Or did I want to finish this stupid map? I turned off my phone and put it in my underwear drawer. And that actually made me feel a little bit better. Because avoiding stress was the first step in reducing stress. Then I gathered all my map materials and got to work. I started by tracing the base for my mountain range. My hand shook a little, because I wanted all of my range to line up perfectly and look amazing on my first try.

It basically took forever. And after I finished tracing, I decided to label everything. Because I figured it would be easier to do that while everything was still flat.

I found it really hard to keep my handwriting nice. Because I wasn't used to working with a brush pen. When my mom finally knocked on my door, I thought she was going to talk more about her toilet phone. But she actually said, "Time for dinner." And that blew my mind a little bit. Because that meant I'd been working for hours.

I staggered out of my room and sat at the table. I was relieved to see a giant pizza.

"I was so scared it was going to be rice," I said.

"You don't like rice?" my dad asked. "I didn't know that."

"Don't, Perry," my mom said.

"Don't say that I don't like toilet-water rice?" But then after I said that I figured out my mom didn't want me to mention her phone.

"Toilet-water rice?" my dad said. And then he looked straight at my mom and said, "You did *not* drop your phone in the toilet again."

And I couldn't believe my dad had said the word *again*, because that meant that my mom had a serious problem.

"This is so gross," I said. Because in addition to the toilet-water discussion, there was also a lot of tension at the table.

"It barely got wet this time," my mom said.

"Why can't you keep it in your purse until you're finished?" my dad asked.

Wow. This was way too much information.

"I can't believe the man who accidentally flushed the car keys at a rest stop in Nevada on our honeymoon is judging me," my mom said.

"My pants didn't have pockets!" my dad said.

And while this arguing was taking place, I grabbed two slices of pizza and went to my room. Because I did not need to hear about problems between my parents that had happened at a rest stop in Nevada before I was born.

I decided to finish eating my pizza and wash my hands before I touched my map. Because I didn't want to get any grease stains on it. Because Mr. Falconer was such a tough grader I bet I'd get marked down for those.

After my hands were clean enough to perform surgery, I started making my cuts. I needed multiple pieces for each mountain. And even though I had special scissors, it was still difficult to slice through the cardboard.

I wanted to listen to music, but I didn't want to get my phone out of the drawer. So I fiddled with the station finder on my clock radio until I found an upbeat station that I'd never listened to before. When it came time to start gluing my pieces together, I located the bottle of glue that would dry the quickest. Digging around in our pantry and our garage, I was surprised by how different the drying times were for glue. A white bottle of glue I found near the freezer bags took eighteen hours to set. And a yellow pasty bottle of glue I found in my mom's craft room took two hours. But the label on a small yellow tube of glue I found in the garage stated that it bonded instantly. So I chose that for my map. Because I needed speed.

It was almost midnight before I'd finished my map. Luckily, my labeling strategy had worked perfectly. So once it was glued, I didn't have to label anything else. My map was complete. I set it on the bedside table next to me.

When I turned off my light that night, I tried not to think about what Venice and Leo and Derby and Anya were doing. Because I'd find out soon enough. I figured that Principal Hunt was going to want to meet with us as soon as school started. On any other night, that realization would have kept me from sleeping. But because I was exhausted from all my map building, I slipped right to sleep as soon as I got under my covers. I mean, it happened in an instant. I closed my eyes and I was gone.

The next morning I still felt tired and a little delirious. I swatted at my alarm clock and accidentally knocked it onto the floor. When I leaned over to pick it up, I was really surprised to feel something hard and sharp pressing against my cheek. It felt like a book. Except when I tried to move it, it stayed stuck. It wasn't until I climbed out of bed and stood in front of my mirror that I realized my topographic map was attached to the side of my face. I mean, it took me a second to realize I wasn't dreaming and that this was really my map. And that it was seriously stuck to me.

"Help!" I cried. Because I suddenly remembered that the glue package had said it could bond metal to metal in seconds. And so I worried that this topographic map might be permanently pasted to my cheek area.

First my mom entered my room. Then my dad.

"What's on your face?" my dad asked.

"Oh my gosh," my mom said, gasping and looking away.

That really freaked me out. Because she never looked away from anything. Even Mitten Man's hairballs. I mean, this was a person willing to reach her hand into a mall toilet.

"It's my topographic map!" I said.

"Why did you glue it to your face?" my dad asked.

Then he picked up a small bottle of glue from the dresser.

"Please tell me you didn't use this, Perry," he said.

He seemed so angry that even though I was on a truth-telling campaign, I decided to follow his command. "I didn't use that."

He and my mom looked a little bit more relieved. But then he pinched the top of the bottle and got a worried look on his face again.

"Then why is the cap off?" he asked.

And so I answered honestly. "Because I used it."

"Perry," my mom snapped. "You just told us that you didn't use any of it."

I could feel tears rolling down my cheeks. "That's because Dad told me to tell him that."

My dad tried to set the superglue bottle down on the dresser, but it stayed stuck to his finger. He shook it really hard. But it stayed pasted to him. My mom reached over and pulled it off his skin.

"Where did you even find this?" he asked.

"The garage," I answered. Because that was where we kept important heavy-duty items, like hammers, and fire extinguishers, and ice melt. So I figured it would have the best glue.

"I think nail polish remover will get this off," my mom said.

"No way!" I screamed. Because I liked my face. And I didn't want to put chemicals on it. Plus, I needed to turn my map in today. And I was pretty sure nail polish remover wouldn't improve it. And might possibly smear or even remove my labels.

"We need to call Dr. Turtle," my mom said.

"Should I cancel work?" my dad asked.

I couldn't believe how serious things had gotten. I didn't have time to go to my pediatrician. I had to get to school. And turn in my map. And find out my outcome. Because Principal Hunt had said that was happening today.

"I can take Perry," my mom said. "We don't both need to go."

My dad gently tugged at the northwest corner of my map.

"Ouch!" I said. "Don't do that. You'll rip off my face." And that was when I really started to cry. Because my situation felt unfixable.

My dad let go of my map and exhaled a loud breath. "You shouldn't have done this, Perry."

"I understand that," I said, wiping my nose with my pajama sleeve and inspecting my map in the mirror. Luckily, it looked like only the Boise Mountains were glued directly to my cheek. The valley didn't have any glue on it. Neither did any of the rivers. So that part I could almost wiggle my finger underneath.

"Did you fall asleep next to your map?" my mom asked, still trying to figure out how I'd managed to do this.

"Apparently," I said with a sniffle, holding back more tears.

My dad got on his phone and dialed Dr. Turtle's office. "They've got to have somebody on call."

"I really don't want to miss school," I said. Because it felt really important to learn what was going to happen to me. And turn in my map.

"You can't go to school with a map on your face," my mom said.

I looked in the mirror again. "Is there going to be a giant red mark when we get this sucker off?" I asked. Because I didn't want to look weird. Even if it would be temporary.

"It probably depends on how they remove it," my mom said.

"Really?" I heard my dad say. "The emergency room?"

I got tremendously scared when I heard those words, and I started crying again. Because that meant I had to go to the hospital. And that was where people went with serious medical problems. Had my topographic map become a serious medical problem? My dad walked back into the room. He looked a little pale.

"This is no joke," my dad said. "This is a serious problem."

"No!" I screamed. Because I didn't want to have a serious problem that involved my face *and* my homework *and* the emergency room.

"Let's leave it alone and maybe it will fall off on its own," I suggested. Because watching nature shows and eating snacks on the couch and being filled with hope seemed like a way better way to spend the morning than going to the emergency room.

"We need to get dressed," my dad said. "I'll have Maryann push my schedule back."

This was when I realized my situation was very terrible. Because my dad never pushed his schedule back. Except one time when he dislocated his knee.

I tried to gently separate some of the mountain range from my skin.

"Don't do that," my dad said. "You could scar your face."

And when he told me this I cried even harder. Because I didn't want a scarred face. I wanted my own face. Without a map on it.

"Everybody change and let's go," my dad said. "Move it."

Tragically, I was only able to change my pants to go to the hospital, and I had to wear my turquoise pajama top with maraschino cherry juice stains on it. Because the neck area wouldn't go over my head while a map was glued to me.

When we walked through the revolving door, I started to

feel more panicked than ever. Because I saw somebody with a washrag against her head and it looked bloody. My mother guided me to the check-in window.

"My daughter superglued a cardboard map to her face," she said. "Our pediatrician told us to come to the emergency room."

"Tell them it's worth ten percent of my grade," I whimpered. I really wished I'd signed up for Idaho History next semester. My life would have been so much easier.

"Fill this out and leave your insurance card," the woman said.

I looked at the woman with my uncovered eye. She seemed very sympathetic.

"We'll get you in right away," she said. "Dr. Salak will fix everything."

I followed my mom to a chair and sat between my parents. I could feel tears rolling out of my eyes and down my face.

"Okay, honey," my dad said. "This might sound harsh, but if you cry, you're going to smear your river labels."

And that was one of the saddest things anybody had ever told me. I looked at him with my only available eye and said, "This really sucks."

"It'll be over before you know it," my dad said. "Once, a cat scratched your mom in the eye. And its claw nicked her cornea and she had to wear a patch and we sat in this exact waiting room. And look how well things turned out. Moments like this feel awful, but they end. Right?" My dad looked at my mom for confirmation.

She continued to fill out the paperwork. "I don't know

why you'd bring that up. I had to wear that stupid patch for a month and my eye ended up getting infected."

My dad grimaced at that response and rubbed my back. "I forgot that part."

I whimpered a little bit. "Do you think they'll be able to save my map?"

My dad nodded. "Absolutely."

"Phil," my mom said in a tense voice. "Don't write checks you can't cash." Then my mom looked at me and said, "If your map gets ruined, we'll make a new one together."

But that didn't thrill me. Because I felt I should only have to make my map one time. After my mom turned in the papers we didn't have to wait long at all.

"Perry Hall," a nurse called from the hallway.

I raised my hand and stood up.

"Poor thing," the nurse said. "Does it hurt? Or does it primarily just annoy you?"

"I'm not sure," I said, trying not to cry any more.

"Don't worry," she said. "Dr. Salak is the best."

I nodded as she led me to a cushioned table behind a curtain. Then she did a bunch of things quickly. She took my temperature. And my blood pressure. And she inspected the map with a superlong stick with a cotton tip on the end of it.

"I think bacitracin can fix this," she said. "But I'll let the doctor make that call."

This worried me because bacitracin sounded like a terrible medicine that probably smelled and stung and I didn't want to have that stuff touch me.

"We should have helped her," my mom said. "I was distracted by my phone. I feel awful."

I shook my head. "It's okay. It was my homework. I should have worked on it sooner."

I felt my mom hug me a little. "You are such a trouper."

I was pretty relieved when Dr. Salak showed up, because things with my parents were feeling really mushy.

"So I hear you've run into problems with a homework assignment?" Dr. Salak said.

I was surprised that she wore cute blue clogs and silver hoop earrings. Because I thought all doctors wore ugly white shoes and zero jewelry.

"It's worth ten percent of my grade," I explained, pointing to my map.

"We think she fell asleep next to it," my mom said.

"We didn't know she was using superglue," my dad offered. "We keep it in the garage. She really had to look for it."

Dr. Salak put her hands up in front of her like she was surrendering. "No blame here. I just want to find a pain-free way to save this map and this beautiful face."

"Thank you," I said, smiling. Because getting compliments was always pleasant. Even in the emergency room.

"Here's what we're going to do," Dr. Salak said, grabbing another long stick with a cotton tip. "We'll apply bacitracin to the impacted areas. We'll let that sit for an hour. Then we'll be able to remove the map."

"Will bacitracin feel like a deadly chemical to me?" I asked. "I mean, will it burn?" Because an hour was a long time to let a deadly chemical burn your face.

"You won't feel anything. It doesn't even smell," Dr. Salak said. "It's just very gooey and effective."

But I still felt very anxious. "Will its goo smear my river labels?" I asked.

Dr. Salak smiled and shook her head. "I should be able to keep it away from any labeled areas."

And it was like Dr. Salak was magic. Because she seemed to have the power to fix everything.

Applying the bacitracin was a totally painless experience. Sitting for an hour with my parents on the cushioned table was a little bit tougher.

"You can go to work," my mother said.

"It's fine. Maryann already pushed everything back," my dad said. "Can I get anyone anything to eat from the vending machine?"

That was a great idea. I was surprised nobody had suggested that when we were in the waiting room staring at it and all its awesome junk food. "I'll take a pack of powdered-sugar doughnuts," I said.

"No," my mother said. "They'll get everywhere. You can have a granola bar."

I don't know why my mom was being so harsh. I mean, I was in the emergency room. If they offered powdered-sugar doughnuts in the vending machine, I figured the hospital was fine with them getting everywhere.

"Three granola bars?" my dad said.

"And a soda?" I asked.

My mother sighed. "You really don't need that much sugar this early in the morning."

I couldn't believe my mom was acting like such a mom.

"Okay," my mom said. "But nothing with caffeine."

"Orange soda, please," I said.

My mom sat in the chair across from me hanging her head a little. "I should probably call Piper, but I don't have a phone."

"I left mine in my underwear drawer," I explained. It bummed me out that Piper had basically blown off all my major problems and told me that I was in charge of fixing my own life. Because turning to her for advice had made me feel cared for.

"That's too bad," my mom said. "I bet Venice will want to hear all about this."

"Yeah," I said. But thinking about Venice didn't feel awesome either. Because the amazing feeling I'd had all day yesterday after I'd spilled the truth had begun to fade. Sitting in this sterile room made me think of school. And I wasn't sure how Venice was going to feel about me when I got back there. I was pretty sure that Leo was going to get suspended for bringing a weapon to school. But I also didn't think that was totally my fault. Because I didn't know a chain was a weapon. I worried that Venice would blame me for that. I worried that things were going to feel even more different. Because if we got our staff lanyards suspended, would she blame me for that, too?

"I hope I haven't missed any important calls. The tree cutter was going to get back to me with a quote," my mom said. Then she stood up and started pacing. "I feel so marooned without a phone."

"Yeah," I said. But I thought it was sort of good timing. Because as long as my mom's phone was in a box of rice on the refrigerator, it meant Principal Hunt couldn't call her. And whatever happened, whether I got in trouble or whether nothing happened at all, I thought it would be ideal for me to tell my mom about things before my principal. Because I would probably phrase it better.

When my dad came back into the room he had three granola bars and a package of doughnuts and a steaming cup.

"No soda?" I asked. Because I hardly ever got to drink orange soda.

"Better. It's hot chocolate!" he cheered.

And I didn't even know you could get that out of a vending machine.

"You'll probably need a straw," my dad said, carefully handing me the cup.

"Thanks," I said.

"I see you bought the doughnuts," my mom scolded.

"I figured we should live a little," my dad said.

It must have taken me an hour to eat my doughnuts, because when I was finished Dr. Salak returned.

"Okay," she said in a cheery voice. "Let's save this map."

She took her fingers and pressed my cheek away from the cardboard. She only had to do this about four times until the map came off.

"Voila!" she said, handing me my map. "A total success."

But I immediately touched my face and felt a patch of glue, so I didn't feel like it had been a total success.

"You can get rid of that with soap and water," Dr. Salak said. "It might take a couple of days. But gentle scrubbing should do it."

And at first I misunderstood and I thought she'd told me

that I had to gently scrub my face for two days. "We're going to need to buy a lot more soap," I said to my mom.

"Don't overdo it," Dr. Salak warned. "I wouldn't wash that area more than three times a day. You don't want to irritate the skin."

She was right. I didn't want to do that.

"Thank you so much," my mom said.

"You're a real map saver," my dad said. But both my mom and I cringed at that.

And before I could talk more with Dr. Salak, she shook my hand and told me to have a nice day.

"That was a fast exit," I said. Because I thought she could've talked to me a little bit more.

"I think she's also dealing with a serious head wound," my mom said.

"Yeah. I think I saw a woman going into labor on the way to the vending machine," my dad said.

And I guessed that all made sense. Because a pregnant woman going into labor with a head wound sounded pretty dramatic.

On the drive back home I tried to stay in my stress-free place. But my mind kept thinking about Derby and Venice and Leo and Anya and all my problems.

"Were you really popular in middle school?" I called from the backseat.

"Your mom was extremely popular," my dad said. "She was on the dance squad and was student body vice president."

"That was high school," my mom corrected.

Our neighborhood zoomed past us as we drove home.

"It sounds like you were super popular," I said.

"It didn't feel that way," my mom said. "I just felt busy."

"Oh," I said. Because I definitely understood that feeling.

"Are you thinking about Derby?" my mom asked.

And rather than admit that I was mostly thinking about myself, I said, "Sort of."

"Who's Derby?" my dad asked. "Is he a boy you like?"

"Bleh," I said from the backseat. Because even if I did like Derby that way, which I didn't, it was gross for my dad to say it.

"Being in Yearbook has really thrown Perry into a new social group," my mother said.

We pulled up into the driveway and my dad parked the car and turned around to look at me.

"You shouldn't stress out about being popular. My experience is that the kids who were most popular at your age don't amount to much. It's the nerds and the geeks who really become successful."

"But you just said that Mom was popular," I said with a frown. Because it sounded like he was saying harsh things about her.

"He's saying that being popular now doesn't matter," my mom said. "The important stuff comes later."

"But what even made you popular?" I asked. "How does that happen?" Because I really felt that I owed it to Derby to help him.

She shrugged. "People liked me and I liked them back."

I dragged myself into the house. With that kind of advice it seemed pretty unlikely that I'd be able to help Derby climb any social ladders.

When we got into the house I zoomed straight to the bathroom to inspect my cheek. I could see a crusty spot where the glue remained.

My mom and dad sneaked up behind me to take a look too.

"I hope you're not worried that a glue spot will make you unpopular," my mom said. "I'm sure it will be gone in a day or two."

"You look beautiful," my dad said. "And if there is a spot, I bet your mom will help you cover it up with makeup."

I stayed in front of the mirror and stared at it. The spot actually wasn't that big. It was smaller than a dime. But it felt pretty noticeable. If Venice and I weren't in a weird place right now, I'd take a picture of my patchy glue skin and send it to her and ask her what she thought.

But I wasn't sure I should do that. Because I was sort of afraid of her right now. I didn't want her to be mad at me. And I was pretty sure she would be. Because if she'd gotten me into this much trouble, I was sure I'd be upset for a while.

19

The Calls

I was probably the only sixth grader in the history of the world who left her phone in an underwear drawer for almost an entire weekend. But that was exactly what I did. I guess I was in denial and I wanted to stay there. Because when you're in denial, your problems aren't right in front of your face. They stay hidden. Because you don't know what any of your texts say. Also, you haven't listened to your voice mails so you don't know if any of your friends have yelled at you.

I think taking their child to the emergency room had reminded my parents how short life was, because suddenly they wanted to accomplish all the yard work they'd been putting off for weeks.

"We'll be thanking ourselves in October," my dad said. "When all the hard stuff is done."

I held a rake and a lawn bag and waited for further instructions.

"Do you see the difference between this vine and the

clematis?" my dad asked, pointing to some overgrown plants clinging to the lattice attached to the house.

"The vine is a vine and the clematis has dead flowers on it?" I said.

My dad lifted his sunglasses up so I could see his eyes and he smiled at me. "Exactly. The vine is a monster and we want to stamp out its existence, and the clematis is a perennial and we're on the same team."

"Okay," I said, yanking out a big piece of it.

"Stop," my dad said. "Those are the poppies."

But I didn't feel too bad about ripping out the poppies, because my dad hadn't even told me they were there.

"Okay," he said. "I'll take care of the vine. Why don't you rake leaves?"

And that seemed like a good idea, because I was already holding the rake. The saddest thing about yard work was raking the side lawn. Because that was where my bedroom was. And Mitten Man liked to sit in the window and watch birds. But today instead of birds he was watching me. And he looked really miserable and he kept meowing at me. Because he didn't understand that he was an indoor cat.

When I heard my dad's phone ring, I didn't suspect it was my principal calling to ruin my life. It wasn't until I heard the rotten sound of my dad saying her name that I realized this was happening.

"Anita Hunt?" my dad said. "I didn't expect to hear from you on a Sunday. Is your back crown acting up?"

And I was pretty sure that Principal Hunt's back crown was not acting up.

"Really?" my dad said.

And I was dying to know what Principal Hunt was saying.

"No. Perry didn't go to school on Friday because she was in the emergency room," he said. "No. No. She's fine now."

And I sort of felt like this was my one chance to run and get away. But I didn't take it, because my mom joined us. And I figured she would just chase me down. She did have a background in track.

"Yes," my dad said. "Perry's mom is right here. And so is Perry. Let me put you on speakerphone."

I glanced at my dad's phone and then at my rake. "I should probably get back to work." I turned to leave before this conversation could turn dangerous, but my dad put his hand on my shoulder.

"I was hoping to schedule a conference with you," Principal Hunt said.

My mind flashed back to the dead, balding deer. My knees felt shaky. Nobody should be forced to be in that room. Even the deer.

"I was hoping this could happen before Perry starts detention," Principal Hunt added.

And that was basically the worst thing I'd ever heard come out of my dad's speakerphone.

"Detention?" my mother said. She looked at me very harshly. And I just sort of made a sad and surprised face. Because I was pretty sure that hearing about my detention on speakerphone was much more terrible for me than her.

"Um," my dad said, staring up at the sky. "I've got a pretty full schedule next week. When does Perry's detention start?"

"Monday. Five lunches," she said. "I've left several messages on your wife's phone and emailed her. But I haven't heard anything back."

"She likes to step away from technology on the weekends," my dad said, frowning at my mom.

I felt relieved that he didn't mention the toilet phone drama.

"What did Perry do?" my mom blurted out. But I thought that was pretty rude to assume I was automatically guilty of something. Even though maybe in this case I was.

"There's been some confusion regarding school resources concerning Perry and other members of Yearbook," Principal Hunt said.

"I have been very confused about school resources," I said, hoping that would soften what was coming next.

"What kind of resources?" my dad asked. Because he still didn't understand I was in serious trouble.

"Is she overusing paper towels?" my mom asked. She looked at me and wagged her finger. "You need to tone it down with that," she whispered at me.

But I didn't even think that made sense. Piper had stolen at least four rolls. When it came to the paper towels, I was using them at a normal rate.

"We can pay for any excessive use," my dad said. "Sometimes Perry overdoes it."

And it was very hard to watch my parents misunderstand what was being said.

"Actually, it's more serious than paper towels. Perry and three other students accessed a supply closet that's normally locked," Principal Hunt said.

"You got into a school supply closet?" my dad asked. "Did you take something?"

I couldn't believe my dad automatically assumed I was a thief. But I decided to stay quiet. And not answer any questions until Principal Hunt was through explaining things.

"On Thursday, they borrowed a folding ladder in an attempt to take photos of another student from an aerial position," Principal Hunt said.

I just kept looking at my shoes and my garden gloves. My life would have been so much better if I was still doing awful yard work.

"I told you *not* to use that dangerous ladder again!" my mother snapped. "You said you wouldn't."

"You knew Perry was breaking into the supply closet at her school?" my dad asked.

"Please, let me finish," Principal Hunt said.

And I was glad that at least one person's voice was remaining calm.

"This isn't entirely Perry's fault," Principal Hunt explained.

And I liked the way that sounded.

"I believe that the oversight of Yearbook staff has been a little too relaxed this semester," Principal Hunt said. "I've met with Ms. Kenny, and we've both agreed that there need to be some changes."

"Wow," my mom said. "This is all coming out of left field."

"Perry, have you told your parents anything about what happened on Thursday?" Principal Hunt asked.

Both my parents looked at me and I felt very uncomfortable. I mean, what normal person would want to volunteer such horrible news to their parents? "I haven't had time to do that yet. I have been in the hospital."

"I can meet with you on Monday," my mom said. "Give me a time and I'm there."

My mom took Principal Hunt off speakerphone so they could decide on a time. And my dad kept looking at me in this sad and upset way. I felt pretty strongly I should mention the chain to him before Principal Hunt mentioned it to my mom. Because if she referred to it as a weapon, and didn't mention it was just a chain, my parents were going to think I'd turned into a total thug.

"What's going on?" my mom asked as she marched over to join us.

"Um," I said. Because I wasn't sure where to start. "Remember Derby?" I asked.

And that was when I tried to explain things as best I could. "I was tired of the popular kids treating the dweebs like they were zeroes. So I tried to get Derby into the What's Hot section by getting him to pose as a hot-looking sixth grader. But it was harder than I thought. And I borrowed a ladder. And I'm not sure any of my pictures make him look hot enough."

My parents kept looking at me like I was crazy. Then my dad got the wrong idea and said, "Is somebody bullying you?"

And that didn't even make sense. Because this wasn't about that.

"I'm trying to make Derby popular," I said. "But it's impossible. And now my life feels ruined. Also, Venice's boyfriend accidentally brought a weapon to school."

And that was probably not how I should have mentioned that, but it was how it came out.

"It was just a chain," I explained. But that didn't seem to calm my parents down.

My mother covered her mouth. "I can't believe you didn't say anything about this."

But that felt a little unfair considering I had spent several hours completing my map and had been in the emergency room. "I was waiting to learn my outcome. That was supposed to happen on Friday."

"Perry, you need to go to your room while your mom and I have a talk," my dad said.

"Okay," I said. "But please remember that almost all of what happened was an accident. And I was only trying to rescue a nerd from being a nerd. If I thought things would end this badly, I never would have tried to do anything."

I was no longer in denial. I had to face the facts: My life wasn't going very well. Also, I needed to face another fact: It was time to check my phone. Here's the thing about facing reality when your life is going terribly—it's very hard to do it. I looked at my phone for a long time before I had the courage to power it back up.

I knew once I turned it on that anything could have been waiting for me. Venice could have left me a bunch of mean messages. Or worse, Venice could have been so hurt and angry that she hadn't left me any messages at all.

I finally pushed the button. I was really happy to see that I'd missed a bunch of calls and that I had five new text messages. Four were from Venice and one was from Anya. And I had five new voice mails. They were all from Venice. I decided to listen to those messages first.

Thursday 12:01 p.m.

Voice mail #1: I'm not sure where you are. It's lunch.
Did you go home? Okay. Leo took the blame for the
chain. It's not fair. He is so amazing. I hope he doesn't
get in real trouble. I need to go talk to him. Call me
later. Also, Derby looked great in Leo's jeans. I mean,
until today I never realized Derby had a butt. It's cute.

After listening to this message, I took a deep breath. So
far, Venice didn't hate me. I mean, what she said about Derby's butt was alarming, but she was probably under a ton of
stress and wasn't thinking clearly.

Thursday 4:42 p.m.

Voice mail #2: Are you gonna call? Leo is here. We can
talk and figure out plans. Derby doesn't hate us. He
said his class loved watching stuff through the window.
Somebody thought the chain was a meteor hammer.
Which is a deadly weapon. He said everybody was
talking about it. Do you think I'm mad at you? I'm not.
I'm mad at Anya. She's so terrible.

This message was better than the first message. Venice liked me and maybe taking Derby's picture had worked
after all.

Thursday 8:02 p.m.

Voice mail #3: Leo left. I'm worried about tomorrow.
Where are you? If you don't call me back I'm going to
have my mom call your mom. That's right. I'm going to
mom-call you.

Oh, that was such a sweet message. Venice and I never mom-called each other. She must've been super worried about me.

Friday 12:01 p.m.

Voice mail #4: It's lunch. WHERE ARE YOU? Principal Hunt came to Yearbook and changed everything! Leo is suspended. Anya isn't the boss anymore. Also, Derby borrowed another pair of Leo's pants. His butt looked cute again. I mean, he just seems much more normal than before. Did you tell him to act that way? Because suddenly he's a much cooler version of Derby.

Wow, Venice needed to quit looking at Derby's butt ASAP.

Friday 3:06 p.m.

Voice mail #5: Anya found me. She told me tons of crazy stuff about you and showed me a bunch of your texts. What happened to you? We're supposed to be best friends. Quit being a jerk and call me when you remember how to tell the truth. And why aren't you calling me back? It's starting to feel like we're dunzo.

Anya had shown Venice my text messages! She was so evil. It was like she wanted Venice to hate me. And *dunzo*? Those words sent a chill through me. How could Venice think we were that? She was such a sweet person. I couldn't even imagine her thinking it. I really needed to call her. But before I did that, I decided to deal with my text messages.

I was hoping that maybe she'd texted me an apology

about suggesting we were dunzo when we were clearly still best friends. I only had to read five texts. I figured I could do that in no time. It wasn't like five text messages were going to kill me.

Thursday 12:02 p.m.

Venice

You vanished. Come back.

Thursday 4:01 p.m.

Venice

You suck.

Thursday 9:01 p.m.

Venice

Text me back before I die.

Friday 3:07 p.m.

Venice

Should I believe Anya?
Are you a backstabber?

Friday 3:09 p.m.

Anya

Load up the spaceship with the rocket fuel.

Wait. All of Venice's messages made sense. But Anya's was super weird. Was it a threat? It sounded really threatening. Or did it? I decided to look it up on the Internet. Because I felt like it was a quote from something. I typed the phrase into my search bar.

"Load up the spaceship with the rocket fuel" was a terrible quote made by the Ultimate Warrior, who was a crazy-looking wrestler with freakishly tanned muscles and tons of frightening face paint. But what Anya sent was only part of the quote. The Ultimate Warrior went on to say, "Dig your claws into my organs. Stretch into my tendons. Bury your anchors into my bones for the power of the Warrior will always prevail."

That definitely was a threat. But why did Anya only send me part of it? It only took me a couple of seconds to figure it out. Anya knew she'd get in trouble for sending me a threatening text. So instead she sent me a weird text that she knew I would research on the Internet. How did I know for sure that was what was happening? Because I knew how Anya's terrible brain worked. And she thought the Internet was my "thing," because I'd told her that during our first photo critique. So she'd set up a trap. She was so sneaky. I decided to keep researching the Ultimate Warrior to see what else I could find.

It was awful! He had four signature moves: atomic drop, gorilla press drop, leaping shoulder block, and multiple clotheslines. Plus, he had a brutal finishing move called the ultimate splash. I needed to see what that looked like.

My poor eyes! I watched as one giant wrestler dove on top of another giant wrestler and pinned him to the ground. And there was a bunch of yelling. And slapping. And struggling.

And shirtlessness. And sweating. I watched it three more times. I knew what Anya was doing. She was sending me a terrible message. In her eyes, this wasn't over. In her eyes, I'd started a war. I guess this was what happened in middle school when you confessed everything to the principal and you got the meanest photographer you'd ever met demoted in Yearbook. What was I supposed to do now? How did you move forward after you started a war with a brutal eighth grader and you still had to build a yearbook together?

I decided to solve this problem later and text Venice. Because I wanted to make things normal again with her.

Me.

> We are not dunzo! Do you think your mom will let you come over?

Then I stared at my phone forever and waited for a reply. I jumped a little when my mom opened my door, because I wasn't expecting to see her for a while.

"I've got bad news," she said.

And that seemed like a really unfair thing to tell me. Because my whole life had become bad news.

"Mrs. Garcia called," she said. "She's grounded Venice from her phone for a week. So you should stop texting her."

I looked down at my own phone.

"And I'm going to need to take that too," she said.

But that didn't seem right. Just because Venice was grounded from her phone shouldn't mean that I was grounded from mine.

"Mom," I tried to argue.

But she held her hand out like a crossing guard asking me to stop.

"You've put your dad and me on quite a roller coaster," she said. "I mean, we've gone from the emergency room to detention in no time flat."

When my mom summarized everything that had happened, she made my life sound awful. And she didn't even know about most of it.

"But I need to fix some things," I said.

My mom shook her head. And then I saw my dad enter my room too.

"Me too," he said. "Let's take a bag of gravel and go fix the bare spots in the driveway."

It was like my parents weren't thinking about what I needed. They were only thinking about our yard area.

"Move it," my dad said in a serious voice. "We're burning daylight."

I stood up, surrendered my phone, and marched out of my bedroom. My life had become a countdown to detention. I had no idea what to expect when I got to school tomorrow.

20

The New Crew

On the morning I had to go back to school, I felt lucky and unlucky at the same time. Lucky: Glue patch on my cheek was 95 percent gone. Unlucky: Topographic map was getting turned in late. Lucky: My cute winter snowflake sweater was clean and ready to wear. Unlucky: Mitten Man had thrown up on the ankle boots I wore with that sweater. Lucky: I no longer cared about what I wore because my life felt totally ruined, so I decided to wear whatever I touched next. Unlucky: I was holding my orange Hamburg Hoodie.

When I saw my mom's phone out at the kitchen table, I really freaked.

"That thing is way too close to our breakfast!" I said. Because it was basically six inches away from a stack of steaming pancakes.

And my dad agreed with me. "Considering that phone's recent plunge, it probably shouldn't be at the breakfast table."

"Exactly," I said, poking at my pancakes.

"Are you worried about detention?" my dad asked. "I think you're the first person in our family to get detention."

And that felt like a horrible thing to say to me. Because it meant I was the worst member of our family.

"I'm worried about everything," I explained. "I don't even know if Mr. Falconer will accept my map."

"Don't worry about that. I wrote a note that I want you to give to your Idaho History teacher," he said. "It outlines our visit to the emergency room and formally requests that he accept your map with no penalty to your grade. I wrote it on my official dental office letterhead."

"This is a long letter," I said, glancing through all five paragraphs.

"On TRAC your teacher's late policy states that you must turn in a signed letter on official letterhead from the doctor in order to receive credit for an assignment the day you return to school."

I barely remembered reading that. I thought that presenting him with my hospital ID wristband would be enough, so after my mom cut it off me, I'd stashed it in my backpack. "Thanks," I said, carefully folding the letter into a crisp square.

"If that man gives you any grief about turning in that map late, I want him to call me," my mom said really energetically. "I'll tell him what's what."

I did not want my mom talking to any of my teachers and telling them what was what. "I think Dad's note will work," I said. Then I pulled myself away from the table and put on my backpack.

As I walked to school that morning I developed certain expectations about what I would find once I got there. I expected Anya to hate me. And I expected Sabrina and Sailor to feel similarly. I expected Venice to be upset with me, but to possibly still like me. I expected Leo to be suspended. I expected Derby to feel betrayed, but I also expected him to bounce back pretty quickly. He didn't strike me as the kind of person who held a grudge. And I guess I expected everybody else to be in the dark about things. Because was some weird thing that happened in Yearbook really a big enough deal to upset the entire workings of my middle school?

It turned out that it was. I knew things were bigger and worse than I'd expected as soon as I got close enough to the school to see the posters. They were everywhere.

VOTE FOR FLETCHER

WHAT'S HOT
—BAYLOR KITTS—
4EVER!

NOBODY IS HOTTER THAN REECE

FORGET FRO-YO-ROCKY IS HOT HOT HOT

And the weirdest poster of all was one that said:

DERBY! DERBY! DERBY!
—ARGH

As I walked through the school's front doors I saw signs everywhere. They were all plastered with campaigns for hot stuff. Hot songs. Hot movies. Hot pizza places. And hot students. What was happening? There weren't too many signs for eighth and seventh graders. I mean, I saw a couple of big ones for Reece and Fletcher. And the one out front for Rocky DeBoom. It was the competition for sixth graders that seemed to be overflowing with candidates.

It felt a little unreal walking to my locker. Because I couldn't believe that these signs were approved. But each and every one of them had a red triangle at the bottom that said OFFICE APPROVED. It was so unbelievable.

I went to my locker and opened it, and about a dozen pieces of paper tumbled out. It took me a second to realize they were notes. I opened up the first one and was stunned by what I saw.

YOU SUCK! (bare butt + fart cloud)

Was that a fart cloud?

I thought maybe that note was left in my locker by mistake. But then I saw on the outside it said:

For Perry Hall.

I felt really terrible, standing by my locker, holding a bunch of notes that I was pretty sure all told me I sucked and had obscene drawings on them. I mean, it suddenly felt like the whole school hated me *and* thought I was a terrible person. How was that possible? Then something really horrible happened. I mean, it was so bad I almost peed myself out of sadness right there in the hallway before the warning bell rang. I recognized Venice's handwriting on one of the notes. She'd written it with her purple pen. I sniffed the ink to make sure it was hers. And what I smelled broke my heart. Because I'd given her that pen, so I knew exactly what it was supposed to smell like. Fresh wild huckleberries. And it did.

I wasn't sure what to do with all the hate notes. As much as I didn't want to read them, I thought they might contain useful information, so I shoved a few in my pockets and put a couple more inside my Yearbook notebook. Then I carefully removed my map from my backpack before cramming everything else into my locker and slamming the door. I swear I could feel people looking at me. But I didn't know why they were doing that. It didn't feel like they were looking at me because I was popular. It felt like they were looking at me because I was a freak. And it felt rotten. I kept my head down and tried to walk as fast as I could toward Yearbook. But I felt somebody bump me and I looked up. It was Rocky DeBoom. He had knocked into me on purpose. He wanted to hand me something.

"Be a lifesaver. Vote Rocky," he said, handing me a piece of candy wrapped in plastic.

And before I could even answer, he was walking down the hallway saying that to somebody else. He sounded like a robot. "Be a lifesaver. Vote Rocky. Be a lifesaver. Vote Rocky." I shoved the candy into my pocket and kept going. And somebody else came up to me. Sabrina!

"Are you headed to detention?" she asked, really casually.

"What?" I said. Because how did she even know about my punishment? "That doesn't start until lunch."

"I can't believe you guys got a week," Sabrina said, looking as surprised as I felt.

And when she said the word *guys* I worried that Derby was in there too.

"How many of us got detention?" I asked. Because it seemed like good information to have before I showed up.

Sabrina's eyes got big with surprise. "You don't know?" she asked. "Venice didn't tell you?"

And I was tempted to tell Sabrina about Venice being grounded. And me being grounded. But it just didn't feel like her business. I mean, instead of *me* telling Sabrina stuff, I felt like *she* should be telling me stuff.

"What's going on?" I asked. I was surprised by the sound of my own voice. I mean, it sounded pretty desperate. "Why all these posters? Are we voting as a school for What's Hot?"

Sabrina glanced over her shoulder. "Anya will kill me if she sees me talking to you." She frowned at me really sympathetically and then applied some lip balm. "You should ask Venice. I mean, if she's still talking to you."

And then Sabrina took off very, very fast.

I decided that instead of looking for Venice, who possibly hated me, I should probably turn in my topographic map. I flipped around and headed to Mr. Falconer's room.

As soon as I got there, I saw something surprising, amazing, and disturbing. Derby Esposito. It made me incredibly happy to see that he was sitting exactly where he belonged, right by the windows in his Idaho History classroom. He saw me walk in and he waved. And that wasn't even the disturbing thing. Derby was dressed in a weird green outfit. It looked like he was trying to be a dragon or something. It was like he'd decided to ignore all the great advice Leo and Venice and I had given him. He looked like a super dweeb in a super-dweeb costume. Also, he was wearing a cardboard sign that said VOTE DERBY. It was crushing. I mean, what happened to Leo's borrowed jeans? Why wasn't he emphasizing his cute butt?

I waved back to him, and felt super deflated. Because if there had been a small chance that somebody would vote for Derby for What's Hot, it was over now. Because why vote for somebody for the What's Hot section who wants to be unpopular? I mean, there was nothing hot about dressing like a lizard.

I saw Mr. Falconer adjusting his Idaho flag at the back of the classroom, and I sheepishly approached him with my map.

"Sorry this is late," I said. "I was in the hospital."

And then I gathered all my medical evidence, including my hospital bracelet, and tried to hand it to him.

"I don't need any of that, Perry," he said. "Just your map."

And that worried me. Because I felt certain that meant I was going to get a huge markdown for turning it in late.

"Um," I said. "I have an excused absence. I was in the emergency room."

I considered telling him that the map had been glued to my face and had been removed by a doctor, but then I worried he'd inspect it closer for leftover bacitracin and possibly lower my grade. He was that tough.

"I heard you, Perry," Mr. Falconer said. "It's not a problem."

But I worried that he meant it wasn't a problem for him, but getting a lower grade was a problem for me. "But I want full credit."

Mr. Falconer quit fiddling with his flag fringe and looked at me. "I'm not going to penalize you if you have a medical reason for not being in class."

And that sounded pretty refreshing. Because that was exactly what I had been worried about.

"Oh," I said.

"Your map looks great. I'll need to check it for all the rivers, but based on what I see, it looks like you're headed toward an A."

That was fantastic news. It was like Mr. Falconer wasn't the beast of a grader I thought he was. He was just normal.

"You'd better get to class," he said. "You don't want to be late."

But I wasn't sure he was right.

I left his room and aimed myself toward Yearbook. I really hoped Venice would be happy to see me.

Venice was sitting next to Anya and it just looked so weird. I mean, didn't we all hate one another?

Ms. Kenny waved for me to come to her desk. I was prepared for the worst.

"How are you feeling?" she asked.

And instead of saying something polite I just said the truth. "Stressed."

She smiled when I said that and then tilted her head. "Last week was a doozy. For everyone." And then she touched my arm in a very kind way and said, "Don't be stressed. Everything is going to be okay."

I hadn't realized Ms. Kenny was such a nice person.

"There's been a little bit of a shake-up," she said. "I feel that the photography team has gotten behind."

And I felt like I should defend my team, even though Anya was a part of it. "We've met all our goals on the main calendar."

Ms. Kenny glanced over at the main calendar. There was a lot more red marker on it than I remembered.

"We edited it," she explained. "I think adding a member to your team could amp things up and get you back on track."

But what I heard when she said that was that she thought we were failures.

"Javier is going to join you," she said.

"Javier?" I asked. "But he's on the business side."

"Don't sell Javier short. He's going to be a tremendous asset."

I looked over at Javier. I didn't like the idea of growing

the photography team. I preferred to shrink it. And kick out Anya.

"Go back to your table, and start setting your photography goals," Ms. Kenny said. "I expect you to turn in your new calendar by the end of class."

I walked back to my table and sat down two seats away from Venice. Because I didn't want to crowd her.

"Okay," Javier said. "I'm ready to go gangbusters on this calendar."

I watched Anya roll her eyes and scowl at Javier. I almost felt bad for him. Because Anya was probably going to make his life miserable. I glanced at Venice. She smiled at me. I couldn't figure out why she was smiling at me if she was also mad at me. Maybe her note wasn't hate mail. I mean, why should I assume the worst?

"Perry?" Javier said. "Perry?"

"Um," I said. "Yeah."

"You're not writing anything," he said. "I'm assigning the football and basketball games. Also, we're going to photograph the teachers Wednesday during lunch. You need to write that down."

"Sure," I said.

"I mean, in a perfect world, we'd shoot them this week, but, well, you guys are all in detention and I don't think I could do it myself."

Anya's mouth dropped open and she glared at Javier and then looked over at Venice and me. It did seem sort of rude to rub it in our faces that we had detention.

Then Javier hijacked everything and started going day by

day until Thanksgiving, outlining all the work he expected from us. It was sort of a nightmare. I mean, he started giving us assignments that were due on Saturdays.

"That's a gigantic workload," Venice said when Javier mentioned that we should turn in all student portraits, including retakes, before Columbus Day.

"Things will slow down after winter break," he argued.

"How are things going over here?" Ms. Kenny asked as she pulled up a chair.

"We're nailing down the data," Javier said. "And divvying up the work."

But I didn't think that was what was happening. I thought we were just being bossed around. Luckily, my eyes started to wander and I noticed Venice writing something.

Have you read my note?

I shook my head.

DON'T

But that made me really want to read it.

Meet me in the craft corner.

I looked up at her and smiled.

As soon as we met in the craft corner she gave me a hug.

"This is a nightmare," she said.

"Don't worry. Javier will probably do most of the work," I said. Because it seemed like he was willing to do that.

"Derby looked terrible today. Even his butt," Venice said. "It's like he wants to be a dweeb."

And it was like Venice finally understood that Derby wasn't going to change. "Derby is Derby," I said.

Venice gave me another hug. "When Anya showed me those texts I thought we were dunzo."

I stopped hugging her and looked her right in the face. "Don't even say that word."

She chewed her lip a little bit and then Venice asked me a terrible question. "All that stuff Anya said about you, how much of it was true?"

I patted Venice on the back. "Anya is psycho," I said. "Let's just forget about all that stuff."

"But the texts you sent," Venice said. "Those were real, right?"

And I really hated having to admit that they were. What was I thinking? How could I treat my best friend like that?

"They were," I said. "I'm sorry. I think I got manipulated by a psycho person." And I wasn't trying to dodge responsibility when I said that. I really thought that was the case.

"Yeah," Venice said. "We should probably avoid Anya."

"Totally," I said. "Do you forgive me?"

Then Venice said the best words ever. "Of course." And she gave me a final hug.

"What's in your pockets? How come you're making crunching sounds?" Venice asked.

"Hate notes," I said.

"Don't read them," Venice said. "I bet Anya wrote most of them."

I didn't know what to do with them. I figured I'd throw them away at home, so that nobody else would see them. Nobody's life needed hate mail. People need the opposite.

21

Detention

As soon as I arrived at detention I felt out of place. I didn't recognize the three boys at the back. They must've been eighth graders. Because they were huge and one of them either had a very dirty lip or a mustache. The only other people in the room were Anya and Venice. They sat on opposite sides of the room. I felt frozen in fear. Should I sit next to Venice? Or were there rules about that? What was she reading? Why wouldn't she look up at me?

"Perry Hall," Mr. Hackett said in a loud booming voice. "We have assigned seats in the classroom. You can take your sack lunch and sit in front of Daren."

But I sort of wanted to learn more about my punishment. I mean, what were the rules? Shouldn't Mr. Hackett tell me what I was allowed to do while I sat in front of Daren? Also, who was Daren?

"Um," I said, looking around.

"She doesn't know who Daren is," Anya said in a snotty voice.

But I actually found that helpful. Because it was true. The boy with the mustache raised his hand. And so I carefully walked toward him.

"You better not fart on me," he said.

Nobody had ever said anything so rude to me before. Especially not in front of a teacher. It was almost like he was expecting me to pass gas. I sat down in the chair and looked up to the front of the room.

Poot. Poot. Poot.

I felt my chair moving and flipped around.

"She's farting," Daren said. "It smells like rotten eggs back here."

I wanted to die. He was acting like a bully. Was this what detention meant? Was I going to have to spend five lunches in here with these goons?

"Stop moving her chair," Venice snapped. "That is so old."

And even though we were in a terrible place surrounded by terrible people, eating soggy sandwiches, at least we were on the same team again.

"Here are the rules," Mr. Hackett said. "Eat your lunch in silence. No talking. No disruptive noises. You can quietly work at your desks until lunch is over. If you need something, raise your hand and wait for me to call on you. Any violation of these rules will result in additional detentions."

He sounded like he meant business. I opened my sack lunch and pulled out my sandwich. I needed to remember not to pack my lunch last in my backpack so it would be on top of my books, because basically my entire lunch was flatter than it should've been.

I heard everybody chewing. I could even hear Daren swallow. It was *that* quiet in the room. It didn't take me long to finish my lunch, because I wasn't very hungry and I hadn't packed much. I felt super jealous of Anya when she pulled out a package of mini doughnuts. She was so smart. Because eating those would make detention feel a thousand times better. I glanced over at Venice to see how she was handling things and noticed she was reading a comic book. It bummed me out to realize that everybody else had done a much better job planning for detention. The only thing I'd brought was what I'd already eaten. I guess I hadn't realized how punishing sitting in silence with rule-breaking yo-yos would be. I started to fold my chip bag into very small squares.

I heard somebody raise a hand.

"Ryker," Mr. Hackett said. "Do you have a problem?"

"The new girl is folding her chip bag and it's making a disruptive noise," Ryker said.

That really surprised me. Because I thought my chip bag was making a medium amount of noise.

"Please throw out your trash," Mr. Hackett said.

But I didn't even move. Because I wasn't totally sure he was talking to me. Because didn't we all have trash?

"Now, Perry," Mr. Hackett said. "If I have to ask you again, you get another day of detention."

I heard Anya make a happy smirking sound. It really felt awful to feel her rooting for my downfall. Because even though I thought she was a psycho control freak, I didn't want her life to get stuck in detention forever. As I walked to throw my trash away, I realized that getting sent to the garbage can was actually a good thing. Because as I walked I heard a crunching sound and I remembered all the notes in my pocket. I'd never felt so lucky to have something to read. Even if some of it might be hateful messages that contained rude images.

I hurried back to my desk and pulled out the first note.

I hate you! You ruined Yearbook! I hope you move!

This note did not contain any rude images. And I was pretty sure it was from Sailor, because she dotted her *i*'s with clouds. And so did the author of this note.

I pulled out the next note and it was the terrible one with the fart bubble, so I just moved on to the next note. This one was the one from Venice.

When you lie to me over and over again and refuse to answer your phone or respond to your emails it makes me feel like our friendship is a joke. We're DUNZO!

And even though Venice and I had already made up, it made me a little sad to read that note. She should have never ever written the word *dunzo* to me. I looked up and frowned at her back.

The next message looked very dark on the outside. When I unfolded it I realized that it was a picture. I got worried that somebody had image-edited a photo of me to look ridiculous or freakishly ugly. But it wasn't a picture of me at all. It was a picture of Derby. What I saw totally blew me away. It was a terrible picture of him. I mean, his face looked all twisty with fear. And one of his shoulders was out of focus because it looked like he was turning to run. And Anya was standing right next to him laughing. And there was a giant snake in it. And at the bottom I could see it was printed from a Split Pic account. And that it had over three hundred hits. And somebody had written on it.

Ha. Ha. Ha. Dweeb 4ever

I flipped around in my chair and glared at Anya. She'd done this. She'd recognized that Derby was actually becoming a tiny bit more popular and she couldn't take it. She realized that a bunch of people might actually vote for him to be the What's Hot sixth grader and she got extra mean. I wanted to confront her with the photo right then and there. But I didn't want to break any detention rules and end up with more detention.

"Perry," Mr. Hackett said with his booming voice. "Turn back around."

And I was so startled that I almost fell on the floor. I could hear Anya snicker again and it just crushed me. Because why did she care so much about making unpopular kids stay unpopular? Couldn't she relax and let Derby have a moment of glory?

I kept flipping through the notes. And I actually think Sailor wrote more than one. Anya probably told her to. But I didn't even care anymore. I kept thinking about that awful picture I'd taken of Derby. What an unlucky person. He looked so awkward. It was almost like he was a cartoon. I kept looking at the picture. It was amazingly bad. I couldn't even believe I'd taken it.

When I had two notes left I felt pretty relieved I hadn't gotten more offensive images. Then I read them.

I can get you more skate passes if you want them.
And my mom moved to a house near yours.
I practically follow you home every day.
If you want to walk together we could.

That was so crazy for Hayes to write me that. Because if I hadn't used any of the skate passes he'd given me, why should he be giving me more? And he basically confessed to stalking me. I was totally going to run this by Piper. Because I had no idea what to do when it came to guys. Especially when they wrote me notes.

When I got to the last note I almost thought it was a joke.

I need your help. Do for me what you did for Derby.
People like him now. I want to know what that feels like.
I know you're trying to get a great picture of him in
the yearbook. I want that too. Please. Drea Quan

It was nuts that Drea had written to me. Because I'd probably made Derby's life worse. Yes, maybe a few more people liked him. But thousands of people were looking at a terrible picture and laughing right at his scaredy-cat face. I folded up all the notes. I needed to start accepting that nerds were nerds for a reason. And there was no way to change that. And Drea needed to accept that too. I couldn't help her. I couldn't help anyone.

Sixth grade was so much harder than I thought it would

be. And now that Javier was part of the photography team and setting the schedule it was only going to get harder. When the bell finally rang I didn't even move. I just felt so sad and stunned by everything. It was like no matter how hard I tried I couldn't change anything. No matter how hard I tried, Anya always got what she wanted.

22

What If

"You are in so much trouble," Piper said when I swung open the front door after school. She walked toward me in her wedge sandals, yoga pants, and flowy blue shirt.

"Hasn't Mom calmed down?" I asked. Because I thought her meeting with the principal had been in the morning.

"She did, and then the principal emailed her this. She's on the phone with her now." Piper lifted her own phone and showed me the dreaded Derby snake photo. It was up to five thousand hits.

Piper looked at me like she felt sorry for me. "How was detention?"

But I thought that was a pretty terrible subject to talk about.

"Don't ask," I said. "My world is crumbling."

"Yeah. I tried to explain things to Mom so she'd understand what you were trying to do," Piper said. "That you wanted to rescue that nerdy kid."

"Did it work?" I asked.

"Getting that photo was a game changer," she said. "Now Mom thinks you're mean."

"But I'm not," I said. "I know the snake photo sucks. I didn't send that out. I tried to take an awesome photo of Derby. I mean, he looked pretty good. And if the janitor hadn't interrupted us, he'd have looked totally awesome."

"Ladders. Chains. Janitor. Nerds. Detention. Your life sounds hard," Piper said. "Sixth grade wasn't like this for me at all."

I just stared at Piper. I couldn't believe she'd come all this way to insult me. My life was bad enough.

"We dressed Derby in cool clothes. And we had amazing props," I tried to explain. "We were really close to making this whole thing work."

Piper pointed to a picture of her wearing her track uniform hanging on the wall. They'd won the state championship that year and she was standing next to a giant gold trophy.

"How come you don't want to be in track?" she asked. "Those girls were awesome. You need to drop Yearbook."

I stared at the photo of my thin-legged sister in her yellow shorts. "But running makes me feel like I'm going to die," I explained.

"Yeah, it always feels like that until the endorphins kick in. You just need to run more," Piper said. "Seriously, Yearbook is killing you."

And I sort of knew that Piper was right. But I wasn't a quitter. Was I? I couldn't drop Yearbook. Could I?

I took Piper's phone and really studied the picture. It was pretty clear that Derby was going to be a nerd forever. And this picture sealed that fate. And it wasn't just a terrible picture of Derby. It was a terrible picture in general. I mean, in addition to Derby's knobby shoulder, the diamond design on the snake was completely out of focus.

"I know that psycho Anya probably sent it," Piper added.

I looked at Piper. It felt really amazing to have her standing in the living room with me. I had no idea that Piper could be such a supportive and awesome sister.

"As soon as Mom gets off the phone, I need to pick up my soup and hit the road," Piper said.

Which was sad to hear because I wanted her to stay and help me fix my life.

"We're voting for What's Hot on Friday," I said. "Do you think I should try to take another picture of Derby and put that on a Split Pic account and see if that helps anything?"

Piper looked horrified. "You need to stop taking pictures of Derby immediately. Seriously. This kid lacks all photogenic qualities. And all your meddling has only made his life worse."

That was a harsh reality check.

"I guess I need to ride it out," I said.

"Exactly," Piper said. "And call Venice. I mean, now is the time where you should be leaning on your friends."

"Oh," I said, shaking my head. "We can't talk. We're grounded from our phones."

"Use a landline," Piper said with a shrug.

And that seemed pretty brilliant. Even if it meant I'd have to find Venice's home phone number.

When my mom came into the living room after finishing her phone call with Principal Hunt, she looked a little dazed. "I am so glad middle school only lasts three years," she said.

"College is way worse than middle school," Piper said. "It costs a ton and you have to pay your own electric bills."

My mother looked at me in a very disappointed way. "What you're doing. You need to stop doing it."

But that didn't make total sense. Because I was sitting on the couch.

"It's not all her fault," Piper said. "You never should have bought her that terrible orange hoodie. Ever since she wore it her life has gone downhill. It's cursed."

And then I realized I was wearing it again and had had a pretty miserable day, and it was easier to talk about that hoodie than everything else that was wrong in my life, so I added, "Yeah. We should burn this."

"We're not burning your school clothes," my mom said.

"That's a mistake," Piper added. "Because that thing might start cursing the rest of her clothes. Where was it even made?" Piper rooted around near my neck until she found the tag. "Bangladesh!"

"Stop it, Piper," my mother said. "We're not having another debate about working conditions in foreign factories."

"All I'm saying is that's an unlucky orange hoodie," Piper said. "And Perry's popularity has plummeted since she wore it."

And even though I was pretty sure that Piper was trying to distract my mom from what the principal had said with this conversation, I was starting to believe what Piper was saying. Because it seemed true. A cursed hoodie from Bangladesh could have destroyed my popularity.

"I can't do this right now," my mom said. "I need to get to the bank before it closes."

Then she grabbed her purse and looked at me with her disappointed face again. "Piper, the soup is in the fridge. Perry, there's a burrito in the freezer you can heat up."

And I knew my mom must be furious with me. Because that burrito had been in our freezer all summer. It was probably a life-risking event to even heat it in the microwave.

Slam.

"I don't know what to tell you," Piper said. "Track was awesome. We ate a ton of junk food and got to ride the bus to tournaments all over the state."

I already knew Piper's life was better than mine. It always had been. This wasn't what I needed to hear. I swallowed hard and held back tears. Piper went into the kitchen and ladled a bowl of soup for me from her giant plastic container.

"Here," Piper said. "That burrito looks lethal."

I felt a tear roll down my cheek. After the terrible day I'd had, being instructed by my own mother to eat deadly food really broke my heart.

"If I were you, I'd stop feeling sorry for myself and get on the phone with Venice," Piper said.

"Don't you want to talk to me?" I asked. Because I thought Piper might have some good advice.

"I've actually got a study group tonight. It's for my English class."

"So you're leaving me?" I said.

"I can't fail out of college," Piper said.

She handed me the bowl of soup and kissed the top of my head. "Don't give up yet. People might actually vote for Derby for the What's Hot section."

But I just rolled my eyes when Piper said this. Because it felt like an empty and untrue thing to say.

"That picture is so weird that it's sort of amazing. Plus, there's a snake in it. I mean, Bobby even liked it."

"He did?" I asked.

"Stranger things have happened," Piper said.

I watched her carry her soup container to the door.

"Say something else to cheer me up," I said.

Piper smiled as she opened the door. "That photo shows pure and genuine fear. His face is priceless. And the prissy girl next to him really accentuates his sincerity. It's not all bad."

The burning sensation behind my eyeballs that was making me cry started to fade.

"I just hate to see Yearbook dragging you through the bummer pit," Piper said as she slipped out the door. "If Derby wins, yay for nerds. If he doesn't, then that's life."

Piper made everything sound so simple.

I got up from the couch and opened the cupboard where my mom kept a list of important phone numbers. Toward the bottom I saw Venice's mom's name, Lola Garcia. I grabbed the kitchen phone and called the number.

"Hello?" a voice said. It sounded like Victor.

"Is Venice there?" I asked.

"Venice!" a voice shouted. "Phone!"

I could hear the sound of footsteps running across a linoleum floor.

"Hello?" she said.

"I'm not going to give up," I said. "That picture isn't as bad as it looks."

"Victor actually loves that picture. He said it looks raw and hilarious."

And I didn't even know whether looking raw was a good thing or a bad thing.

"Maybe Derby can win this," I said.

"It's a long shot," Venice added. "I mean, his face does look weird."

Mitten Man weaved between my legs and I picked him up so he could walk around on the counter and lick the butter. Ever since I'd started Yearbook and tried to change how middle school worked, I'd really neglected him.

"But the photo is hot. People are looking at it. Everybody knows who Derby is. Even college kids," I said.

"You're right," Venice said.

"This election could change everything."

"And Javier seems like he's going to keep Anya in her place."

I paced in the kitchen. "Our lives might not be as terrible as they feel."

"Friday is going to be huge," Venice said.

And I knew she was right. Because that was the day of the election.

"What if he wins?" I asked.

"Then we don't stop," Venice said.

"We'll find other nerds," I said.

"We'll get their pictures in the yearbook," Venice said.

"Will Javier let us do that?" I asked.

We both paused. Leo was such good friends with Javier. We could probably convince Javier to do anything.

"I feel hopeful," Venice said in a happy voice.

"I feel that way too," I said.

Mitten Man had eaten way too much of the butter, so I picked him up and held him to my chest. My life wasn't as terrible as I had thought it was. This could work. Rocky Mountain Middle School might change. We didn't have to be stuck with what we had.

"Derby can do this," Venice said. "Especially if he wears normal pants and shows off his butt more. Do you think I should tell him that?"

Wow. I wanted Venice to feel upbeat about stuff, but I didn't want her to lose her mind. "At this stage, it's too risky to give anyone a butt compliment."

"You're right," Venice said. "You're totally right."

I heard Mrs. Garcia calling for Venice.

"Gotta go!" Venice slammed down the phone.

It didn't bother me that she'd basically hung up on me, because I didn't think she was technically allowed to talk to me. I thought of something else I needed to do. I grabbed a pair of scissors from the junk drawer and headed to my room.

I pulled off my Hamburg Hoodie and tried to ignore all the orange fuzz balls it had left on my T-shirt underneath. Then I didn't even hesitate. I started cutting it into ribbons. Piper was right. Some clothes were cursed. And the whole reason I had even bought this hoodie was because other kids were wearing them. And Piper was also right about me picking the wrong color. Other than sunsets and soda, I didn't even like to see the color orange. Suddenly, it was as if my hoodie was a symbol. It wasn't who I really was at all. It wasn't even close. And wearing it had made me feel like a fake. A phony. A fraud. And this wasn't how I wanted to feel. This wasn't who I wanted to be.

After I destroyed it, I wadded the shredded strips into a ball and tossed it up in the air. Mitten Man turned into a wild beast and dove at several pieces. Clearly, I should have done this for him weeks ago. As I watched Mitten Man remain in attack mode and jump around my room, I kept picturing that photo of Piper on our wall. Those things mattered. Everybody should have a frameworthy moment in middle school. Even the nerds. And when those nerds were old and in college and looking at those photos, I wanted them to feel the same way Piper did when she looked at her photo. Happy.

Couldn't Venice and I do that? I mean, it was the right thing to do, wasn't it? And we both wanted this *so bad*. And so did other people. Like Drea Quan. The longer I thought about it, the more certain I became. Having already faced what we'd faced in Yearbook, and dealt with what we'd dealt with in the first month of middle school, if anyone could fix this situation, it was me and Venice Garcia.

Acknowledgments

I am very lucky. So many people helped me make this book a book. Thank you, Sara Crowe, for always being there, and for encouraging me to quit drinking diet soda. And thank you to my brilliant editor, Wendy Loggia, who gently guided this book into a much better version of itself. I'm serious when I end my emails to you saying "I love your brain." So many talented people at Random House made sure this book looked amazing, and I appreciate all they've done, especially Kate Gartner. Buckets of thanks go to my husband, Brian Evenson, for providing the time I needed to make writing possible. And thanks to my son, Max, for helping me stay in shape by mercilessly requesting that I chase him around the table, down the hallway, into the kitchen, and back to the table. I'd also like to thank my teachers at North Bonneville Junior High (now known as Rocky Mountain Middle School). It's been many, many years since I walked those hallways, but they still live inside me, and in my stories.

MORE FUN READS
by KRISTEN TRACY!

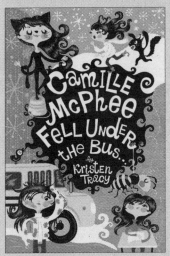